I0656833

Kate Sanborn

Home Pictures of English Poets

for fireside and schoolroom

Kate Sanborn

Home Pictures of English Poets
for fireside and schoolroom

ISBN/EAN: 9783337255428

Printed in Europe, USA, Canada, Australia, Japan

Cover: Foto ©Andreas Hilbeck / pixelio.de

More available books at **www.hansebooks.com**

HOME PICTURES

OF

ENGLISH POETS,

FOR

FIRESIDE AND SCHOOL-ROOM.

NEW YORK:
D. APPLETON AND COMPANY,
90, 92 & 94 GRAND STREET.
1869.

PREFACE.

THE writer, in the following Sketches of our best English Poets, from old Father Chaucer to the short-lived Burns, has attempted to interest the young student by making of each life a story as well as a lesson.

It has been her aim to introduce these men of genius familiarly to her readers, that they may shake hands as good friends through the medium of a book.

The style is intentionally informal and colloquial, in order to attract those who might neglect elaborate works on English Literature, and to lead them to a more thorough and extensive exploration in the same direction.

K. A. S.

HANOVER, N. H., *September* 10, 1868.

CONTENTS.

CHAUCER.

"Dan Chaucer, well of English undefyled,
On Fame's eternal bead-roll worthy to be fyled."

SHINING brightly in the twilight period of English literature, appears the name of GEOFFREY CHAUCER. · He is often called *Dan* Chaucer, as in the quotation ; a title of respect, originally "Don"* or Lord. Southey says, that the line of English poets begins with him, as that of English kings with William the Conqueror. He is styled the "Father of English poetry;" "the loadstar of the language," and extolled as

"The *morning-star* of song, who made
His music heard below ;

* From the Latin Dominus.

> Dan Chaucer, the first warbler, whose sweet breath
>   Preluded those melodious bursts, that fill
> The spacious times of great Elizabeth
>   With sounds that echo still."

The poets before him are almost forgotten, and you could not even read their rhymes without some study; so much does the old English differ from our own. A short lyric from an unknown poet of the thirteenth century will show the state of the English language at that time. The theme is the uncertainty of life:

> " Winter wakeneth all my care;
>   Now these leaves waxeth bare.
> Oft I sigh and mourn sare,
>   When it cometh in my thought.
> Of this world's joy, how it goth all to nought.
> Now it is and now it n'is (is not).
> All so it ne'er n'were I wis;
> That many men saith sooth it is,
> All go'th but Godes will.
> All we shall die, though us like ill.
> All that grain me groweth green,
> Now it falloweth all by-dene (fadeth presently),
> Jesu help that it be seen,
>   And shield us from hell;
> For I n'ot (know not) whither I shall,
>   Ne how long here dwell."

Those early days in " Merrie England " were the days of feudalism, which, you know, is the exact reverse of republicanism, the government of which we are now so proud. The twelfth and thirteenth · centuries saw the height of the feudal system, and the commencement of its decline. In our country the basis of honor and power is the *people*, but in theirs it was the *king*, from whom all classes took their power, and on whom they were dependent, while the common people were mere slaves, to do his bidding.

Society was divided into nobles and serfs. Under the great barons were lesser barons, under these the yeomen, each owing military service to the class above them. The barons lived in strong castles, in plenty and wealth; the poor in miserable hovels, often nothing but mud cottages, with rotten thatches. Very few houses had windows, only loopholes to look from, and chimneys were rare. The fire was usually placed in an iron grate in the centre of the room, the smoke escaping at the open, blackened roof. At meals, the family were seated before the table was laid, with hands carefully washed, as forks were unknown, and fingers had to be freely used. Travelling minstrels would often come in during the meal, and were well supplied with food and wine, for the songs they sung and the stories they told. They danced as well as sung, and were experts in the art of legerdemain; always welcome at the marriage feast, or other gay festivals.

> "Merry it is in halle to here the harpe,
> The minstrelles synge, the jogelours carpe."

They often received handsome and costly gifts; for instance, a certain earl gave to his host's minstrels, "gowns of cloth of gold, furred with ermyne, valued at 200 franks." Masques and brilliant pageants, tournaments, archery, hunting, and wrestling, were the amusements of the age.

A *hawk* was the symbol of nobility. Enormous prices were paid for these birds, and men of rank were seldom seen without one or more of them, taking them even to war and to church. They bequeathed their favorite falcon, in their wills, to their dearest friend, and a pathetic tale is told of a young nobleman, who, after sacrificing every thing in pursuit of a haughty dame, resolved to dress his hawk for her dinner, as the last and greatest proof of his love. Chaucer's poems are full of allusions to the art of hawking; one of them, indeed, "The Parliament of Love" is quite devoted to that subject.

Much cannot be said for the morality of the age. The monks were too often corrupt and gluttonous hypocrites; the barons spent much of their time in feasting and fighting; and the poor, with their rough garments seldom changed by night or day, grew sullen and reckless.

A writer of those times describes a poor ploughman and his half-starved family. The man is in rags from head to foot; "his ton (toes) toteden (peeped) out," and his oxen are so starved that men might "reckon each a rib."

Here is a touching picture, as we know the distress was real:

> " His wife walked him with
>   With a long goad
>   In a cutted coat,
>   Cutted full high;
> Wrapped in a winnow sheet
>   To wearen her from weathers.
> Barefoot on the bare ice,
> That the blood followed.
> And at the land's end layeth
>   A little crumb bowl.
> And thereon lay a little child
> Lapped in clouts;
> And twins of two years' old,
>   Upon another side.
> And all they sungen one song
> That sorrow was to hear;—
> They crieden all one cry,
>   A careful * note.
> The simple man sighed sore
> And said, "Children be still."

Chaucer, though a close student of books (or rather manuscripts written on parchment, for books were then

---

* Full of care.

almost unknown), was a great lover of nature, as may easily be seen from his writings. Early poetry, like venison, has a flavor of the wild-woods; its very words are redolent of nature.

Bacon says, that what we call antiquity, was really the youth of the world, and Chaucer's poetry seems to breathe of a time when humanity was younger and more joyous-hearted than it now is. "The first great poet of any country has this advantage, that he converses with Nature directly, without an interpreter, and his utterances are not so much the *echo* of hers as in very deed her living voice; carrying in them a spirit as original and divine, as the music of her running brooks, or of her breezes among the leaves." For this reason Chaucer's rhymes are still the freshest and greenest in our language, disfigured as they are by the coarseness of the times and obsolete spelling.

Chaucer had a child's love for birds. Some of his best lines are descriptions of them and their sweet songs, and he could not bear to see them imprisoned. He says:

> "Where birds are fed in cages,
> Though you should day and night tend them like pages,
> And strew the bird's room fair and soft as silk,
> And give him sugar, honey, bread, and milk;
> Yet had the bird, by twenty thousand-fold,
> Rather be in a forest, wild and cold;
> And right anon let but his door be up,
> And with his feet he spurneth down his cup,
> And to the woods will hie, and feed on worms.
> In that new college keepeth he his terms,
> And learneth love of his own proper kind—
> No gentleness of home his heart may bind."

Like a child, too, he mourned over the decline of the charming illusions that, in his early days, had such power in the land. But the elf-haunted glades were so scorched by the stern *limitour* (or friar licensed to beg within cer-

tain *limits*) that all the fairies were driven away, and
danced no more at midnight on the moonlit greensward.
There is something so comically pathetic in Chaucer's
way of telling of this change, that I must give you his own
words :

> " In olde dayes of the King Artour,   .
> All was this lond ful filled of faerie ;
> The elf-queen, with her jolly compaynie,
> Danced ful oft in many a grene mede,
> But now can no man see non elves mo,
> For the great charitee and prayeres
> Of limitoures, and other holy freres,
> That searchen every land and every streme.
> This maketh that there ben no faeries,
> For ther as wont to walken as an elf,
> *Ther walketh now the limitour himself.*"

He lived in stirring times and an illustrious age, the
brightest ornament of the reigns of Edward III. and
Richard II., the one the ablest, and the other, perhaps, the
weakest of all the English sovereigns.

WICKLIFFE, the first translator of the *whole* English
Bible, was his contemporary, and I am sure a few words in
regard to this great teacher and reformer will not be
thought a useless digression.

The Bible was to the mass of the people a sealed book,
locked up in a dead and foreign tongue. Wickliffe commenced his " Apology " for his noble work in this way :
" Oh Lord God ! sithin at the beginning of faith so
many men translated into Latin, and to great profit of
Latin men, let one simple creature of God translate into
English for profit of Englishmen." Of course, the
priests raged at this innovation, and abused him without
mercy. They complained that " the Gospel is made vulgar, and laid more open to the laity, and even to *women*
who could read, than it used to be to the most learned of
the clergy and those of the best understanding. And so

the Gospel jewel or evangelical pearl is thrown about and trodden under foot of swine." They openly rejoiced at his death, which occurred in 1384, and the far-famed Council of Constance, which also condemned Huss and Jerome to the stake, determined, thirty years later, to wreak their vengeance on his *bones*, which by their decree were taken up and burned, and the ashes thrown into the waters of a brook which runs into the Avon. · A poet of a later day thus alludes to this sacrilege:

> · "The Avon to the Severn runs,
> The Severn to the sea,
> And Wickliffe's dust shall spread abroad
> Wide as those waters be."

"Quaint old Thomas Fuller" also remarks that "the ashes of Wickliffe are the emblems of his doctrine, which are now dispersed all the world over."

From this sturdy, unconquerable, outspoken, great-hearted reformer, our poet learned · not only lessons of wisdom, but those religious doctrines which he ever after supported, though a Catholic by birth and education. There is much uncertainty about his early life, but we have good reason to believe that his father was a wealthy London merchant, and that his childhood was spent in that city. In the "Testament of Love," his longest prose work, we find these words: "Also the citye of London, that is to me so dere and swete, in which I was forth growen, and more kindly love have I to that place than to any other in yerth." He studied at Cambridge, and perhaps at Oxford also.

His first poem, "The Court of Love," was written while at college, when only eighteen. An entry in some old register of the Inns of Court, stating that "Geoffrey Chaucer was fined two shillings for beating a Franciscane friar in Fleet Street," is the only recorded event of his supposed law studies in the Inner Temple.

In some way he obtained the patronage of John of Gaunt, Duke of Lancaster, and so well played the courtier's part, as to gain honor, preferment, position, and, above all, after eight years of faithful courtship, the hand of one of Queen Philippa's maids of honor, sister-in-law to the duke.

In 1372, he was sent on an important mission to Genoa, and during this embassy visited Petrarch in Northern Italy, who told him the story of "Patient Griselda," which he afterward wove into the "Canterbury Tales."

> "I woll tell a tale which that I
> Learned at Padowe of a worthy clerk,
> As preved by his wordes and his werk ;
> He is now dead and nailed in his chest ;
> I pray to God so yeve his soul rest.
> Francis Petrarch, the laureat poet,
> Highte this clerk, whose rhethoricke sweet
> Enlumined all Itaille of poetrie."

How pleasant, in this prosy, matter-of-fact age, to look back to the fourteenth century, and picture the meeting of those master-minds !

Chaucer's path was now onward and upward, brightened by frequent tokens of royal favor ; not empty praise merely, but gold and silver, were generously given to the court poet by the brave old king. His cup was full of blessings, but, like other mortals, he was destined to trials and disappointment.

When King Edward died, in 1377, Chaucer lost his best friend. For several years all went well; but at last Richard quarrelled with the Duke of Lancaster, and Chaucer nobly sided with his patron. He was accused of joining in a riot in London, and was obliged to flee to the Continent. There he remained nearly two years, with his wife and children, "becoming at last almost penniless, through generosity to his fellow-exiles, and the failure of supplies from home, where his agents had treacherously appropriated his rents." Perhaps it was at this time he addressed these verses to his purse:

"TO MY PURSE.

"To you, my purse, and to none other wight,
 Complain I, for ye be my lady dere;
I am sorry now that ye be light,
For certes, now ye make me heavy chere:
Me were as lefe be laid upon a bere,
For which unto your mercy thus I crie,
Be heavy again, or else mote I die.

"Now vouchsafe this day, or it be night
That I of you the blissful sound may here,
Or see your color like the sunne bright;
That of yellownesse had never peere,
Ye are my life, ye be my herte's stere,
I ween of comfort and good companie,
Be heavy again, or else mote I die.

"Now purse, thou art to me my live's light
And saviour, as downe in this world here;
Out of this town helpe me by your might;
Sith that you will not be my treasure,
For I am slave as nere as any frere,
But I pray unto your curtesie,
Be heavy again, or else mote I die."

Literature had been confined to the *monasteries*, but Chaucer was a good-humored man of the world, a traveller, courtier, and scholar, and brought it to the market. The best part of his life was given to the translation of poems from the French and Italian, and it was not until the age of sixty that he commenced the " Canterbury Tales," to which he owes his fame. They were never finished, but the story-tellers are talking yet, and their voices, echoing from the past, tell us how the Englishman of the fourteenth century spoke, dressed, and acted, giving, with more fidelity than any painting, the follies, vices, and customs of the age.

> " Old England's fathers live in Chaucer's lay
>   As if they ne'er had died. He grouped and drew
>   Their likeness with a spirit of life so gay,
>   That still they live and breathe in fancy's view,
>   Fresh beings, fraught with time's imperishable hue."

Chaucer's plan was to describe in narrative poetry the men and manners of his day. This he does in his rugged tongue, with much quiet humor and keen satire, marred at times by the coarseness then too common.

Lowell says of him : " His narrative flows on like one of our inland rivers, sometimes hastening a little in its eddies, seeming to run sunshine — sometimes gliding smoothly, while here and there a beautiful, quiet thought, a pure feeling, a golden-hearted verse, opens as quietly as a water-lily, and makes no ripple."

He represents a company of pilgrims on a visit to the shrine of Thomas à Becket at Canterbury. They all happen to lodge at the Tabard Inn, at Southwark—strangers to each other, thirty-two in number, if we include the story-teller himself, and the jolly, corpulent host of the Tabard, Harry Bailey, who, having often travelled the road before, proposes to go with them as guide, and at the same time suggests that the journey would seem less tedious if each were to tell a story as they ride—a supper to be given on their return to the one who had been most entertaining.

> " In Southwark, at the Tabard as I lay,
>   Redy to wenden on my pilgrimage
>   To Canterbury, with full devout corage,
>   At night was come into that hostelrie,
>   Wel nyne and twenty in a compayne
>   Of sondry folks, by aventure i falle
>   In felawschipe, and pilgrims were they alle,
>   That toward Canterbury wolden ryde."

This simple plot is the string upon which these pleasant stories are strung, and the number of personages in this motley but attractive cavalcade gave the poet a fine opportunity to describe the various classes of society. Every member of the party has a separate and individual interest, each character is a perfect picture in itself, each traveller represents a class, and in the entire company the whole society of that age stands again before us just as it was.

The Tabard Inn, under the name of *Talbot*, is still pointed out in London, opposite Spurgeon's Tabernacle, as the very place where these pilgrims met five hundred years ago. But this seems rather improbable, as I write it, so I will add "they say," and a hope that you and I may some day see that venerable "hostelrie."

As examples of our poet's humor, satire, and power, we have here a lawyer described as the busiest of mortals, with the sly addition,

> "And yet he *seemed* besier than he was;"

and, after an imposing list of the doctor's medical authorities, a droll line tells us that his study was but "litel on the Bible." But his severest satire is reserved for the monks and priests, with whom he is no more in love than when he beat the friar in Fleet Street, and their hypocrisy and lack of spirituality are described with zest.

He tells us of a "gentil pardonere" or seller of indulgences, who, brimful of pardons, came from Rome all hot, who carried in his wallet the Virgin Mary's veil, and a part of the sail of St. Peter's ship, and in a glass he had "pigges bones" for relics, and with these he made more money in a day than the poor parson did in two months.

His description of the parson, a simple man of God, is considered one of the best :

> "A good man there was of religion,
> That was a poore parson of a town,
> But rich he was of holy thought and werk;

He was also a learned man, a clerk,
That Christe's gospel truly woulde preach:
His parishens devoutly would he teach.
Benign he was and wonder diligent,
And in adversity full patient.
Wide was his parish, and houses far asunder,
But he ne left nought, for no rain nor thunder,
In sickness and in mischief to visit
The farthest in his parish much and lite,
Upon his feet, and in his hands a staff;
This noble ensample to his sheep he yaf,
That first he wrought and afterward he taught.
To drawen folk to heaven with fairness,
By good ensample, was his business;
But it were any person obstinate,
What so he were of high or low estate,
Him would he snibben sharply for the nones;
A better priest I trow that no where none is.
He waited after no pomp or reverence;
He maked him no spiced conscience;
But Christe's lore and his apostles twelve
He taught, *but first he followed it himselve.*"

I would like to give you the whole description of the
pretty Prioresse—

"That of her smiling was full simple and coy."

" Full well she sang the service divine,
Entuned in her nose full sweetly.

At meate was she well y-taught withal,
She let no morsel from her lippes fall.

But for to speaken of her conscience,
She was so charitable and pitous,
She would weep, if that she saw a mouse
Caught in a trap, if it were dead or bled;
Of smale hownds, had she that she fed
With wasted flesh and milk and wastel bread,
But sore wept she if one of them were dead;
Or if men smote it with a yerde smart,
And all was conscience and tender heart."

Though she had renounced the world and its pleasures, she had not given up all womanly love for ornaments, for

> "Of smale corall about hire arm she bare
> A pair of bedes gauded all with grene,
> And thereon hung a broche of gold ful shene,
> On whiche was first y-written a crowned *A*,
> And after, Amor vincit omnia."

How different is his description of the wife of Bath, a plain, vulgar, full-faced, well-dressed dame, who rode her horse like a man; had spurs on her feet, and a hat on her head as "broad as a buckler: "

> "In all the parish, wif ne was there none
> That to the offring bifore hire shulde gon;
> And if there did, certain so wroth was she
> That she was out of alle charite.
> Her coverchiefs (head-dress) weren ful fine of ground,
> I dorse swere they weyden a pound,
> That on the Sonday were upon hire hede;
> Her hosen weren of fine scarlet rede.
> Full straite iteyed, and shoon ful moist and newe;
> Bold was hire face, and fayre, and red of hew.
> She was a worthy woman all hire live,
> Husbands at chirche dore, had she had five."

But of course I do no justice to these mental photographs by clipping here and there, and you will enjoy looking up these shrewd and skilful pictures. The original plan of Chaucer would have required at least sixty tales, with prologues, interludes, local descriptions, and side-scenes. Only twenty-four stories were completed; these contain 17,000 lines, and his other works exceed this number. It may give a better idea to mention that "Paradise Lost" contains but 10,575 lines, and the whole of Virgil but 12,497. The Tales are written both in prose and poetry, are both serious and comic, to suit the person from whom they came. "The Clerke's Tale" is perhaps the best of all, which Chaucer owned he had taken from Petrarch, and

Petrarch confessed that he had borrowed from Boccaccio, who remodelled it from some old legend. It deserves to be told in yet better language, by some poet of our own day.

Dryden and Pope have modernized some parts of Chaucer's great work, but not the best. The former says of him, "He is a perpetual fountain of good sense." Emerson accuses Chaucer of being a "huge borrower," using "poor Gower" (an author of that time) "as if he were only a brickkiln or stone quarry, out of which to build his house." This may be very true, but it is hard to criticise severely the genius who borrows indifferent material and makes it immortal.

His Tales remained in manuscript form for seventy years, and were then published by Caxton, the first printer of England.

In regard to the personal appearance of Chaucer himself, but little is known. "His common dress consisted of red hose, horned shoes, and a loose frock of camlet reaching to the knee, with wide sleeves, fastened at the wrist."

A miniature introduced, as was the fashion of those times, into one of the most valuable manuscript copies of his works, gives him a pleasant, thoughtful, and somewhat abstracted countenance. As a young man, he was handsome, elegant, and graceful, his mouth, especially noticed for its beauty of color and outline. But, toward the end of his life, he grew rather corpulent, and always walked with downcast face, as if absorbed in meditation. When called on in his turn to amuse the pilgrims by a story, he is rallied by honest Harry Bailey, who was not a slender man himself, on his obesity and studious air; and the amiability with which the poet receives these jokes, proves him a true gentleman as well as a fine writer.

Listen for a moment to the burly landlord:

"What man art thou ? quod he,
Thou lookest as thou woldest find a hare ;

For ever on the ground I see thee stare.
Approach near, and loke merrily.
Now ware you sires, and let this man have room,
He in wast is shape us well as I.
This were a popet in an arm to embrace
For any woman and fair of face;
He seemeth elveisch by his countenance,
For unto no wight doth he dalliance."

Crowned with plenty and content, enjoying a quiet, happy old age, warmed once more by the sunshine of royal favor, Chaucer spent his last and best days writing his greatest work in a pleasant home at Woodstock, receiving a liberal pension and a pitcher of wine daily from the cellar of the king.

He died in 1400, and was buried in Westminster Abbey, in what is now called the "Poet's Corner." It is said that he repeated in his last moments the "Balade made by Geoffrey Chaucer upon his dethe bed, lying in his great anguisse." Here is a portion of it, with the modern spelling:

"Fly from the crowd, and be to virtue true,
    Content with what thou hast though it be small;
To hoard brings hate, nor lofty thoughts pursue,
    He who climbs high endangers many a fall.
Envy's a shade that ever waits on fame,
    And oft the sun that rises it will hide;
Trace not in life a vast expansive scheme,
    But be thy wishes to thy state allied.
Be mild to others, to thyself severe,
    So truth shall shield thee or from want or fear."

Chaucer was the type of his age, a connecting link between the days of chivalry and the great Reformation, uniting in his character the knight and the Christian.

The first poet, like the snow-drop, the harbinger of spring, attracts all eyes and wins all hearts. Those who followed Chaucer admired and imitated him. They called his words "the gold dew-drops of speech," and himself "superlative in eloquence," "the chief poet of Britain," "the first finder of our fair language."

Wordsworth speaks of

> "That noble Chaucer, in those former times,
> Who first enriched our English with his rhymes;
> And was the first of ours that ever broke
> Into the Muses' treasures, and first spoke
> In mighty numbers, delving in the mine
> Of perfect knowledge."

He first introduced the heroic metre into our language, and his vigorous Anglo-Saxon was inlaid with such a number of Norman-French words, that contemporaries complained that he imported a "wagon-load of foreign words." A French accent is often necessary to make the rhythm perfect.

His principal works, besides the "Canterbury Tales," are "The Flower and the Leaf," "Troilus and Creseide," "Romaunt of the Rose," and "The House of Fame." Pope, in his "Temple of Fame," has imitated the last poem to some extent.

His poetry exhibits a rare combination of *opposite* excellences—"the sportive fancy, painting and gilding every thing with the keen, observant, matter-of-fact spirit, that looks through whatever it glances at; the soaring and creative imagination,.with the homely sagacity and healthy relish for all the realities of things; the unrivalled tenderness and pathos, with the quaintest humor and the most exuberant merriment; the wisdom at once and the wit; the all that is best, in short, both in poetry and prose at the same time."

Henry Reed says: "You look at him in his gay mood, and it is so genial that that seems to be his very nature, an overflowing comic power, or rather that power touched with thoughtfulness and tenderness — '*humor*' in its finest estate. And then you turn to another phase of his genius, and with something of wonder, and more of delight, you find it shining with a light as true and natural and beautiful into the deeper places of the human soul— its woes, its anguish, and its strength of suffering and of heroism. In this, the harmonious union of true tragic and comic powers, Chaucer and Shakespeare stand alone in our literature; it places them above all the other great poets of our language."

Most persons have the idea that Chaucer was a remarkable poet for the age in which he lived, but that now "he is dead and buried in a literary as well as a literal sense," regarding his works as relics of an almost barbarous age. But those who are willing to master the difficulties of his style will be amply rewarded. "It will conduct you," to use the beautiful words of Milton, "to a hill-side; laborious, indeed, at the first ascent, but else so smooth, so green, so full of goodly prospects and melodious sounds on every side, that the harp of Orpheus was not more charming."

Leigh Hunt has given us the story in exquisite prose of the "glorious, sainted Griselda." He says: "The whole heart of Christendom has embraced her. She has passed into a proverb; ladies of quality have called their children after her, the name surviving (we believe) among them to this day, in spite of its *griesly* sound; and we defy the manliest man of any feeling to read it in Chaucer's own consecutive stanzas (whatever he may do here) without feeling his eyes moisten." And then follows his version:

"At Saluzzo, in Piedmont, under the Alps—

'Down at the root of Vesulus the cold'—

there reigned a feudal lord, a marquis, who was beloved by his people, but too much given to his amusement, and an enemy of marriage; which alarmed them, lest he

2

should die childless, and leave his inheritance in the hands
of strangers. They, therefore, at last sent him a deputa-
tion which addressed him on the subject; and he agreed
to take a wife, on condition that they should respect his
choice wheresoever it might fall.

"Now, among the poorest of the marquis's people—

> 'There dwelt a man
> Which that was holden poorest of them all :
> But highé God sometimé senden can
> His grace unto a little ox's stall ;
> Janicola, men of that thorp him call ;
> A daughter had he fair enough to sight,
> And Grisildis this youngé maiden hight.'

Tender of age was 'Grisildis' or 'Grisilda' (for the poet
calls her both); but she was a maiden of a thoughtful
and steady nature, and as excellent a daughter as could
be, thinking of nothing but her sheep, her spinning, and
her 'old poor father,' whom she supported by her labor,
and waited upon with the greatest duty and obedience.

> 'Upon Griseld', this pooré creáture,
> Full often sith this marquis set his eye,
> As he on hunting rode peráventure ;
> And, when it fell that he might her espy,
> He not with wanton looking of folly
> His eyen cast on her, but in sad wise
> Upon her cheer he would him oft avise.'

"The marquis announced to his people that he had
chosen a wife, and the wedding-day arrived : but nobody
saw the lady; at which there was great wonder.   Clothes
and jewels were prepared, and the feast too; and the marquis, with a great retinue, and accompanied by music, took
his way to the village where Griselda lived.

"Griselda had heard of his coming, and said to herself, that she would get her work done faster than usual, on
purpose to stand at the door, like other maidens, and see

the sight; but, just as she was going to look out, she heard the marquis call her; and she set down a water-pot she had in her hand, and knelt down before him with her usual steady countenance.

"The marquis asked for her father; and, going in-doors to him, took him by the hand, and said, with many courteous words and leave-asking, that he had come to marry his daughter. The poor man turned red, and stood abashed and quaking, but begged his lord to do as seemed good to him; and then the marquis asked Griselda if she would have him, and vow to obey him in all things, be they what they might; and she answered trembling, but in like manner; and he led her forth, and presented her to the people as his wife.

"The ladies, now Griselda's attendants, took off her old peasant's clothes, not much pleased to handle them, and dressed her anew in fine clothes, so that the people hardly knew her again for her beauty.

> ' Her hairés have they combed that lay untresséd
> Full rudély, *and with their fingers small*
> A coroune on her head they have ydresséd,
> And set her full of nouches * great and small.
> Thus Walter lowly, *nay but royally,*
> Wedded with fortunate honesty ; '

and Griselda behaved so well and discreetly, and behaved so kindly to every one, making up disputes, and speaking such gentle and sensible words—

> ' And couldé so *the people's heart embrace,*
> *That each her lov'th that looketh on her face.*'

"In due time the marchioness had a daughter, and the marquis had always treated his consort well, and behaved like a man of sense and reflection; but now he informed her that his people were dissatisfied at his having raised

---

* *Nouches*—nuts ?—buttons in that shape made of gold or jewelry.

her to be his wife; and, reminding her of her vow to obey him in all things, told her that she must agree to let him do with the little child whatsoever he pleased. Griselda kept her vow to the letter, not even changing countenance; and shortly afterward an ill-looking fellow came, and took the child from her, intimating that he was to kill it. Griselda asked permission to kiss her child ere it died; and she took it in her bosom, and blessed and kissed it with a sad face, and prayed the man to bury its ' little body' in some place where the birds and beasts could not get it. But the man said nothing. He took the child, and went his way; and the marquis bade him carry it to the Countess of Pavia, his sister, with directions to bring it up in secret.

"Griselda lived on, behaving like an excellent wife; and four years afterward she had another child, a son, which the marquis demanded of her, as he had done the daughter, laying his injunctions on ·her at the same .time to be patient. Griselda said she would; adding—as a proof, nevertheless, what bitter feelings she had to control—

> ' I have not had no part of children twain ;
> But first, sickness ; and after, woe and pain.'

The same 'ugly sergeant' now came again, and took away the second child, carrying it like the former to Bologna; and twelve years after, to the astonishment and indignation of the poet, and the people too, but making no alteration whatsoever in the obedience of the wife, the marquis informs her, that his subjects are dissatisfied at his having her for a wife at all, and that he had got a dispensation from the pope to marry another, for whom she must make way, and be divorced, and return home; adding, insultingly, that she might take back with her the dowry which she brought him. Woefully, but ever patiently, does Griselda consent; not, however, without a tender exclamation at the difference between her marriage-

day and this: and as she receives the instruction about
the dowry as a hint that she is to give up her fine clothes,
and resume her old ones, which she says it would be impossible to find, she makes him an exquisite prayer and
remonstrance, in which she says:

' Let me not like a worm go by the way.
Remember you, mine owen lord so dear,
I was your wife, though I unworthy were.'

"She leaves her beautiful home in the simplest garb
possible, without one word of complaint for her tyran-
nical husband, who is thus testing her love.

"The people follow her weeping and wailing; but she
went ever as usual, with staid eyes, nor all the while did
she speak a word. As to her poor father, he cursed the
day he was born. And so with her father, for a space,
dwelt 'this flower of wifely patience;' nor showed any
sense of offence, nor remembrance of her high estate.

"At length arrives news of the coming of the new
marchioness, with such array of pomp as had never been
seen in all Lombardy; and the marquis, who has, in the
mean time, sent to Bologna for his son and daughter, once
more desires Griselda to come to him, and tells her that
as he has not women enough in his household to wait upon
his new wife, and set every thing in order for her, he must
request her to do it; which she does with all ready obedience, and then goes forth with the rest to meet the new
lady. At dinner, the marquis again calls her, and asks
her what she thinks of his choice. She commends it
heartily, and prays God to give him prosperity; only
adding, that she hopes he will not try the nature of so
young a creature as he tried hers, since *she has been
brought up more tenderly, and perhaps could not bear it.*

' And when this Walter saw her patience,
Her gladdé cheer, and no malice at all,

And he so often had her done offence,
And she aye sad * and constant as a wall,
Continuing aye her innocence over all,
This sturdy marquis 'gan his hearté dress
To rue upon her wifely stedfastness.'

He gathers her in his arms, and kisses her; but she takes
no heed of it, out of astonishment, *nor hears any thing
he says :* upon which he exclaims, that, as sure as Christ
died for him, she is his wife, and he will have no other,
nor ever had; and with that he introduces his supposed
bride to her as her own daughter, with his son by her
side; and Griselda, overcome at last, faints away.

' When she this heard, aswooné down she falleth
For *piteous joy ;* and, after her swooning,
She both her youngé children to her calleth,
And in her armés, piteously weeping,
Embraceth them, and tenderly kissing
Full like a mother with her salté tears
She bathed both their visage and their hairs.

' Oh ! such a piteous thing it was to see
Her swooning, *and her humble voice to hear !*
" *Grand mercy !* Lord, God thank it you (quoth she),
That ye have savéd me my children dear:
Now reck † I never to be dead right here,
Since I stand in your love and in your grace,
No force of death, ‡ nor when my spirit pace.

" O tender, O dear, O youngé children mine !
Your woful mother weenéd steadfastly,
That cruel houndés or some foul vermín
Had eaten you: but God of his mercy
And your benigné father. tenderly
Hath done you keep; " and in that samé stound
All suddenly she swapped adown to ground.

' *And in her swoon so sadly holdeth she*
Her children two when she 'gan them embrace,

---

* *Sad ;* composed in manner; unaltered.   † *Reck ;* care.
‡ *No force of death ;* no matter for death.

That with great sleight and great difficulty
The children from her arm they 'gan arrace,*
Oh! many a tear on many a piteous face
Down ran of them that stooden her beside;
Unnethe abouten her might they abide."

That is, they could scarcely remain to look at her, or stand still.

"And so, with feasting and joy, ends this divine cruel story of Patient Griselda; the happiness of which is superior to the pain, not only because it ends so well, but because there is ever present in it, like that of a saint in a picture, the sweet, sad face of the fortitude of woman."

---

* *Arrace* (French, *arracher*); "pluck."

THE TABARD INN.

SP·N·SER.

" That gentle bard,
Chosen by the Muses for their page of state,
Sweet Spenser, moving through his clouded heaven,
With the moon's beauty and the moon's soft face."

AFTER the " Morning-Star " came a long, dark night, instead of the bright dawn, and for more than one hundred and fifty years no great poet appeared.

With Chaucer, our literature and language had made a " burst " which they were not able to maintain.   He has, by Warton, been well compared to some warm, bright day in the very early spring, which seems to say that the winter is over and gone.   But its promise is deceitful; the full bursting and blossoming are yet far off:

" Old Chaucer, like the morning-star,
To us discovers day from far;
His light those mists and clouds dissolved,
Which our dark nation long involved;

> But he, descending to the shades,
> Darkness again the age invades."

It was, indeed, a dark and stormy period, an age of change and revolution, without progress, a desert-tract of time, a blank in our literary history. No form of government, no creed was safe; life and property were nowhere protected. Yet England was in a better condition than any other country in this respect.

How could men improve in such dreadful days? the crown claimed by rival kings, the people divided into factions, causing that civil war

> " Which sent, between the red rose and the white,
> A thousand souls to death and deadly night ! "

How could men be merry or wise, when the bells in the church-steeples were not heard for the sound of drums and trumpets, and their voices were daily hushed by battle-cries and the crackling of fagots? for the best men of the day were burned for heresy.

But at last there came a blessed change. The dark ages, with all their gloom and horror, passed away, and the dawn came on. Henry VII. ascended the throne in 1485, and from that time the people began to enjoy peace and prosperity.

SPENSER now appeared, to clasp hands with Chaucer over the black abyss that parted them, uniting the fourteenth and sixteenth centuries by their sweet minstrelsy. That was the " golden age " of English literature, in the reigns of Queen Elizabeth and James I. The great men of the world, its lights and teachers, come in *clusters*, and it is a well-known fact that a period of peculiar literary glory often succeeds a great national revolution.

Lowell says " the world is only so many great men old," and we find so many men of genius and wisdom in this century, that the " ball or sphere " (as the geographies say) on which we are revolving so swiftly, yet so quietly, must have added several years to its life during those brilliant days when Spenser, Shakespeare, Bacon, Hooker, Raleigh, Coke, and Sidney, were. busy with tongue and pen at court, the bar, and pulpit.

Queen Bess was very fond of *mythology*, which, of course, made it popular with her subjects ; and fables, fiction, strange concerts, and whimsical pageants, were the order of the day. When she passed through a town every display in her honor consulted this fancy. Mercury was her herald, Cupid her special attendant, and the Penates, or household gods, guarded her abode. 'Tis even said that the *cooks* learned to be expert mythologists, and tempted her dainty palate with Ovid's wondrous metamorphoses, done in confectionery, and immense loaves of plum-cake, on which were embossed, in elaborate icing, the destruction of Troy and other historical events. Handsome pages, dressed like wood-nymphs, peeped from every bower to pay their obeisance to their virgin queen, and stupid footmen gambolled over the lawns, arrayed like satyrs.

Though chivalry, as a political or social system, had ceased to exist at this period, though the joust and tournament had lost their ancient splendor, yet the chivalric *character*, "high thoughts seated in a heart of courtesy," still modified the manners of the higher classes.

Such were the influences surrounding EDMUND SPENSER, the greatest poet between Chaucer and Shakespeare. He was born in London, in 1553, and speaks in one of his poems of

"Merry London, my most kindly nurse,
That to me gave this life's first native source."

His parents were poor, though his father belonged to an old and honorable family, and he was obliged to enter

Cambridge as a "sizar," or charity student, the name derived from the *size* of the portion of bread and meat
allowed to them.

Chaucer, you remember, did not develop his best
powers until late in life, resembling

> "The aloe-flower,
> That blooms and blossoms at fourscore;"

but Spenser was a poet from his boyhood—"at home in
the temple of the Muses, as the child Samuel was in the
temple of God"—and, like the young prophet, he conse-
crated his youth with religious exercises to letters and
poesy. His intimate companion at Cambridge was Gabriel
Harvey, who was his firm friend through life, exerting no
small influence upon his fortunes.

After taking his degree, he went to the north of England, whether to visit a friend or in the capacity of a tutor
is not certain. He remained, at any rate, long enough to
fall in love, and be rejected.

Poets have often been compared to the nightingale,
"singing with a thorn in her breast," and Spenser's fame,
like so many others, had its root in a deep sorrow. "A lady,
whom he calls Rosalind, made a plaything of his heart,
and, when tired of her sport, cast it from her. She little
knew the worth of the jewel she had flung away. 'The
sad, mechanic exercise of verse' was balm to the wounded
poet, who poured forth his tender soul in 'The Shepherd's
Calendar.'" The name at once suggests scenes of rural
life, where

> "Every shepherd tells his tale
> Under the hawthorn in the dale,"

or pipes his tender song,

> "In shadow of a green oak-tree,"

marking with red letters those days made bright by the

smiles of his true-love. But instead, we have a series of twelve long and rather prosy eclogues,* named after the twelve months of the year, written in such an antiquated style, that even then an explanation of the obsolete words followed each eclogue, and the shepherds, instead of sighing over the charms of some Chloe or Phyllis, discuss, in a solemn way, the comparative merits of the Protestant and Romish Churches.

He aimed at originality in the form of his work and its language, and the change from the beaten path was no improvement; but, notwithstanding these faults, the "Calendar" was considered an extraordinary production, placing Spenser among the highest poetical names of the day, and attracting for him the notice and patronage of the great.

Through his friend Harvey he had been introduced to Sir Philip Sidney, and, under the grand old oaks in the beautiful park at Penhurst, the ancestral mansion of the Sidneys, Spenser is said to have completed this poem. He seemed to fear the criticism of envious or evil tongues, and dedicated it to his young patron, "Maister Philip Sidney—worthy of all titles, both of learning and chivalry" —under a *feigned name :*

> " Goe, little booke, thyself present,
>   As childe whose parent is unkent,
>   To him that is the president
>   Of noblenesse and chivalrie.
>   And if that *Envie* bark at thee—
>   As sure it will—for succour flee,
>   Under the shadow of his wing."

A life of Spenser, however brief, would be incomplete without some notice of this accomplished friend, the em-

---

* Pastoral poems.

bodiment of so many graces and virtues, whom Elizabeth considered " the jewel of her court "—

" The courtier's, soldier's, scholar's eye, tongue, sword:
The expectancy and rose of the fair state,
The glass of fashion and the mould of form,
The observed of all observers."

Noble, brave, beautiful, good, learned, and generous, his life on earth was far too short to show half his worth, but he will ever be remembered with tenderness, pride, and regret.

He was killed in a skirmish near Zutphen in 1586, while assisting Holland to throw off the Spanish yoke. Riding to the field of battle, he met an old general, the marshal of the camp, too lightly equipped for safety, and with his usual generosity insisted that he should take all his armor but his breastplate. His kindness killed him, for, unprotected himself, he soon received a fatal wound. Overcome with thirst from excessive bleeding, he called for drink. It was brought to him immediately; but the moment he was lifting it to his mouth, a poor soldier was carried by mortally wounded, who fixed his eyes eagerly upon it. Sidney, seeing this, instantly delivered it to him, with these memorable words, "Thy necessity is greater than mine."

His last hours were spent in serious conversation upon the immortality of the soul, in sending kind wishes and keepsakes to his friends, and in the enjoyment of music. All England wore mourning for his death, and volumes of laments and elegies were poured forth in all languages. His whole life was a poem. Lord Brooke, his most intimate friend, said of him: "Though I lived with him, and knew him from a child, yet I never knew him other than a man with such steadiness of mind, lovely and familiar gravity, as carried grace and reverence above greater years. His talk was ever of knowledge, and his very play tended to enrich the mind."

Lord Buckhurst said, "He hath had as great love in this life and as many tears for his death, as ever any had."

Cowper calls him "a warbler of poetic prose," and although he wrote a few pretty sonnets, his literary reputation rests on his prose works; the "Arcadia," a mixture of the heroic and pastoral romance, much admired at that time, and the "Defence of Poesy," a short treatise written in 1581, "to combat certain notions of the Elizabethan Puritans, who would fain, in their well-meant but mistaken zeal, have swept away the brightest blossoms of our literature, along with pictures, statues, holidays, wedding-rings, and other pleasant things."

I will give a short extract from the "Defence of Poesy:"

"Now therein—(that is to say, the power of at once teaching and enticing to do well)—now therein, of all sciences—I speak still of human and according to human conceit—is our poet the monarch. For he doth not only show the way, but giveth so sweet a prospect into the way, as will entice any man to enter into it. Nay, he doth, as if your journey should lie through a fair vineyard, at the very first give you a cluster of grapes, that, full of that taste, you may long to pass further. He beginneth not with obscure definitions, which must blur the margent with interpretations, and load the memory with doubtfulness; but he cometh to you with words set in delightful proportion, either accompanied with, or prepared for, the well-enchanting skill of music; and with a tale, forsooth, he cometh unto you with a tale which holdeth children from play, and old men from the chimney-corner; and pretending no more, doth intend the winning of the mind from wickedness to virtue, even as the child is often brought to take most wholesome things, by hiding them in such other as have a pleasant taste. For even those hard-hearted evil men, who think virtue a school name, and know no other good but *indulgere genio,* and therefore despise the austere admonitions of the philosopher, and feel not the inward reason they stand upon, yet will be content to be delighted; which is all the good-fellow poet seems to promise; and so steal to see the form of goodness—which, seen, they cannot but love ere themselves be aware, as if they had taken a medicine of cherries. By these, therefore, examples and reasons, I think it may be manifest that the poet, with that same hand of delight, doth draw the mind more effectually than any other art doth. And so a conclusion not unfitly ensues, that as virtue is the most excellent resting-place for all worldly learning to make an end of, so poetry, being the most familiar to teach it, and most princely to move toward it, in the most excellent work is the most excellent workman."

But to return to Spenser. Sidney urged him to try something higher and better than this pastoral, but ten years passed before his great work, the "Faërie Queene," appeared. In 1582 he received a grant of land in Ireland from the queen, having previously spent two years there as secretary to Lord Grey; but this was no great gift, as by the conditions he was obliged to *live* on it, which really banished him from England. Neither Queen Bess, nor her treasurer, Lord Burleigh, were ever very generous in their treatment of this poet, of whom they should have been so proud. Spenser had in some way given offence to Burleigh, and his best friends were of the opposite party, so his powerful influence was constantly against him. The queen once promised Spenser one hundred pounds for a poem, but when it was done Burleigh said "that sum was beyond all reason." "Give him reason then," said her majesty. But the ill-used bard received just nothing at all, as this stanza will show:

> "It pleased your grace, upon a time,
>   To grant me reason, for my ryme,
>   But from that time until this season
>   I've heard of neither ryme nor reason."

He grew nervous and sad over this lack of kindness, and in one of his poems, called "Mother Hubbard's Tale," complains of the miseries of a courtier's life:

> "Full little knowest thou, that hast not tride,
>   What hell it is, in sueing long to bide;
>   To lose good days, that might be better spent;
>   To waste long nights in pensive discontent;
>   To speed to-day, to be put back to-morrow;
>   To feed on hope, to pine with feare and sorrow;
>   To have thy Prince's grace, yet want her Peeres;
>   To have thy asking, yet waite manie yeares;
>   To fret thy soul with crosses and with cares;
>   To eate thy heart through comfortlesse dispaires;
>   To fawn, to crouche, to waite, to ride, to ronne,
>   To spend, to give, to want, to be undone."

Sir Walter Raleigh, who you remember was so polite or politic as to throw his rich plush cloak over a muddy spot for the queen to pass over (by which he gained many good suits), visited Spenser at Kilcolman Castle, in the summer of 1589. Charmed by his rhymes, he persuaded him to go with him to England, and soon the first three books of the "Faerie Queene" saw the light, the noblest allegorical poem in our language. Every one was delighted with what he modestly calls "a simple song." It is said that Spenser sent to Sidney the ninth canto of his poem. On reading a part of the allegory of despair, he ordered his steward to give the writer fifty pounds; as he read further he doubled it; and with another stanza he added another fifty pounds, and bade the messenger depart, lest his gifts should exhaust his treasury. The queen, to whom he had dedicated his work, rewarded him with an annuity of fifty pounds.

I hardly know how to give a clear idea of the poem in a few words. It is a long fable, full of hidden meaning, and the scene is laid in an imaginary land of chivalry. His purpose was "to fashion a gentleman or noble person in vertuous and gentle discipline." Each book of the poem is allegorical of some virtue, such as temperance, friendship, courtesy; each defended by its own knight. We read of brave knights, captive ladies, guarded by dragons, besieged castles, witches, enchanters, and fairies. It is a " dark conceit," as the poet says; and is not read with great interest now, as we do not care much for the perfect knights and fair damsels of so long ago. We do not read it with pleasure, because it is not natural, it is not real life, and he might have chosen a better theme. Spenser's imagination was wonderful, and as a descriptive poet he has never been excelled.

His style was vivid, earnest, clear, but without one bit of humor; he failed, when he tried to be amusing. "We look in vain in the 'Faerie Queen' for flashes of wit and humor, for profound observations on life and manners, for the varied lights and shades of character, or the pungent flavor of satire. Nor has he that vivid energy of passion which concentrates a world of meaning into a few burning words, and penetrates to the heart's core with the quick, irresistible energy of lightning. His poetry is a pure creation of the *fancy*. He transports us into an ideal world, in which shapes of perfect beauty and grace are contrasted with forms of hideous or loathsome deformity. We walk upon a new earth and beneath a new heaven, where the light that shines is a 'light that never was on sea or land.'"

His genius was "pictorial." Campbell calls him the "*Rubens*" of English poetry. I will quote a little from this poem, that you may have a better idea of his style.

In describing Una, a beautiful maiden, he says:

> " Her angel's face,
> As the great eye of heaven shined bright
> And made sunshine in the shady place,
> Did never mortall eye, beholde such heavenly grace ? "

He uses a fine metaphor to depict fear:

> " And troubled blood, through his pale face was seen,
> To come and goe with tidings from the heart,
> As it a running messenger had been."

His description of repose is also beautiful:

> " Sleepe after toyle, port after stormy seas,
> Ease after pain, death after life, doth greatly please."

Spenser sometimes describes a landscape which might adorn Paradise itself:

> " It was a chosen spot of fertile land,
> Emongst wide waves sett a little nest,
> As if it had by nature's cunning hand
> Been choycely pickt out from all the rest,
> And laid forth for ensample of the best.
> No dainty flowre or herb that growes on ground ;
> No arborett with painted blossomes drest,
> And smelling sweete, but there it might be found,
> To bud out fair and her sweet smels throwe all arounde ;
> No tree, whose branches did not bravely spring,
> No branch, whereon a fine bird did not bravely sit,
> No bird but did her shrill notes bravely sing,
> No song, but did contain a lovely ditt,
> Trees, branches, birds and songs, were framed fitt
> For to allure fraile mind to careless ease."

Two stanzas on the ministry of angels are too beautiful to be omitted :

> " And is there care in heaven ?   And is there love
> In heavenly spirits to these creatures bace,
> That may compassion of their evils move ?
> There is : else much more wretched were the case
> Of men then beasts : But O ! th' exceeding grace
> Of Highest God that loves his creatures so,

And all his workes with mercy doth embrace,
That blessed Angels he sends to and fro,
To serve to wicked man, to serve his wicked foe!

"How oft do they their silver bowers leave
To come to succour us that succour want!
How oft do they with golden pineons cleare
The flitting skyes, like flying pursuivant,
Against fowle feendes to ayd us militant!
They for us fight, they watch and dewly ward,
And their bright squadrons round about us plant;
And all for love and nothing for reward:
O, why should Hevenly God to men have such regard!"

Spenser was not merely a great poet, but a Christian philosopher, who never omitted, in glowing picture or fanciful allegory, the lessons of morality and holy living which, like the hidden meaning in our Saviour's parables, pervade and glorify the whole.

"Great injustice is done to Spenser, when, bewildered with the mazes of his inexhaustible creation, or by the brightness of his exuberant fancy, we see in the 'Faerie Queene' nothing more than a wondrous fairy tale, or a gorgeous pageant of chivalry. Beyond all this, far within it, is an inner life, and that is breathed into it from the *Bible*. It is the great sacred poem of English literature."

"I dare be known to think," said Milton (addressing the Parliament of England), "our sage and serious Spenser a better teacher than Scotus or Aquinas." John Wesley, in giving directions for the clerical studies of his Methodist disciples, advised them to combine with the study of the Hebrew Bible and the Greek Testament the reading of the "Faerie Queene." And Keble, the poet of the "Christian Year," described this poem as "a continued, deliberate endeavor to enlist the restless intellect and chivalrous feeling of an inquiring and romantic age on the side of goodness and faith, of purity and justice." It is written in a peculiar versification, which Spenser first used, and which has since been styled the "Spenserian stanza." He added a *ninth* line to the "ottava rima," or eight-lined Italian stanza, a measure full of music and rhythm, in that flowing language, but very difficult to write with pleasant effect in English.

But Spenser has wielded this complicated instrument with such consummate mastery and grace, that the rich, abundant melody almost oppresses the ear with its overwhelming sweetness. Like the soft undulation of a tropic sea, it bears us onward dreamily, with easy swell and falls, by wizard islands of sunshine and of rest, by bright phantom-peopled realms, and old enchanted cities.

We will now return to his private life. He married at about the same period of life as Chaucer—forty-one or two. His wife was the fair "Elizabeth" to whom he addressed one hundred sonnets, rather too artificial to be pleasing, and for whom his most melodious notes were sung in his "Epithalamion," "the sweetest marriage-song our language boasts." Let me give you her picture:

> " Loe! where she comes along with portly pace,
>   Like Phœbe, from her chamber of the East,
>   Arysing forth to run her mighty race,
>   Clad all in white that seems a virgin best,
>   So well it her beseemes, that you might weene
>   Some angell she had beene.
>   Her long loose yellow locks, like golden wyre,
>   Sprinckled with perles and perling flowers atweene,
>   Doe like a golden mantle her attyre,
>   And being crowned with a garland greene,
>   Seeme like some mayden queene.
>   Her modest eyes abashed to behold
>   So many gazers as on her do stare
>   Upon the lowly ground affixed are.
>   Ne dare lift up her countenance too bold,
>   But blush to hear her prayses sung so loud,
>   So farre from being proud.

Nathless doe ye still loud her prayses sing,
That all the woods may answer, and your echo sing.

Behold, whiles she before the altar stands,
Hearing the holy priest that to her speaks,
And blesseth her with his *happy hands*,
How the red roses flush up in her cheeks,
And the pure snows, with goodly vermeill staine
Like crimson dyde in grayne;
That even the angels, which continually
About the sacred altar doe remaine,
Forget their service, and about her fly,
Oft peeping in her face, that seems more fayre
The more they on it stare.
But her sad eyes still fastened on the ground,
Are governed with goodly modesty,
That suffers not one look to glaunce awry,
Which may let in a little thought unsound.
Why blush ye, Love, to give to me your hand?
The pledge of all our band—
Sing ye sweet angels, Alleluya sing!
That all the woods may answer and your echo ring!"

The next few years were full of happiness, in his Irish castle, now made bright by the love of wife and children. It was a beautiful home by the shaded banks of the river Mulla. "Soft woodland and savage hill, shadowy river-glade and rolling plough-land, were all there to gladden the poet's heart with their changeful beauty, and tinge his verse with their glowing colors."

But alas! how soon the dark clouds of sorrow and death swept over this lovely scene! In 1598 he was driven from his home by the Irish rebellion, and, his castle being burned by the mob, one of his children perished in the flames.

Crushed by grief and poverty, he died soon after in London at the early age of forty-five, on the 16th of January, 1599. He was buried by the side of Chaucer, with great pomp, in Westminster Abbey. His pall was borne by poets, and mournful elegies, with the pens that wrote them, were thrown into his grave.

Lowell says, "The rare nature of Spenser was, like a Venice glass, meant only to mantle with the wine of sunniest poesy. The first drop of poisonous sorrow shattered him."

In character he was gentle, sensitive, affectionate, and *good* as well as *great*, one of the few whose life needs no apology.

> "More sweet than odors caught by him who sails,
>   Near spicy shores of Araby the blest,
> A thousand times more exquisitely sweet
>   The freight of holy feeling which we meet
>   In thoughtful moments, wafted on the gales
>   From fields where good men walk,
>   And bowers wherein they rest."

DESTRUCTION OF SPENSER'S CASTLE.

SHAKESPEARE.

"In Stratford-upon-Avon,
  Where the silent waters flow,
  The immortal drama woke from sleep,
  Three hundred years ago."

You remember that before Spenser appeared, the country was disturbed with civil wars; the times were out of joint, and all was darkness and ignorance. But with time came light, and the age of Queen Elizabeth, made famous by its many great men, is considered the most brilliant in English history. High above all other names that adorn this period stands that of SHAKESPEARE, the greatest literary genius the world has ever known.

Very little can be learned with any certainty of this wonderful man—so little, that some have tried to prove that no such person ever lived—and one or two books have been published lately, endeavoring to prove that what are called Shakespeare's plays were really written by Lord Bacon. But we cannot believe this, and although it is indeed strange that few of his contemporaries ever mentioned him, and that he never alluded to any of the events which occurred during his lifetime, we still cling with faith to the few names, dates, traditions, and anecdotes, which may or may not be true, but are all we have to tell us of the personal Shakespeare we love to believe in.

Rev. James Freeman Clarke, in his address at the tercentenary celebration of Shakespeare's birth, shows us how easily critics might do away with the little evidence we have on this subject. He says: "If it should be thought desirable to treat Shakespeare as critics have treated Homer, Moses, and Christ, and deny his existence, they have an excellent opportunity and ample means for their destructive analysis. As they have proved to their satisfaction that the books of Moses are composed of innumerable independent historical fragments, carefully joined together, and so are a *Mosaic* work only in the artistic sense; as they have taken away Homer, and left in his place a company of anonymous ballad-singers, so that we are able to settle the dispute between the seven cities which claimed to be his birthplace by giving them a Homer apiece, and having several Homers left; as these able chemical critics have analyzed the Gospels, reducing them to their elements of legend, myth, and falsehood, with the smallest residuum of actual history, so much more easily can they dispose of the historic Shakespeare.

"See, for example, how they might proceed. They might say, How can Shakespeare have been a real per-

son, when his very name is spelled at least in two different
ways in manuscripts professing to be his own autograph,
and when it is found in the manuscripts of the period
spelled in every form, and with every combination of letters
which express its sound or the semblance thereof? One
writer of his time calls him *Shake-scene*, showing plainly
the mythical origin of the word.

"He is said to have married, at eighteen, a woman of
twenty-six, which is not likely, and her name also has a
mythical character—'Anne Hathaway'—and was probably derived from a Shakespeare song, addressed to a lady
named Anne, the first line of which is—

'Anne hath a way, Anne hath a way.'

"If he were a living person, living in London in the
midst of writers, poets, actors, and eminent men, is it
credible that no allusion should be made to him by most
of them? He was contemporary with Sir Walter Raleigh,
Edmund Spenser, Lord Bacon, Coke, Burleigh, Hooker,
Queen Elizabeth, Henry IV. of France, Montaigne, Tasso,
Cervantes, Galileo, Grotius, and not one of these, though so
many of them were voluminous writers, refers to any such
person, and no allusion to any of them appears in all his
plays. He is referred to, to be sure, with excessive admiration by the group of play-writers, among whom he is supposed to move, but as there is not in all his works the
least allusion in return to any of them, we may presume
that the name Shakespeare was a sort of *nom de plume* to
which were referred all *anonymous* plays.

"If such a man existed, why did not others out of this
circle say something about his circumstances and life?
Milton was eight years old when Shakespeare died, and
might have seen him, as he took pains to go and see
Galileo, who was born in the same year with Shakespeare.
Oliver Cromwell was seventeen years old when Shake-

3

speare died; Descartes twenty years old; Rubens, the artist, thirty-nine years old. None of them have heard of him, though Rubens resided in England, and painted numerous portraits there.

"The critic might add that there is something quite suspicious in his being said to have been born and to have died on the same day of the month—April 23d—and in the fact that Cervantes was said to have died on the same day as Shakespeare, and Michael Angelo in the same year. The year of his birth, he might add, seems to have some mythical significance, since Calvin is said to have died, and Galileo to have been born, each in 1564.

"Many great events occurred in his supposed lifetime, to none of which he has alluded, as the battle of Lepanto, the Bartholomew massacre, the defeat of the Spanish armada, the first circumnavigation of the world, the gunpowder plot, the deliverance of Holland from Spain, the invention of the telescope, and the discovery thereby of Jupiter's satellites. In an era of the great controversy between the Roman and Protestant religions, no one can tell from his works whether he was Catholic or Protestant. Unlike Dante, Milton, and Goethe, he left no trace on the political or even social life of his time."

I have quoted thus at length that you may gain, in a general way, some idea of the age, its great men and great events, and also see how plausible arguments can be brought to bear on the wrong side of any subject.

Whately reasons in this fallacious way (merely for the sake of the argument), and makes it very evident that such a man as Napoleon never existed; while Froude defends the character of Henry VIII. in good earnest, making him a high-toned patriot, a noble monarch, an exemplary father and husband, instead of the bloody tyrant, the modern Blue-beard, that he has appeared to our prejudiced minds, and De Quincey, going further yet, honestly tries to prove that *Judas Iscariot* was a well-meaning man, a loyal, though mistaken, subject of his Divine Master. But, in spite of all this eloquent logic, the name of Judas Iscariot will still be the blackest upon the page of human history; Henry VIII. will still be branded as the bad husband, the pseudo-Protestant; Napoleon will still be the hero of Marengo and Austerlitz, and, with due deference to Miss Bacon and Judge Holmes, every one will still prefer to believe that Shakespeare was *himself*, and not somebody else.

He was born at Stratford-upon-Avon on the 23d of April, 1564, the oldest of six children. It has been discovered that his father's name was John, and that he was either a glover, a farmer, a butcher, or a dealer in wool! How little thought that rustic sire, whose business is such a matter of doubt, as he gazed upon his baby-boy,

"Mewling and puking in his mother's arms,"

that devotees from every clime, through every age, would make pilgrimages, as to a sacred shrine, to that homely chamber where "the sweet bard of Avon" first saw the light! Of his mother we only know that her name was Mary Arden, and that she possessed, when married, a pretty little fortune, which soon disappeared.

Rowe, Shakespeare's first biographer, says: "His family, as appears by the register and public writings relating to the town, were of good figure and fashion there, and are mentioned as gentlemen."

His father, up to the year 1574, was a man of considerable estate and position. But in 1578 he had by some misfortune become so poor that he was not obliged to pay taxes, and William, after the age of fourteen, was obliged to earn his own bread. We are told that he attended the grammar-school in his native town, and, as usual, there are various stories of his rank there. But alas! we know nothing certainly. No merit-roll was kept, no record of his jokes and frolics.

Equally various and unsatisfactory are the stories of the way in which the next few years were employed. One author says, "He understood Latin pretty well, for he had been in his younger days a schoolmaster in the country." Another represents him as assisting his father in slaughtering animals, and says that when William killed a calf he would do it in a high style,. and make a speech. But I do not believe the young poet ever wasted any eloquence in an elegy on a dying calf.

Some wise critics think that his dramas furnish abundant proof that he was a lawyer's clerk. But if we judge from this, we may as well say that he pursued all the learned professions, besides working occasionally at every other occupation in life. Married at the early age of eighteen, he could have had but little time to devote to learning or labor.

He is said to have been driven from his home, by a prosecution for deer-stealing, by Sir Thomas Lacy, but his friends deny the charge. One writer proves, first, that the offence was too mild to compel flight; second, if he did steal the deer, it was not a moral offence; and third, *Lacy never kept deer !* This is too much like the famous case of the borrowed iron kettle, which was found broken when returned. The defendant's counsel maintained, first, that the kettle was cracked when it was borrowed; second, that it was used with the greatest care; third, that he never had the kettle !

The early history of Shakespeare reveals a rollicking, frolicking, passionate, and headstrong boy, and the morals of the people among whom he was brought up did not tend to his sobriety. Bedford, a neighboring village, was famed for its beer. The people of the surrounding towns were divided into classes, known as topers and sippers, and used to challenge each other to drinking-bouts. Shakespeare was at the head of the Stratford party, and the crab-tree underneath which the tired revellers bivouacked for the night, on their return from their tipsy frolics, was for a long time after known as "Shakespeare's Tree."

At the age of twenty or twenty-three he went to London. Some say that, on his arrival in that great city, he held gentlemen's horses at the door of the theatre for a small fee; others, that he filled the lowest place among the actors, being merely the call-boy or prompter's attendant. We hear of him as an actor in 1589, and, soon after, he commenced writing, remodelling old dramas. The success of his plays was immediate and great, filling the theatres to overflowing.

In England, at this time, the drama took the place now filled by the newspaper and novel, or, as Emerson says, it was "ballad, epic, newspaper, caucus, lecture, punch, and library, at the same time." The land swarmed with strolling players, ordinary carts carrying stage and actors about the country. There were *fourteen* theatres in and near London. The top was open to sun and rain, and the people sat on benches. There was but little scenery, but placards would be hung up on which were written, "A Castle," "A Country House," "A Temple," and the audience were obliged to *imagine* these objects.

His talent as an actor was not remarkable; the ghost in "Hamlet" and Adam in "As You Like It" were his favorite parts. "But his magic pen has taught us almost to forget that he ever was an actor, nor can we, without a violent stretch of fancy, realize our greatest poet stalking slowly with whitened cheeks across the boards, or tottering in old-fashioned livery through a rudely-painted forest of Arden."

He also owned shares in two theatres, and was constantly adapting and altering old plays, and writing new ones. He soon became known, and gained wealth and troops of friends. The wits of that day used to meet at some public house to enjoy each other's company, and drink wine and ale. Ben Jonson and Shakespeare had many brilliant word-combats, which set the table in a roar.

The famous " Mermaid Tavern " was the favorite resort of Shakespeare, Jonson, Beaumont, and Fletcher, and other great spirits of the time. Beaumont speaks of these merry meetings in a sonnet to Jonson:

> " What things have we seen
> Done at the Mermaid! heard words that have been
> So nimble, and so full of subtle flame,
> As if they every one from whence they came,
> Had meant to put his whole soul in a jest,
> And had resolved to live a fool the rest
> Of his dull life."

Jonson, who appreciated Shakespeare both as friend and antagonist, said of him,

> " He was not for an age, but for all time."

In writing for the stage, he borrowed in all directions, using freely whatever suited his purpose. For instance, Malone has computed that out of 6,043 lines in Henry VI., only 1,899 are entirely his own.

But (to quote from Emerson's essay) " Shakespeare knew that *tradition* supplies a better fable than any invention can. If he lost any credit of design, he augmented his resources; and at that day our petulant demand for originality was not so much pressed. There was no literature for the million. The universal reading, the cheap press, were unknown. A great poet, who appears in illiterate times, absorbs into his sphere all the light which is anywhere radiating. Every intellectual jewel, every flower of sentiment, it is his fine office to bring to his people; and he comes to value his memory equally withh is invention. He is therefore little solicitous whence his thoughts have been derived; whether through translation, whether through tradition, whether by travel in distant countries, whether by inspiration; from whatever source, they are equally welcome to his uncritical audience. Nay, he borrows very near home. Often men say wise things as well as he; only they say a good many foolish things, and do not know when they have spoken wisely. He knows the sparkle of the true stone, and puts it in high place wherever he finds it."

You may like to see a few stanzas from the old ballad where Shakespeare undoubtedly found the story on which he built his great drama of "The Merchant of Venice." It is called

"GERNUTUS, THE JEW OF VENICE.

" The bloudie Jew now ready is
    With whetted blade in hand,
To spoyle the bloud of innocent,
    By forfeit of his bond.

" And as he was about to strike,
    In him, the deadly blow;
' Stay,' quoth the Judge, ' thy crueltie,
    I charge thee to do so.

" 'Sith needs thou will thy forfeit have,
    Which is of flesh a pound;
See that thou shed no drop of bloud,
    Nor yet the man confound.

" ' For if thou do, like murderer
    Thou here shalt hanged be;
Likewise of flesh see that thou cut
    No more than 'longs to thee.

" ' For if thou take either more or lesse
    To the value of a mite,
Thou shalt be hanged presently,
    As is both law and right.'

" At the last he doth demand
  But for to have his owne :
' No,' quoth the judge, ' doe as you list,
  Thy judgement shall be showne.

" ' Either take your pound of flesh,' quoth he,
  ' Or cancell me your bond.'
' Cruell judge,' then quoth the Jew,
  ' That doth against me stand ! '

" And so with griping, grieved mind
  He biddeth them farewell :
Then all the people praysed the Lord,
  That ever this heard tell.

" Good people, that doe heare this song,
  For trueth I dare well say,
That many a wretch as ill as hee
  Doth live now at this day,

" That seeketh nothing but the spoyle
  Of many a wealthy man,
And for to trap the innocent,
  Deviseth what they can.

" From whome the Lord deliver me,
  And every Christian too,
And send to them like sentence eke,
  That meaneth so to do."

No wonder that his brother actors were jealous and envious of the man who had the genius to transform this old ballad of thirty verses into the " Merchant of Venice," and whose plays were " most singularly liked " by Queen Elizabeth. The complaint of one of them has been preserved. He said, " There is an upstart crow, beautified with our feathers, that, with his tiger's heart wrapt in a player's hide, supposes he is as well able to bombast out a blank verse as the best of you ; and, being an absolute *Johannes Factotum*, is, in his own conceit, the only *Shake-scene* in a country ! "

While Shakespeare was thus living in London, charming the public, enraging his rivals, and astonishing all, his family remained quietly at Stratford, in the old home with his parents.

His marriage does not seem to have been a happy one. Mistress Anne probably *had-a-way* that was neither soothing nor agreeable to the poet, who used to run away from his gay and busy life for a few days each summer to pet his favorite child Susanna, and have a romp with the twins, Hamnet and Judith. His son died at the age of twelve, and in the next year, 1597, he purchased the finest house and grounds in the town, called New Place, and fitted them up handsomely, that he might have a comfortable home to which he could retire when weary of the excitements of a city. It was in this garden he planted the mulberry-tree of which Garrick has sung so enthusiastically :

> "Behold this fair goblet! 'Twas carved from the tree,
> Which, O my sweet Shakespeare, was planted by thee!
> As a relic I kiss it, and bow at thy shrine,
> What comes from thy hand must be ever divine.
> All shall yield to the mulberry-tree;
>   Bend to thee
>   Blest mulberry!
>   Matchless was he
>   Who planted thee,
> And thou like him, immortal shalt be.

> "The oak is held royal, is Britain's great boast,
> Preserved once our king, and will always our coast;
> But of fir we make ships, we have thousands that fight,
> While one, only one, like our Shakespeare can write.

> "Then each take a relic of this hallowed tree;
> From folly and fashion a charm let it be;
> Fill, fill to the planter the cup to the brim—
> To honor the country, do honor to *him*."

Irving tells us, in his own delightful style, of the

various relics he found at the birthplace of Shakespeare; "There was the shattered stock of the very matchlock with which Shakespeare shot the deer, on his poaching exploits. There, too, was his tobacco-box; which proves that he was a rival smoker of Sir Walter Raleigh; the sword also with which he played Hamlet; and the identical lantern with which Friar Lawrence discovered Romeo and Juliet at the tomb! There was an ample supply also of Shakespeare's mulberry-tree, which seems to have as extraordinary powers of self-multiplication as the wood of the true cross; of which there is enough extant to build a ship-of-the-line. .

"The most favorite object of curiosity, however, is Shakespeare's chair. It stands in the chimney-nook of a small gloomy chamber, just behind what was his father's shop. Here he may many a time have sat when a boy, watching the slowly-revolving spit with all the longing of an urchin; or of an evening, listening to the cronies and gossips of Stratford, dealing forth churchyard tales and legendary anecdotes of the troublesome times of England. In this chair it is the custom of every one that visits the house to sit; whether this be done with the hope of imbibing any of the inspirations of the bard, I am at a loss to say, I merely mention the fact; and mine hostess privately assured me, that though built of solid oak, such was the fervent zeal of devotees, that the chair had to be new-bottomed at least once in three years. It is worthy of notice also, in the history of this extraordinary chair, that it partakes something of the volatile nature of the Santa Casa of Loretto, or the flying chair of the Arabian enchanter; for, although sold some few years since to a northern princess, yet, strange to tell, it has found its way back again to the old chimney corner."

An old minister, who afterward lived at "New Place," actually *cut down* that "blest mulberry!" because it attracted so many visitors. I wonder if Garrick's ghost did not haunt him after that act of vandalism!

The year 1612 is given as the date of Shakespeare's return to his Stratford home. Perhaps failing health led him to seek repose, for he lived only a few years after the change, having died on the 23d of April, 1616, his fifty-second birthday. He was buried in Stratford church, and his grave was at first marked by a plain stone, with an inscription, said to be written by himself. Here is a fac-simile of the inscription :

> " GOOD FREND FOR IESVS SAKE FORBEARE,
> TO DIGG THE DVST ENCLOASED HEARE :
> BLESE BE Y .MAN Y SPARES THES STONES,
> AND CVRST BE HE Y MOVES MY BONES."

This singular epitaph has prevented his remains from being placed in Westminster Abbey, and reveals, it is thought, his belief in the resurrection of the body.

Some unknown artist executed a statue of the poet, sitting beneath an arch, with a desk before him, and a pen in his hand. This was colored to the life, eyes light hazel; hair and beard of an auburn tinge, with a scarlet doublet and black gown. All the busts of Shakespeare are said to be taken from this.

In his will, written a short time before his death, we find a careful, loving remembrance of many of his old comrades, to each of whom he gave some token of his regard, generally a ring. But to his wife there was nothing left but the "second best bed, with the hangings"! Poor Anne! termagant and virago though she may have been, one cannot help pitying a woman handed down to immortality in that fashion. She would certainly have been "more honored in the breach than the observance."

You notice that one of the pictures illustrating this sketch represents the great dramatist reading one of his plays to Elizabeth. This is not an historic *fact*, but one of those traditions that have been created by later writers to embellish his life. Yet he was undoubtedly popular with Elizabeth and James, who attended the theatre where his plays were acted. Some writer says, that Queen Elizabeth was so well pleased with the admirable character of Falstaff in the two parts of "Henry IV." that she commanded him to continue it for one play more, and to show him *in love*. This is said to be the occasion of his writing the "Merry Wives of Windsor," but there is no proof of this.

We *are* certain, however, that Queen Bess, true to her sex, was not averse to receiving a graceful compliment, and, among her wily, flatterering train of courtiers, there was not one who could compete successfully in this respect with the once obscure playwright, who, by the might of his unaided genius, eclipsed them all. As a proof of this, read Cranmer's prophecy at the christening of the infant Elizabeth, in "King Henry VIII.:"

> "Let me speak, sir,
> For Heaven now bids me; and the words I utter
> Let none think flattery, for they'll find them truth.
> This royal infant (Heaven still move about her!)
> Though in her cradle, yet now promises
> Upon this land a thousand thousand blessings,
> Which time shall bring to ripeness. She shall be
> (But few now living can behold that goodness)
> A pattern to all princes living with her,
> And all that shall succeed: Sheba was never
> More covetous of wisdom, and fair virtue,
> Than this pure soul shall be; all princely graces
> That mould up such a mighty piece as this is,
> With all the virtues that attend the good,
> Shall still be doubled on her; truth shall nurse her;
> Holy and heavenly thoughts still counsel her:
> She shall be loved and feared: Her own shall bless her;
> Her foes shake like a field of beaten corn,

And hang their heads with sorrow; good grows with her;
In her days, every man shall eat in safety
Under his own vine, what he plants; and sing
The merry songs of peace to all his neighbors;
God shall be truly known; and those about her
From her shall read the perfect ways of honor,
And by those claim their greatness, not by blood.

  .   .   .   .

She shall be, to the happiness of England,
An aged princess; many days shall see her,
And yet no day without a deed to crown it.
Would I had known no more! but she must die;
She must; the saints must have her—yet a virgin;
A most unspotted lily shall she pass
To the ground, and all the world shall mourn her."

Richard Grant White, the most thorough Shakesperian scholar and critic in this country, tells us that he has found but ONE passage in praise of woman, in the whole of Shakespeare's writings, and this he calls "cold and conceitish." You will find the passage in "Love's Labor's Lost:"

" From women's eyes this doctrine I derive,
   They sparkle still, the right Promethean fire;
   They are the books, the arts, the academies
   That show, contain, and nourish all the world."

Praises of particular women are numerous, but not of the sex; and, on the other hand, there is no lack of sharp censure. Yet Shakespeare's women are at once the noblest, loveliest, and truest to nature, that have ever been described. This incongruity is owing partly to the influence which his unhappy marriage had upon his mind, and partly to the state of society at the time. He never indulged in the impossible, and judged of women as they were judged by the world in his day.

Henry Giles says: "Shakespeare's women are no fictions, no coinage of a heated brain, drunk with the fumes of réverie, when the realities of society are lost in the loneliness of woods, or the realities of day forgotten in the fantasies of midnight. They are no such attenuated illusions as are thus created—mixture of sunshine and vapor, shapes of mist and moonlight—that play for a moment on the feelings, gleam dimly across the imagination, then leave no trace on the memory or affections. Shakespeare's women are drawn from *life*—drawn as nature makes them in substance, soul, and form. Each has the individualism of reality—the distinctness of personal existence."

Freeman Clarke says that "this creative, *unifying* power of imagination also causes Shakespeare's characters to differ from those of all other writers. *His* unfold from a living centre; *theirs* are moulded from without. His *grow* like a plant from its seed; theirs are carved like a statue from a block of marble. Therefore, Shakespeare's characters are like so many real human beings added to mankind. We refer to them as illustrations of human nature, as examples of human conduct, just as we should to real beings. It is not so with the creations of any other writer. Take the characters of Scott, of Schiller, of Goethe; they are not quite persons. They are abstractions; they owe something to costume, to circumstances. Take an everyday man, and educate him in the middle ages as a knight, and you have Ivanhoe; take the same man, and let him be brought up in Scotland, in the days of John Knox, and you have Halbert Glendinning. In all Goethe's characters you get a glimpse of Goethe himself; in all of Scott's you catch the twinkle of the sheriff's eye. But each one of Shakespeare's men and women is as distinctly, though often as slightly, individualized as the two leaves of neighboring trees—almost the same, yet forever immutably different."

Collier says that "so true and subtile an interpreter of the human soul, in its myriad moods, has never written novel, play, or poem. The door of his fancy opened as if of its own accord, and out trooped such a procession as the world had never seen. The bloodiest crimes and the broadest fun were there; the fresh, silvery laughter of girls and the maniac shriekings of a wretched old man; the stern music of war, and the roar of tavern rioters, mingled with a thousand other various sounds, yet no discordant note was heard in the manifold chorus."

Most great writers show themselves in their works, but Shakespeare has painted all faces, from the king to the beggar; sages and sots; saints and sinners; heroes and villains; yet we cannot say that the poet himself sat for a single picture in the whole gallery.

No other English writer has been so often reviewed, so often quoted, so closely criticised, so highly commended.

Voltaire gives the following account of " Hamlet:" " It is a gross and barbarous piece, which would not be endured by the vilest populace of France or Italy. Hamlet goes crazy in the second act; his mistress goes crazy in the third. The prince kills the father of his mistress, pretending to kill a rat. They dig a grave on the stage. The grave-diggers say abominably gross things, holding the skulls of the dead in their hands. Hamlet replies in answers no less disgusting and silly than theirs. During this time Poland is conquered by one of the actors. Hamlet, his mother, and father-in-law, drink together on the stage; they sing, quarrel, fight, and kill each other. One would think this play the work of the imagination of a *drunken savage*."

Hume and the critics of his school undervalued Shakespeare, because they judged every work by classic rules. They put Nature into a strait-jacket, because, in her wildest freaks, she seemed to them a lunatic, and they put Nature's children into a treadmill, because they forgot the strict laws of art. " But human nature is a vagabond itself, maugre the six thousand years of it, and it is this

vagabond feeling in the blood which draws one so strongly to Shakespeare. That sweet and liberal nature blos-
somed with all human generosities."

And now what can I tell you, in a few lines, of his wonderful plays, except to read, re-read, and study them, beginning, perhaps, with the five tragedies—"Hamlet," "Lear,"
"Othello," "Macbeth," "Romeo and Juliet." His thirty-
seven dramas are classed as tragedies, comedies, and histories. Dr. Johnson says, in his preface to Shakespeare's
works: "He that tries to recommend him by select quotations, will succeed like the pedant in Hierocles, who, when
he offered his house to sale, carried a *brick* in his pocket
as a specimen." So I will not attempt the impossibility
of giving a few extracts to show his style. You should be
as familiar with his characters as with those of your home
friends, and the more you read, the more you will find to
admire. He has furnished maxims for every condition of
life, and seems to have known and felt all joys and sorrows.
He has a good moral influence, for he always makes us love
goodness and hate sin. He stands so far above common
mortals, that, judging Shakespeare, is really judging one's
self, and he who can find no charm in his writings must
be very deficient in both head and heart. The influence
of his plays in England and the United States has ex-
ceeded that of all other writings, except the Bible; and
his words will thrill the hearts of future generations down
to the "last syllable of recorded time."

Hazlitt says: "The characteristic of Chaucer is in-
tensity; of Spenser, remoteness; of Milton, elevation; of
Shakespeare, *every thing*."

Many adjectives and epithets have been used to praise
or describe him—such as "honey-tongued," "gentle," "judicious," "myriad-minded," "pleasant Willy," "Nature's
darling," "Fancy's child;" but, as Whipple says, "these
fond but belittling phrases and pet epithets, which other

authors have condescended to shower upon him, are as little appropriate as would be the patronizing chatter of the planet Venus about the dear darling little *Sun*," and nothing can ennoble the name of Shakespeare.

> " Nothing can cover his high fame but heaven;
> No pyramid set off his memories
> But the eternal substance of his greatness."

Let me give, in closing, a few words from Henry Giles : "Some writers we are willing to associate with an age, to associate with a country; with others we will not do this, and we *cannot*. Let Athens have Aristophanes; but even all Greece shall not keep Homer: we give Calderon to Spain; but every nation owns Cervantes: Dante belongs to Italy; Milton belongs to England; but Shakespeare belongs to *man*."

SHAKESPEARE READING HIS PLAYS TO QUEEN ELIZABETH.

MILTON.

"Thy soul was like a star and dwelt apart;
Thou hadst a voice whose sound was like the sea,
Pure as the naked heavens, majestic, free.
So didst thou travel on life's common way
To cheerful godliness, and yet thy heart
The lowliest duties on thyself did lay."

As Shakespeare was walking down Broad Street, London, to the Mermaid Tavern, where he used to meet his friends and make merry over cups of canary, his attention was attracted by a child of six, seated on a doorway, singing a melody, and upon an old-fashioned instrument stretching his tiny fingers in search of pleasing chords. It was a little Puritan boy, with closely-cropped hair, large lace frill about his neck, and closely-fitting black coat; he who, in after-years, was to sing in sublimer strains—

> " Of man's first disobedience, and the fruit
> Of that forbidden tree, whose mortal taste
> Brought death into the world and all our woe."

If any precise critic should ask how I know that this pretty, sweet-voiced boy was ever seen by Shakespeare, I shall have to confess that the scene is but a picture in my own mind, one of the many things that "might have been."

JOHN MILTON was born in London, December 9, 1608. His father, who had been disinherited for adopting the Protestant faith, was an educated man, with a great deal of musical ability, a "scrivener" by profession, his business being very much like that of the modern attorney. Before the invention of printing, the scriveners were penmen of all kinds of writing, often copying literary manuscripts as well as charters and law papers. Chaucer has an epigram, in which he lampoons his scrivener Adam for doing his work badly. At this time the profession was an honorable one. The general aspect of their "shops " was like the offices of modern lawyers; a chief desk for the master, side desks for the apprentices, pigeonholes and drawers for parchments, and seats for customers. They often lent money at a profitable interest. In.the "Taming of the Shrew," a boy is sent for the scrivener to draw up a marriage settlement :

> " We'll pass the business privately and well.
> Send for your daughter by your servant here;
> My boy shall fetch the scrivener presently."

Like most great men, Milton had a good mother, who was famed for her charity, and his home was a happy one, though sobered by the grave Puritanic piety which was then the order of the day. Music took a high place in his father's plan of education, who was himself "a voluminous composer, equal in science, if not in genius, to the best musicians of his age," and under his skilful tuition Milton became an accomplished organist. "Often, as a child, he must have bent over his father, while composing, or listened to him as he played; often at evening, when two or three musical acquaintances would call, the voices in the Spread-Eagle would suffice for a little household concert." Their house took its name from the family coat-of-arms. In his boyhood he studied at home, with a private tutor, whom he loved very much. At ten years of age he was a poet; at eleven, he was a prodigy in the house, as a writer of verses. A portrait of the child at that time still exists. It represents the youthful poet in a striped jacket and richly-embroidered collar; the auburn hair cut close round the head, and the face sweet, amiable, and serious. How proud and fond his parents were of their bright and handsome boy! I imagine that he was sober, dignified, and earnest, with little love of fun or roguery. He is thought to have described himself in this passage from "Paradise Regained:"

> "When I was a child, no childish play
> To me was pleasing, all my mind was set
> Serious to learn, and know, and then to do
> What might be public good. Myself I thought
> Born to that end, to promote all truth
> And righteous things."

At the early age of twelve he often studied until midnight, and, with the imperfect lights then in use, injured his eyes, whose sight he afterward lost, by overtasking them. His great knowledge of the Bible is due to his father and his Puritan teachers. English authors did not, of course, escape his notice. At fifteen he was admitted to St. Paul's school, there also studying too hard, bringing on frequent headaches and increasing the weakness of his eyes. There was much to tempt a mind, so eager for knowledge, in the works of Chaucer, Spenser, Ben Jonson, and Shakespeare, which graced the booksellers' shops where he rambled, and were eagerly conned by him, little dreaming that his writings would one day be placed with theirs. While at this school he wrote a little poetry, and translated the 114th and 136th Psalms into English verse, in a way that won high praise.

In his seventeenth year he went to Cambridge, where he spent seven years, studying hard as ever, and showing great skill in Latin verses. He was at this time extremely handsome, and was, no doubt, raved about by the young ladies of the town. From his beautiful face and slender, elegant form, he was called "the lady of the college," though, I am sure, there was nothing *unmanly* about him. He says himself that he did not neglect daily practice with the sword, and, when armed with it, as he generally was, he was in the habit of thinking himself quite a match for any one, even though much more robust, and of being perfectly at his ease as to any injury that any one could offer him, "man to man." His complexion was fresh and fair as a girl's, and his dark-gray eyes were full of expression, while his long auburn hair, beautiful and curling, flowed to his ruff on both sides his oval face. It is said that, in a long walk one summer's day, he became so tired and heated that, lying down under a tree to rest, he soon fell asleep. Two ladies, foreigners, happened to pass in a carriage, and, charmed by his lovely appearance, alighted for a nearer view. The younger lady, a beautiful girl, drew a pencil from her pocket, and, writing a few lines, placed them in the hand of the handsome youth, her own dainty fingers trembling with emotion. One of his friends, walking by, saw the adventure, and waking him told him the story. Milton opened the paper, and read with surprise a verse from an Italian poet, which said—

"Ye eyes! ye human stars!
Ye authors of my liveliest pangs!
If thus when *shut* ye wound me,
What must have proved the
Consequence had ye been open?"

He tried long and eagerly to find out his fair admirer, but in vain. He could not be called particularly modest; indeed, his self-esteem amounted almost to vanity. He was not, as some one quaintly observes, "ignorant of his own parts." And he had reason to be a little vain. But a boy in years, he was already familiar with the Latin, French, Spanish, Italian, and Hebrew tongues, and was marvellously learned in many directions, besides being well read in all the current literature of the day. In fact, he proved rather a disagreeable pupil for the "fossil professors" at Christ College. He dared to criticise their time-honored methods of teaching as superficial and hackneyed, and they at first treated him harshly, "as a presumptuous and conceited upstart," but learned in the end to appreciate and admire his genius. Speaking of the young men sent to the colleges for education, he says: "Their honest and ingenuous natures, coming to the university to feed themselves with good and solid learning, are there unfortunately fed with nothing else but the scragged and thorny lectures of monkish and miserable sophistry. They are sent home again with such a scholastic bur in their throats as hath stopped and hindered all true and generous philosophy from entering; cracked their voices forever with metaphysical gaggarisms; hath made them admire a sort of formal outside men, prelatically addicted, whose unchastened and overwrought minds were never yet immuted nor subdued under the law of moral or religious virtue, which two are the greatest and best points of learning."

"The conflict between rotten formalism and scoffing infidelity on one side, and earnest living and sincere devotion on the other, which ere long lighted the flames of civil war throughout Great Britain, seems to have already commenced at the university when Milton entered it." And you see that he was already too frank and fearless in expressing his views to be popular. Before he was of age, he had commenced his career as a *controversialist*.

But his whole time was not given to discussions with the "Dons." Christ's College was one of the largest and most comfortable in the university, with a spacious garden, bowling-green, a beautiful pond, and shady walks, in true academic style. Milton's rooms were on the first floor, looking out on the court, and there he read and studied, with very little regard to the usual course. There, too, he wrote, at the age of twenty-one, his grand hymn on the Nativity. In the garden there still stands, preserved with the greatest care, a mulberry-tree, which he planted in 1633, the year in which he entered. Every spring it puts forth its leaves, in all the vigor of youth, and bears delicious fruit in autumn. Its wide-spreading branches are supported by props, and this precious memento is guarded so reverently that it will no doubt send out its sweet blossoms many years longer.

Milton's father had now retired to a quiet parish, about seventeen miles west of London; and, leaving the university at twenty-four, the young poet passed five years in the country in pleasant repose, studying and composing, with no idea that in the future he was to be a leader in reform and a valiant champion of liberty. One of his biographers has given a pleasant description of his new home: "The little village, containing at that time but few families, was quiet, and very beautiful—one of those sweet old English towns in which we desire to lie down and dream—precisely the nook for a speculative thinker or a poet. It was scatteringly built, the houses playing at hide-and-seek among the trees and intervening foliage, with no continuous streets, but only a great tree in the centre of an open space, where three roads met, and suggested that there might be more habitations about the spot than at first appeared, which suggestion was confirmed on looking down one of the roads by the sight of an old church-tower, ivy-covered, and with a cemetery in front, which you entered between two extremely old yew-trees. Here it was that Milton, together with other members of his family, worshipped regularly for five years, during his residence in the hamlet. One could lie under the elm-trees in the lawn, saunter through the green meadows, by the rippling streamlet, from a rustic bridge watch the lazy mill-wheel, or walk along quiet roads, well hedged, deviate into by-paths leading past farm-yards and orchards, or through rich pastures, where horses, cows, and sheep, were wont to graze—an elysium, indeed, for the weary Londoner—a ' Paradise regained ' for the younger Milton."

Don't you suppose that the steady old farmers about Horton parish thought this pale-faced, serious student, who spent his time in scribbling poems, or reading dull books, never caring to swing a scythe or guide the plough, rather a good-for-nothing fellow ? No doubt they thanked their stars, as they saw him wandering with book in hand through the shady lanes, or sitting with pen and paper under his father's elms, that their boys were hard workers and had no such nonsense in their heads.

Though he says he "spent a complete holiday in turning over the Greek and Latin writers" while at Horton, yet Milton·was far from idle, for it was during the first three years of his life there that he composed five of his finest poems—the " Sonnet to a Nightingale," " Arcadles," " Comus " and " L'Allegro," and " Il Penseroso." These poems are unique, and have no seconds of their kind. If he had done nothing else, he would have been immortal.

It is impossible to do the least justice to them by quoting a few lines here and there; and yet I cannot pass them by without a few extracts. The "Masque of Comus" was suggested by the following facts: The Earl of Bridgewater was spending the summer months in his castle near Horton, and it happened that his two sons and his daughter, the Lady Alice Egerton, were benighted and bewildered in Haywood Forest, where the brothers, seeking a homeward path, left the sister alone awhile, in a tract of country inhabited by boorish peasantry. "Such was all the story, simpler than the ballad of the 'Children in the Wood;' and yet it is transfigured into a poem of a thousand lines—a moral drama, showing the communion of natural and supernatural life, the mysterious society of human beings, and the guardian and tempting spirits hovering round their paths; it teaches, with a poet's teaching, how the spiritual and intellectual nature may be in peril from the charms of worldly pleasure, and how the philosophic faith and the Heaven-assisted virtue are seen at last to triumph. The guardianship of ministering angels—their encampment round the dwellings of the just—is finely announced in the opening lines, spoken by the attendant spirit alighting in the wood when the human footsteps are astray:"

> " Before the starry threshold of Jove's court
> My mansion is, where those immortal shapes
> Of bright aerial spirits live insphered,
> In regions mild, of calm and serene air,
> Above the smoke and stir of this dim spot,
> Which men call earth, and with low-thoughted care,
> Confined and pestered in this pinfold here,
> Strive to keep up a frail and feverish being,
> Unmindful of the crown that Virtue gives
> After this mortal change to her true servants,
> Amongst the enthroned gods on sainted seats.
> Yet some there be, that by due steps aspire

4

> To lay their just hands on that golden key
> That opes the palace of eternity ;
> To such, my errand is, and but for such,
> I would not soil these pure ambrosial weeds
> With the rank vapors of this sin-worn mould."

Here are a few more lines, which are most quoted :

> " He that has light within his own clear breast,
> May sit i' the centre, and enjoy bright day ;
> But he that hides a dark soul and foul thoughts,
> Benighted walks under the mid-day sun ;
> Himself is his own dungeon."

> " So dear to Heaven is saintly Chastity,
> That when a soul is found sincerely so,
> A thousand liveried angels lackey her,
> Driving far off each thing of sin and guilt,
> And in clear dream and solemn vision
> Tell her of things that no gross ear can hear,
> Till oft converse with heavenly habitants,
> Begin to cast a beam on the outward shape,
> The unpolluted temple of the mind,
> And tunes it by degrees to the soul's essence,
> Till all be made immortal."

> " How charming is divine philosophy !
> Not harsh and crabbed, as dull fools suppose,
> But musical as is Apollo's lute,
> And a perpetual feast of nectared sweets,
> Where no crude surfeit reigns."

When the fair maiden is at last secured from the
wicked magic which failed to harm her, the good spirit
which guarded her speeds away, with these words:

> " Now my task is smoothly done,
> I can fly or I can run
> Quickly to the green earth's end
> Where the bowed welkin slow doth bend,
> And from thence can soar as soon
> To the corners of the moon.

> Mortals, that would follow me,
> Love Virtue; she alone is free;
> She can teach ye how to climb;
> Higher than the sphery chime;
> Or if Virtue feeble were,
> Heaven itself would stoop to her."

"L'Allegro" can easily be committed to memory, and is so full of beauty, sunshine, and frolic, and pleasant sights and sounds, that its recitation will prove a good recipe for making a sad heart merry.

Milton had at this time no settled plans for the future. He was designed by his father for the church, but he could not sign the articles and indorse the doctrines of the English Church, which was at this time reviving the horrors of the Inquisition, to punish and silence the free speech of the Dissenters.

"The church," he says, "to whose service, by the intention of my parents and friends, I was destined of a child, and in my own resolutions, till, coming to some maturity of years, and perceiving what tyranny had invaded in the church—that he who would take orders must subscribe *slave*, and take an oath withal, which, unless he took with a conscience that would retch, he must either perjure, or split his faith—I thought it better to prefer a blameless silence before the sacred office of speaking, bought and begun with servitude and forswearing."

He had also some thoughts of studying law, but at last decided that his brother Christopher should be the lawyer of the family, and gave himself up to a "ceaseless round of study and reading," with the purpose of doing what he could with pen and tongue to enrich the literature and improve the morals of his age. He said at this time, that he "cared not how late he came into life, only that he came fit," and "perhaps leave something so written to after-times as they should not willingly let it die."

In 1637 he lost his good mother, a woman of rare
talents and virtues, and, without her saintly presence, the
home at Horton seemed sad and desolate. Very soon
after this great sorrow, he learned of the death of one of
his old college-friends, Edward King, who was drowned
while on his way to Ireland. It was for him that
"Lycidas," that beautiful pastoral elegy, was written:

> "Yet once more, O ye laurels! and once more,
> Ye myrtles brown, with ivy never sere,
> I come to pluck your berries harsh and crude;
> And, with forced fingers rude,
> Shatter your leaves before the mellowing year.
> Bitter constraint, and sad occasion dear,
> Compels me to disturb your season due:
> For Lycidas is dead, dead ere his prime—
> Young Lycidas, and hath not left his peer:
> Who would not sing for Lycidas? he knew
> Himself to sing, and build the lofty rhyme.
> He must not float upon his watery bier
> Unwept, and welter to the parching wind,
> Without the meed of some melodious tear."

Depressed by this twofold affliction, and worn by constant study, Milton now felt a longing for travel, and
determined to go abroad. Leaving his aged father in
the care of his younger brother, who had just been
married, he bade adieu to his friends, and to the quiet
rural scenes where he had passed his happiest years, and
sailed from England in April, 1638. After a brief stay in
Paris, Milton journeyed leisurely through Southern France
to Italy, carrying with him letters of recommendation,
which secured for him the distinguished attention which
he so well deserved. His whole journey was one continued ovation. There is enough in Italy to waken the
most prosaic soul; think, then, of Milton, who was as
familiar with its language as his own, who had learned its
glorious legends by heart, and studied its history from his

boyhood! How he revelled in the treasures of art to be found there! They doubtless affected his style in later years, for the arts depend beautifully upon each other, and, feasting on these rare gems in marble and on the canvas, he gained many subjects. for his pen. The thought of writing an epic poem first came to him while there. The frescoes of Michael Angelo, then fresh in the Sistine Chapel, the milder beauties of Raphael, the marble of Bandinelli, who had executed statues of Adam and Eve, had probably great influence in directing his mind to the study of those early scenes of the creation which he has grouped for immortality in the "Paradise Lost." There is much in Milton that is like Michael Angelo, who was the painter of the Old Testament. The style of both was severe and sublime. Both loved to deal with the *primeval* forms of nature, inanimate and human. At Florence he passed an hour at Galileo's villa, received with cordial kindness by the blind old sage. To use his own words: "There it was that I found and visited the famous Galileo, grown old, a prisoner to the Inquisition, for thinking in astronomy otherwise than as the Franciscan and Dominican licensers thought."

While at Rome, the Cardinal Barbesini gave a magnificent concert in his honor, bringing him into the assembly by his own hand.

He was introduced at Naples to Manso, the Marquis of Villa, the patron and biographer of Tasso, who entertained him most hospitably in his own palace, and declared that he had no fault but that of heresy. When he was leaving, Manso gave him this Latin distich:

> "With mind, mien, temper, face, did FAITH agree,
> Not *Anglic*, but an *Angel*, wouldst thou be."

The struggle in England, between Prelate and Puritan, was but a picket-skirmish compared with the great battle

that was raging fiercely over all Christendom, called the
"Thirty Years' War"—a conflict caused by the same question—the freedom of religious thought for the *people*.

Milton made no secret of his opinions, speaking as
boldly at Rome as elsewhere. He was told that snares
were laid for him in that city, by the English Jesuits, and
hints were thrown out of the Inquisition, with advice not
to return. But this warning made no difference in his fear-
lessness of speech. He says: "I had made this resolution
with myself—not indeed of my own accord—to introduce
in those places conversation about religion; but, if inter-
rogated respecting the faith, then, whatever I should
suffer, to dissemble nothing. To Rome, therefore, I did
return, notwithstanding what I had been told; what I
was, if any one asked, I concealed from no one; if any
one, in the very city of the Pope, attacked the orthodox
religion, I, as before, for a second space of nearly two
months, defended it most freely." He was certainly
treated, as he said, with "singular politeness," for it would
have been dangerous for any other person to have upheld
a different faith from the passionate Italians.

He wished to pursue his travels farther, but duty called
him home. In his own words: "While I was desirous to
cross into Sicily and Greece, the sad news of the civil war
coming from England called me back; for I considered it
disgraceful that, while my fellow-countrymen were fighting at home for *liberty*, I should be travelling at ease for
intellectual purposes."

So he retraced his former route through France, arriving in England early in August, 1639, after an absence of
fifteen months. He was now in the prime of life, the full
bloom of manly beauty and accomplishments; unstained
by the vices and license of the Continent. He concludes
his account of his tour in this way: "I again take God to
witness that, in all those places where so many things are

considered lawful, I lived sound and untouched from all profligacy and vice; having this thought perpetually with me, that, though I might escape the eyes of men, I certainly could not the eyes of *God*."

His father had always supported him most generously, but he felt that he should now do something for himself. He therefore took a handsome house in London, where he received his nephews and a few other pupils, "to teach them both knowledge and virtue." These boys were given hard study and spare diet, but had a great affection for their teacher.

At this time he began his work as a *reformer*. No one can read his writings or study his life, without feeling that his first desire was the *freedom*, and through that, the happiness of his country. There was at this time a contest between Charles I. and his people, the one to extend his power, the other to enlarge their privileges. Milton wished for, worked for, and prayed for, a *republic*. His reading of the Bible taught him to defend the oppressed and assail the oppressor, and he wrote boldly in a way that made him many enemies. He also aided the Puritans in their war against the Established Church, which added to his unpopularity.

His "Treatise on the Reformation" was published in 1641, which abounds in stirring passages and attempts to prove that the prelates of the English Church had ever been the foes of liberty, and "that, though at the beginning they had renounced the *Pope*, yet they had hugged the *Popedom*, and shared the authority among themselves; by their six bloody articles persecuting the Protestants no slacker than the pope would have done."

In his prose writings there are passages of great poetic splendor, and a fiery, fervid spirit breathed through all. Macaulay describes his prose as "a perfect field of cloth of gold, stiff with gorgeous embroidery."

He said himself that in prose he always felt that he
was writing with his *left hand*. He was at times too fierce
and severe, and needed the music of verse to bring out all
that was bright and beautiful in his nature.

But these eloquent sentences do not betray any left-
handed awkwardness:

" How the bright and glorious Reformation, by Divine
power, shone through the black and settled night of ignorance and anti-Christian tyranny; methinks a sovereign
and reviving joy must needs rush into the bosom of him
that reads or hears, and the sweet odor imbue his soul
with the fragrancy of heaven. Then was the sacred Bible
brought out of the dusty corners where profane falsehood
and neglect had thrown it; the schools opened, Divine
and human learning raked out of the embers of forgotten
tongues; princes and cities trooping apace to the new-
erected banner of salvation; the martyrs, with the irresistible might of weakness, shaking the powers of darkness, and scorning the fiery rage of the old red dragon.

"Methinks I see in my mind a noble and puissant nation
rousing herself like a strong man after sleep, and shaking
her invincible locks; methinks I see her as an eagle muing
her mighty youth, and kindling her dazzled eyes at the
full mid-day beam; purging and unscaling her long-abused
sight at the fountain itself of heavenly radiance; while
the whole noise of timorous and flocking birds, with those
also that love the twilight, flutter about, amazed at what
she means, and in their envious gabble would prognosti-
cate a year of sects and schisms."

The "Areopagitica" is Milton's greatest prose work;
its theme, the benefits of a free press.

In his thirty-fifth year he married Mary Powell, the
daughter of a Cavalier, after a very short courtship, and
brought her to London. But the young bride, accustomed
to gay beaux and a house full of people, found her new

life rather irksome. She did not fancy the spare diet and the house filled with pupils, and could not endure the dulness and restraints of a scholar's life. So, in a few weeks after their marriage, she went home on a visit and did not return. Milton sent letters and messengers, but in vain, until at last he refused to call her his wife any more, and, to defend his conduct, published four treatises on the subject of "Divorce." In these he argued in favor of polygamy, as allowed in the Old Testament, and nowhere absolutely forbidden in the New. I wonder that he should wish *additional* vexation, after finding one pretty little woman so unruly; but possibly he saw a chance of happiness with one tractable spouse among the half dozen! At the close of a year his wife came back, and, kneeling in tears at his feet, begged forgiveness, which he at last granted, and they managed to live comfortably together. By her he had three daughters, his only children that lived. He had three wives (not all at one time, however!), the last one surviving him several years.

His eyes grew more and more diseased, and at last came total blindness. His enemies regarded this as a punishment for writing against the king. He bore this great trial with rare fortitude and cheerfulness, as his beautiful sonnet on his own blindness will show:

" When I consider how my light is spent
    Ere half my days, in this dark world and wide,
    And that one talent which is death to hide,
Lodged with me useless, though my soul more bent
To serve therewith my Maker, and present
    My true account, lest He, returning, chide:
    ' Doth God exact day-labor, light denied ? '
I fondly ask : but Patience, to prevent
    That murmur, soon replies, ' God doth not need
Either man's work, or his own gifts ; who best
Bear his mild yoke, they serve him best ; his state

Is kingly; thousands at his bidding speed,
And post o'er land and ocean without rest:
They also serve who only stand and wait."

But though he had lost his sight, he retained that fearless spirit which never trembled before pope or king. It
is said that the Duke of York, in the heyday of his honors
and greatness, went to satisfy a malignant curiosity by
visiting Milton, and asked him if he did not regard the
loss of his sight as a judgment for his writing as he had
done. Milton replied, calmly: "If your highness thinks
calamity is an indication of Heaven's wrath, how do you
account for the fate of the king your father? I have
lost but my eyes—he lost his head."

On the duke's return to court, he said to the king,
"Brother, you are greatly to blame that you don't have
that old rogue, Milton, hanged."

"What!" said the king, "have you seen Milton?"

"Yes," answered the duke, "I have seen him."

"In what condition did you find him?"

"Condition! Why he is old, and very poor."

"Old and poor," said the king—"and *blind*, too?
You are a fool, James, to have him *hanged*—it would be
doing him a service. No; if he is poor, and old, and
blind, he is already miserable enough, in all conscience.
Let him live on."

Milton taught his daughters to pronounce half a dozen
languages, without *understanding the meaning of a word*,
and they read much to him. But, I fear, his home-life was
far from pleasant. He had very little sympathy with his
family. His daughters thought it great drudgery to read
to him, and did not hesitate to say so, and he really suffered in other ways from their ill-treatment. They would
sell his books, and advise the servants to cheat him, and
one of them, when told of her father's intention to marry

again, said, " that was no news, but if she could hear of
his death, that would be something."

I can give you a very minute account of the manner
in which he divided his time during the day:

" In his latter years he retired every night at nine
o'clock, and lay till four in summer, till five in winter;
and, if not disposed then to rise, he had some one to sit at
his bedside and read to him. When he rose he had a
chapter of the Hebrew Bible read for him; and then, with
of course the intervention of breakfast, he studied till
twelve. He then dined, took some exercise for an hour—
generally in a chair, in which he used to swing himself—
and afterward played on the organ or the bass-viol, and
either sang himself or made his wife sing, who, as he said,
had a good voice, but no ear. He then resumed his
studies till six, from which hour till eight he conversed
with those who came to visit him. He finally took a light
supper, smoked a pipe of tobacco, and drank a glass of
water, after which he retired to rest."

His public work was now done; his cause had been
defeated, he had been traduced and persecuted. The
King's power has increased, and he was living in poverty,
desertion, and disgrace. Yet his voice was unchanged

> " To hoarse or mute, though fallen on evil days;
> On evil days though fallen, and evil tongues,
> In darkness, and with danger compassed round,
> And solitude; "—

the noble champion of the people's liberty lost not
" one jot of heart or hope," but forgetting his own wrongs,
losses, and woes, devoted his time and talents to writing
his last and greatest poems. Whipple says: "No one can
fully reverence Milton who has not studied the character
of the age of Charles II., in which his later fortunes were
cast. He was Dryden's contemporary in time, but not his

master or disciple in slavishness. He was under the anathema of power; a republican in days of abject servility; a Christian among men whom it would be charity to call infidels; a man of pure life and high principle, among sensualists and renegades. On nothing external could he lean for support. In his own domain of imagination perhaps the greatest poet that ever lived, he was still doomed to see such pitiful and stupid poetasters as Shadwell and Settle bear away the shining rewards of letters. Well might he declare that he had fallen on evil times! He was among his opposites, a despised and high-souled Puritan poet, surrounded by a horde of desperate and dissolute scribblers."

It is pleasant to know that this sad and blind old man, had the consolation of music left him, and to think of him, as playing the organ at twilight, adding to its rich tones, the music of his own sweet voice.

Very peacefully, at midnight, on the 8th of November, 1674, the great Milton closed his tired, sightless eyes, to open them in the light of heaven. He was buried near his father, in the chancel of St. Giles.

"Over his grave, civil and religious liberty clasp hands; science, poesy, and divine philosophy, strew upon it garlands as immortal as his name; while the muse of history, dipping her pencil in the sunlight, sculptures, through proud tears, the scriptural benediction, 'Well done, good and faithful servant; enter thou into the joy of thy Lord.'"

"Paradise Lost," the great Christian epic of our language, was chanted at first to but few hearers. Indeed, Milton had some difficulty in finding a publisher. The poet Waller said: "The old blind schoolmaster, John Milton, hath published a tedious poem on the fall of man; if its *length* be not considered a merit, it has no other."

It is now acknowledged by all to be one of the sublimest monuments of human genius. Homer, Virgil, Dante, and Milton, are the four great evangelists of the human mind, each being in some measure the type of his age. Homer expresses the mythic epoch; Virgil sings of the State; Dante is the embodiment of mediæval Christianity; Milton, the poet of Protestantism. The "Inferno" and "Paradise Lost" are often compared and contrasted. It is enough for me to say, that, while Dante describes minutely and often repulsively the horrors of the lower world, Milton delights in generalizations. He produces effect often by what he leaves *unsaid*, and merely suggested.

"Paradise Regained," an inferior epic written in the same style, was suggested by the question of a Quaker friend, who, after reading the first, said, "Thou hast said much here of 'Paradise Lost,' but what hast thou to say of 'Paradise Found?'"

I might as well try to give you an idea of the grandeur of Mont Blanc, by showing a few rocks from its base, as to hope to impress you with the sublimity of these epics by a few quotations. No one can read them carefully without being amply repaid.

To those who, in studying an author's life, like to see what were the *outward circumstances* that influenced his character and writings, these remarks of Reed's in regard to Milton may be interesting: "The *first part* of Milton's literary life is full of beautiful reflection of the age that had gone before; his genius is then glowing with tints of glory cast upon it by the *Elizabethan* poetry; the *meridian* of it is in close correspondence with the season of the power of the Parliament and Protector, when Milton stood side by side with *Cromwell;* and the *latter period* of it has that of sublime and solitary contrast with the times of *Charles the Second.* The first was the genial season of youth, studious, pure, and happy; the second was of ma-

ture manhood, strenuous in civil strife, and the dubious
dynasty of the Protectorate; the third was old age darkened, disappointed, but indomitable."

Milton's enemies are now forgotten, or at best remembered like the dim shadows of a dream, while his name
and fame as a poet, scholar, and reformer, will endure
until all kingdoms and republics have passed away.

MILTON'S COTTAGE AT CHALFONT.

John Dryden.

DRYDEN.

" Dryden, in immortal strain,
  Had raised the table-round again,
  But that a ribald king and court
  Bade him toil on, to make them sport;
  Demanded for their niggard pay,
  Fit for their souls, a looser lay;
  The world, defrauded of the high design,
  Profaned the God-given strength, and marred the lofty line."

JOHN DRYDEN, who, after Milton's death, was considered the first poet of his time, was born at the parsonage-house of Oldwinkle, All-Saints, August 9, 1631.

Now I could tell you just what Milton liked best for

breakfast, and how he often sat, with one leg thrown over the arm of his chair, when composing ; but of Dryden's daily life we know but little. He belonged to a respectable Puritan family, and was the eldest of fourteen children ; was fitted for college at Westminster, under Dr. Busby, of "birchen memory," who, for fifty-five years, was at the head of that famous school ; then spent seven years at Cambridge, distinguishing himself in no special way at either place. These meagre facts are all we have to tell of his early days at home, at school, and at college.

His first poem, written when only seventeen, appeared in book form, in 1650, with nearly a hundred other elegies, called forth by the sad death of Lord Hastings, " a young nobleman of great learning, and much beloved," who was a victim of the small-pox on the very eve of his intended marriage.

This juvenile effort was absurd and affected, and showed the young poet had but little heart. He raves about the *pustules*, calling them rose-buds and jewels, and at last exalts them into stars—

> " No comet need foretell his change drew on,
> Whose corpse might seem a constellation,"

apparently forgetting the sorrow of the mourners, in delight at his own fine verses. But poetry was in a low state at this time, and the public taste was " detestable." Alliterations, poor puns, and strained allegories, were considered fine writing ; it was only natural that Dryden should follow the general fashion.

His family and friends were all stanch Puritans, and on his going to London, from the university, he was made secretary to Sir Gilbert Pickering, his kinsman, who was at that time Lord-Chamberlain of the Protector's household. His dress of plain drugget, and his manners, homely and serious, plainly proved his parentage, and the in-

fluences that surrounded him. As Hannay expresses it,
" These sable leading-strings were still perceptible in his
walk." But, with all these, Dryden was not a Puritan at
heart. To be sure, when Cromwell died, he lamented the
event in some heroic stanzas; but only two years after,
when the merry monarch, Charles II., was welcomed back
to London, after a disagreeable and rather dangerous experience, hiding in haylofts and stable-yards, disguised as a
servant, to save his worthless life, Dryden approved the rejoicings, the big dinners, flags and trumpets, and wrote
another poem, in the same fulsome strain, celebrating his
return.

For this sudden change he has been called a trimmer
and turn-coat, but has, perhaps, been too severely criticised. One of his defenders exonerates him in these
words: " Puritanism is one way of looking at nature, and,
when *sincere,* of course, a right worshipful one; and the
artistic and literary view of life is a different one! A
man of wit and social sympathies, a lover of the beautiful,
and a humorist, could not be expected to remain a Puritan.
There are sacred birds and singing-birds; trees that utter
oracles, and trees that produce blossoms and fruit for summer afternoons. Young John Dryden followed his bent."
The next few years were spent in writing plays, which
were not especially good, but had just made "a hit," as
they say, with his drama of the " Indian Emperor," dedicated to his beautiful patroness, the Duchess of Monmouth,
when the " Great Plague " broke out in London, and put
a stop to all theatre-going.

Ah! what a sad, sad time in that great city! More
than one hundred thousand died from that terrible disease.
Fires were kept burning night and day in the streets to
stop the infection, but for four months the pestilence raged.
In September of the next year, 1666, a fire broke out in a
baker's shop near London Bridge, which spread and

spread, and burned and burned for three days. Dryden
describes this, and the desperate engagement between the
Dutch and English fleets. This poem, full of flattery to
the king, and which boasts of his countrymen's prowess,
gave him his place among the best poets of the day, but
caused Milton to decide that Dryden was a *rhymer*, and
little more.

In 1670 he was made poet-laureate and historian to
the king, which gave him a handsome income. This may
be considered the most prosperous part of his life. His
" Essay on Dramatic Poesy," published about this time,
proves that he could not only write plays, but defend
them when written. In fact, it was his habit all through
life to write an elaborate argument in prose or verse to
explain his position, telling the world what good reasons
he had for thinking as he did. Having given his time and
talents to the composing of heroic plays, he assumed that
the drama was the highest department of poetry ; and,
because he chose to write in *rhyme*, he argued that blank
verse was inappropriate for the drama. Of course, this
Essay caused a great deal of discussion, few of the poets
or critics of the time agreeing with Dryden. He, too, afterward changed his mind, and went back to the style sanc-
tioned by the great dramatists of the Elizabethan era. He
now engaged to write three plays each year for the king's
company of players, and they evidently appreciated his talents, for, although he really wrote but one instead of three,
they readily paid him the promised sum. But these plays,
twenty-eight in all, were written for *pay*, and to please a
wicked court, and are now considered coarse and contemptible. There never were such profligate times in
England as under Charles II., and Dryden lowered himself by following the public taste. He wanted popularity
and pay, and for this dipped his pen in pollution, and lost
his self-respect.

Whipple says that poverty has been the most fertile source of literary crimes. " Poets are by no means wingless angels, fed with ambrosia plucked from Olympus, or manna rained down from heaven; and men of letters have ever displayed the same strange indisposition to starve common to other descendants of Adam. The law of supply and demand operates in literature as in trade. For instance, if a poor poet, rich only in the riches of thought, be placed in an age which demands intellectual monstrosities, he is tempted to pervert his powers to please the general taste. This he *must* do, or die, and this he should rather die than do; but still, if he hopes to live by his products, he must produce what people will buy—and it is already supposed that nothing will be bought except what is brainless or debasing."

This is more briefly expressed in the old couplet—

" The drama's laws the drama's patrons give,
And they who live to please, *must please* to live."

He then mentions Dryden as a pertinent example of this truth. " The time in which he lived was one of great depravity of taste, and greater depravity of manners. Authors seemed banded in an insane crusade to exalt blasphemy and profligacy to the vacant throne of piety and virtue. Books were valuable according to the wickedness blended with their talent. Mental power was lucrative only in its perversion. The public was ravenous for the witty iniquities of the brain; and, to use the energetic invective of South, laid hold of brilliant morsels of sin, with ' fire and brimstone flaming round them, and thus, as it were, digested death itself, and made a meal upon perdition.' Now it is evident, in such a period as this, a needy author was compelled to choose between virtue, attended by neglect, and vice, lackeyed by popularity. One of Sir Charles Sedley's profligate comedies, one of Lord Rochester's ribald lampoons, possessed more mercantile value than the 'Paradise Lost.' In such a period as this the poet should have descended upon his time, like Schiller's ideal artist, 'not to delight it with his presence, but terrible, like the son of Agamemnon, to purify it.' Dryden was placed in this age, and, for a long period of his life, was its pander and parasite. Yet, had he lived in the reign of George III., he would not have been more immoral than Churchill; had he lived in our day, his muse would have been as pure as that of Campbell. He could not, or would not, learn that it is better to starve on honesty than thrive on baseness. It is hard, says an old English divine, to maintain truth, but still harder to be maintained *by* it."

Ridiculed by some of the wits at court, in a way that cut him keenly, he turned upon them, with all the terrible power of his fierce satire, proving to them and the world that his pen could wound as well as *flatter.* It was in 1681 that he published his great satirical poem of " Absalom and Achitophel," in which, under the thin veil of a Scriptual story, his enemies, the Duke of Monmouth and Shaftesbury, were held up to be ridiculed and scorned. It had a most rapid sale, and even the sufferers themselves had to own his power. "MacFlecknoe" and the "Medal" soon followed. His skill in this kind of "moral portrait-painting" is wonderful, and yet every one must regret that he wasted his great powers in abusing his envious contemporaries.

It is sad, too, to think of him selling himself to the theatre for so many plays a year, when he longed to be writing something better; working for the king, in return for a small pension, irregularly paid; writing any thing for pay, prologues, dedications, translations; yet seldom in comfortable circumstances. Listen to his affecting memorial addressed at this time to the Earl of Rochester:

"I would plead a little merit, and some hazards-of my life from the common enemies; my refusing advantages offered by them and neglecting my beneficial studies, for the king's service; but I only think I merit not to *starve*. I never applied myself to any interest contrary to your lordship's; and on some occasions, perhaps not known to you, have not been unserviceable to the memory and reputation of my lord, your father. After this, my lord, my conscience assures me, I may write boldly, though I cannot speak to you. I have three sons, growing to man's estate. I breed them all up to learning, beyond my fortune, but they are too hopeful to be neglected, though I want. Be pleased to look on me with an eye of compassion. Some small employment would render my condition easy. The king is not unsatisfied of me; the duke has often promised me his assistance; and your lordship is the conduit through which their favors pass. Either in the customs or the appeals of the excise, or some other way, means cannot be wanting, if you please to have the will. It is enough for one age to have neglected Mr. Cowley and starved Mr. Butler; but neither of them had the happiness to live till your lordship's ministry. In the mean time, be pleased to give me a gracious and a speedy answer to my present request of half a year's pension for my necessities. I am going to write somewhat by his majesty's command, and cannot stir into the country for my health and studies till I secure my family from want."

Butler's life of penury and neglect, in contrast with the honors paid him after his death, suggested one of the best epigrams we have :

> " Whilst Butler, needy wretch, was yet alive,
> No generous patron would a dinner give.
> See him, when starved to death and turned to dust,
> Presented with a monumental bust.
> The poet's fate is here in emblem shown :
> He asked for bread, and he received—a stone."

The work to which Dryden alludes was the translation of a pamphlet written in defence of the English Church against the Dissenters, call the "Religio Laici." In 1685, King Charles died, and James II., a bigoted papist, took his place; and all who had any thing to hope from the new monarch, "hastened in sugared addresses to lament the sun which had set, and hail the beams of that which had arisen." Dryden, especially, was anxious to secure the royal favor. He had received little from the reckless, extravagant Charles but "the pension of a prince's *praise*," and had no reason to sorrow immoderately. He at once wrote his "Threnodia Augustalis," in which, after having said all that was decently mournful over the bier of the dead, he tuned his lyre to sing in joyful praise of James.

Now the new sovereign, the most cruel of all the English kings, cared little for verses and much for money, and the poet-laureate suffered the loss of his butt of sack, which had been given him many years. Dryden knew little and cared little about religion, probably being rather skeptical at this time; he *did* care for the wine, and did not wish to lose his pension, so he thought it prudent to become a *papist*. This was considered more politic than pious, by his *enemies* at least. As usual, he defended his opinions, this time in a poetical fable, which exhibited the beasts talking theology in a very able way. This he called "The Hind and the Panther." The Church of England is represented by the Panther, beautiful, but spotted, and the milk-white Hind is the Church of Rome. He speaks thus of the Church he had so lately defended:

> " The Panther, sure the noblest next the Hind,
> The fairest creature of the spotted kind,
> Oh, could her inborn stains be washed away,
> She were too good to be a beast of prey,—
> How can I praise or blame, and not offend;
> Or how divide the frailty from the friend ?

> Her faults and virtues lie so mixed, that she
> Nor wholly stands condemned, nor wholly free."

The Bear and the Wolf figured as Presbyterians and Independents; and various other animals made up the assembly. These learned quadrupeds go to drink at the common brook, and, while wagging their tails and licking their jaws, have long discussions over the merits of their different faiths. But this very singular plot is atoned for by the beauty of the verse, and affords a fine specimen of Dryden's most prominent quality, his power of *reasoning in rhyme.*

James was delighted with his new ally, and added one hundred pounds to his pension, besides restoring the wine; but the revolution of 1688 robbed him of his place, and he was forced once more to write for bread.

Hannay, his enthusiastic defender, says that "the cause of all his embarrassments was, that he took up literature as a profession. He was a man of very good family and connections; and if he had sold himself to making money, the way to do it was surely open enough. Only his instinct made him improve the English language. He would

> ———"join
> The varying verse, the full resounding line,
> The long majestic march and energy divine "—

and he would follow his intellectual instinct! Of course he had a penalty to pay for his independence and his immortality."

He now took some of Chaucer's charming tales, which were seldom read, because few cared to puzzle their brains over the old English, and translated them pleasantly, though increasing rather than diminishing the coarseness which clung to them.

He also translated "Virgil," a work for which he was

not suited and which he did not enjoy, and this heavy task occupied three years. But, although he failed to transfuse into his version the life and soul of the great Latin epic, he has given us a translation still read and admired, as good as any that has ever been attempted.

The "Ode for St. Cecilia's Day," one of the noblest lyrics in our language, was one of his last efforts, and in some respects the best. Scott gives the following anecdote in regard to the short time in which this ode was written:

"Mr. St. John, afterward Lord Bolingbroke, happening to pay a morning visit to Dryden, whom he always respected, found him in an unusual agitation of spirits, even to a trembling. On inquiring the cause, 'I have been up all night,' replied the old bard. 'My musical friends made me promise to write them an ode for their feast of St. Cecilia; I have been so struck with the subject which occurred to me, that I could not leave it till I had completed it; here it is, *finished* at one sitting. And immediately he showed him this ode, which places the British lyric poetry above that of any other nation.'"

Handel, the great composer, set it to music, and it was performed in the Theatre Royal, Covent Garden, with great applause. It is rare to find such talents combined.

Dryden seemed to have no mean opinion of his own production. He says, in writing to his publisher: "I am glad to hear from all hands that my ode is esteemed the best of all my poetry, by all the town. I thought so myself when I writ it; but being old I mistrusted my own judgment."

And when a young friend congratulated him on having produced the finest ode ever written in any language, he replied, "You are right, young gentleman; a nobler ode never *was* produced, nor ever *will!*"

Some of its lines have almost become proverbs, such as:

"None but the brave deserve the fair."

"Sweet is pleasure after pain."

"For pity melts the mind to love."

"Take the goods the gods provide thee."

"War, he sung, is toil and trouble;
Honor, but an empty bubble."

"He raised a mortal to the skies,
She drew an angel down."

He died a poor, neglected man, notwithstanding his many changes and abject flattery, leaving this life on Wednesday morning, the 1st of May, 1700. He died in the Roman Catholic faith, to which he had ever been true, full of resignation to the divine will, "taking of his friends so tender and obliging a farewell as none but he himself could have expressed."

"The death of a man like Dryden, especially in narrow and neglected circumstances, is usually an alarum-bell to the public. Unavailing and mutual reproaches, for unthankful and pitiful negligence, waste themselves in newspaper paragraphs, elegies, and funeral processions; the debt to genius is then deemed discharged, and a new account of neglect and commemoration is opened between the public and the next who rises to supply his room. It was thus with Dryden. His family were preparing to bury him with the decency becoming their limited circumstances, when Charles Montagu, Lord Jeffries, and other men of quality, made a subscription for a public funeral. The body of the poet was then removed to the Physicians' Hall, where it was embalmed, and lay in state till the 13th day of May, twelve days after the decease. On that day the celebrated Dr. Garth pronounced a Latin oration over the remains of his departed friend, which were then, with considerable state, preceded by a band of music, and

5

attended by a numerous procession of carriages, transported to Westminster Abbey, and deposited between the graves of Chaucer and Cowley."

Let us now go back and look at his private life. We know that he was a shy, handsome boy, fond of history and the classics, a great reader, and devoted to the old English ballads. We see him next as a gallant at court, for whose sake

"The blushing virgins died,"

or, giving up the hope of fascinating the gay Lothario, retired to a nunnery. This of course is poetical exaggeration, for, however handsome he may have been, he was always diffident and talked but little. I am glad he enjoyed those early days, for he soon learned the sad truth, that " life is a *strife*," in his own home, as well as with his literary rivals. At the age of thirty-two, he married the Lady Elizabeth Howard, daughter of the Earl of Berkshire. She was proud and odd and ill-tempered, quarrelling with his relations and her own, making him very wretched. Dryden was always very severe on matrimony, and no wonder. Here is an epitaph said to be his, written perhaps as a little relief to his feelings after one of their conjugal squabbles:

"Here lies my wife,
Here let her lie;
Now she's at rest,
And so am I."

But we should have some sympathy for the poor woman, for her eccentricities terminated in insanity, and her last years were spent in an asylum.

Dryden was never a great talker; one of his critics writes for him:

"Nor wine nor love could ever see me gay;
To writing bred, I knew not what to say."

and he has himself very honestly told us: "My conversation is dull and slow; my humor is saturnine and reserved; in short, I am not one of those who endeavor to break jest in company or make repartees."

Neither did he seem to be an epicure. Writing to a lady, declining her invitation to a handsome supper, he said: "If beggars might be chosers, a chine of honest bacon would please my appetite more than all the marrow puddings—for I like them better plain, having a very vulgar stomach." Can't you imagine just how Madam Dryden, fault-finding and foolishly aristocratic, turned up her patrician nose, if she saw that note? She must have been visiting some of her titled friends at that time, for, if she had been at home, no doubt her husband would have gone meekly to the fine dinner and the marrow pudding. His looks, in later years, belied his temperate tastes, for he grew so corpulent that his enemies called him the "Poet Squab;" and his eyes, that had once done such execution among the court beauties, grew sleepy and sunken, while his whole face assumed a florid hue that did not add to his beauty.

His happiest hours were spent at Will's Coffee-House, the great resort of the wits of the town, where he had the royal seat, and his snuffbox was "the fountain of honor." "He was the great literary lion of his day; and no country stranger of any taste for letters, thought his round of London sights complete, unless he had been to Will's Coffee-House in Russell Street, where, ensconced in a snug arm-chair by the fire, or on the balcony, according to the season, old John sat, pipe in hand, laying down the law upon disputed points in literature or politics."

I am afraid that Dryden grew weary of temperance in these days, and that his rubicund visage was owing to his habits, for, during the last ten years of his life, he used to drink to excess with Addison and others, shortening his days, it is said, in this way.

When I think of his rare talents, and the way in which he wasted and degraded them, for the sake of popularity with that wicked court, which never repaid him, I cannot but wish his life had been more like that other " *old John*," who lived in the same city with him, for nearly fifty years ; that noble poet we talked of last, the blind MILTON, neglected but unconquered, who would rather have gone to the stake than shown any sympathy with the follies and vices of his day.

That Dryden admired and appreciated his genius, though he did not adopt his morals, is seen from the following tribute, in which he places Milton above Homer and Virgil:

> " Three poets, in three distant ages born,
>   Greece, Italy, and England did adorn :
>   The first in loftiness of thought surpassed,
>   The next in majesty, in *both* the last.
>   The force of Nature could no further go—
>   To make a third, she joined the other two."

I think he saw his mistake when it was too late, and we are more ready to pity than *blame* when we read a sad strain like this, so full of vain regret :

> " If joys hereafter must be purchased here,
>   With loss of all that mortals hold so dear,
>   Then welcome infamy, and public shame,
>   And last, a long farewell to worldly fame !
>   'Tis said with ease ; but oh, how hardly tried,
>   By haughty souls, to human honor tied !
>   Oh, sharp, convulsive pangs of agonizing pride !
>   Down then, thou rebel, never more to rise !
>   And what thou didst, and dost so dearly prize,
>   That fame, that *darling fame*, make that thy sacrifice.
>   'Tis nothing thou hast given, then add thy tears
>   For a long race of unrepenting years.

'Tis nothing yet, yet all thou hast to give,
Then add those maybe years thou hast to live.
'Tis nothing still; then poor and naked come,
Thy Father will receive His unthrift home,
And thy blest Saviour's blood discharge the mighty sin."

He once spoke very frankly of his strong desire for fame, adding: "For what other reason have I spent my life in so unprofitable a study? Why am I grown old in seeking so barren a reward as fame? The same parts and application which have made me a poet, might have raised me to any honors of the gown."

His old age was far from happy; he was desolate, poor, and obliged to write on distasteful subjects in a mechanical way for daily support.

His habits of composing were very rapid, and he seldom pruned or corrected; his complete works are greater than those of any English poet.

When working hard over his translation of Virgil, he writes to his bookseller about his son, an invalid, who would soon return from Rome: "If it please God that I must die of over-study, I cannot spend my life better than in preserving his."

But light mingled with the clouds in these sunset days, and here is a pleasant story to prove it: Dryden was spending the evening with some friends, when their conversation happened to be directed to the subject of the art of composition, elegant style, etc. So it was agreed that each should write something, and place it under the candlestick for the poet's criticism. Most of the company labored hard, while Lord Dorset, with much composure, wrote two or three lines, and carelessly threw them to the place agreed on. The rest having finished, the arbiter raised the candlestick and opened the leaves of their destiny. In going through the whole, he discovered strong marks of pleasure and satisfaction, but at one, in particular, he seemed in raptures. "I must acknowledge," said he, "that there are abundance of fine things in my hands, and such as do honor to the personages who wrote them; but I am under an indispensable necessity of giving the highest preference to my Lord Dorset. I must request that your lordships will hear it, and I believe all will be satisfied with my judgment : 'I promise to pay John Dryden or order, on demand, the sum of five hundred pounds. Dorset.' "

Dryden's life cannot be considered a failure, though even his warmest friends must regard it with "respectful sorrow." Talents so great as his cannot be concealed by faults of character, or grossness of style. He was a fine reasoner, an able critic, and possessed a wonderful power over language.

Johnson, who was always partial in his opinions, called him the "Father of Criticism," and said, in describing his style, that he did for the English language what Augustus did for Rome—"found it *brick* and left it marble."

No one can help regretting that he did not carry out his favorite plan of composing an epic poem on King Arthur and the Knights of the Round Table, the same subject which Milton once thought of attempting. With such a theme, he would have given us something worthy of his genius.

I must give you a few more lines from his works, just as they happen to strike me in running them over, that you may see how lavishly he scattered gems of thought before that good-for-nothing court—literally casting his "pearls before swine : "

> "Great wits are sure to madness near allied,
> And thin partitions do their bounds divide."

> "But wild ambition loves to slide, not stand,
> And Fortune's ice prefers to Virtue's land."

" Beware the fury of a patient man."

" He trudged along, unknowing what he sought,
    And whistled as he went, for want of thought."

"Errors, like straws, upon the surface flow;
    He who would search for pearls, must dive below."

" Men are but children of a larger growth."

" But Shakespeare's magic could not copied be;
    Within that circle, none durst walk but he."

" Forgiveness to the injured does belong;
    But they ne'er pardon, who have done the wrong."

" This is the *porcelain* clay of human kind."

" Time gives himself, and is not valued."

" Death in itself is nothing; but we fear
    To be we know not what, we know not where."

" Love either finds equality, or makes it."

" That bad thing, gold, buys all good things."

" The secret pleasure of the generous act,
    Is the great mind's great bribe."

" Few know the use of life, before 'tis past."

" When I consider life, 'tis all a cheat,
    Yet, fooled with hope, men favor the deceit;
    Trust on, and think to-morrow will repay;
    To-morrow's falser than the former day;
    Lies worse; and while it says, ' We shall be blest
    With some new joys,' cuts off what we possessed,
    Strange courage! none would live past years again,
    Yet all hope pleasure in what yet remain;
    And from the dregs of life think to receive .
    What the first sprightly running could not give."

" Of no distemper, of no blast he died,
    But fell like autumn fruit that mellowed long;
    Even wondered at, because he dropt no sooner.

> Fate seemed to wind him up for fourscore years,
> Yet freshly ran he on ten winters more;
> Till, like a clock worn out with calling time,
> The wheels of weary life—at last stood still."

He was very ready in extempore composition. Talking one day at his friend's, Mrs. *Creed's*, upon the origin of names and their significance, he bowed to the good old lady, and recited this impromptu:

> " So much religion in *your* name doth dwell,
> Your soul must needs with piety excel.
> Thus names, like well-wrought pictures drawn of old,
> Their owner's nature and their story told.
> Your name but half expresses; for in you
> Belief and practice do together go.
> My prayers shall be, while this short life endures,
> These may go hand in hand, with you and yours;
> Till faith hereafter is in vision drowned,
> And practice is with endless glory crowned."

His assertion that he was not good at repartee, is certainly disproved by his witty reply to his wife, who, in a good-humored mood, wished that she might be a *book*, and so enjoy more of his company:

> " Be an *almanac*, then, my dear,
> That I may change you once a year!"

Lowell, in a recent *North American*, has an able criticism of Dryden, from which I will copy a few sentences:

" In the second class of English poets, perhaps no one stands, on the whole, so high as he; during his lifetime, in spite of jealousy, detraction, unpopular politics, and a suspicious change of faith, his preëminence was conceded; he was the earliest complete type of the purely literary man, in the modern sense; there is a singular unanimity in allowing him a certain claim to greatness, which would be denied to men as famous and more read; to Pope or

Swift, for example; he is supposed, in some way or other, to have reformed English poetry."

I cannot better close this rambling talk than by quoting the words of his biographer, Scott, at the close of his work:

"I have thus detailed the life and offered some remarks on the literary character of John Dryden, who, educated in a pedantic taste, and a fanatical religion, was destined, if not to give laws to the stage of England, at least to defend its liberties; to improve burlesque into satire, to free translation from the fetters of verbal metaphrase, and exclude it from the license of paraphrase; to teach posterity the powerful and varied harmony of which their language was capable; to give an example of the lyric ode of unapproached excellence; and to leave to English literature a name second only to those of Milton and Shakespeare."

5* BURLEIGH HOUSE.

ADDISON.

•

" He taught us how to live, and oh too high
The price for knowledge! taught us how to die."

On the 1st of May, 1672, in the house of a Wiltshire dean, could be heard the cries of a little babe, so feeble and puny that it was christened on the day of its birth, no one daring to hope for its life. This delicate child became a man whom I want you all to love and admire, for his name, given in such sad haste by anxious friends, became one of the brightest and purest in English literature. Joseph Addison's early life was passed at his father's rectory, and of those days we know but little. There is a story which makes him ringleader in a " barring out," which was a mad, impudent frolic of the boys at the close of a term, when they thought it great fun to lock the doors and bar the windows of the school-room, and then jeer and sneer at the poor master standing outside. Another tradition assures us that he once ran away from school to escape a whipping, and hid himself in a wood, where he fed on berries, and slept in a hollow tree, until, after a long search, he was discovered and brought home.

BIRTHPLACE OF ADDISON.

It is hard to believe that so gentle and retiring a man was ever a mutinous runaway, and, whatever his pranks may have been, he must have studied well, for at fifteen he was a fine Latin scholar, and fitted for the university. Tiekell says: "He employed his first years in the study of the old Greek and Roman writers, whose language and manner he caught at that time of life as strongly as other young people gain a French accent or a genteel air." It was at the Charter-house School in London that he met Richard Steele, "a good-hearted, mischief-loving Irish boy," with whom he ever after kept up a warm friendship. Addison's father also liked this frank and lively lad, and approved of the intimacy. Steele, in writing to Congreve, says: "Were things of this nature to be exposed to public view, I could show, under the dean's own hand, in the warmest terms, his blessing on the friendship between his son and me; nor had he a child who did not prefer me in the first place of kindness and esteem, as their father loved me like one of them."

They were also together at Oxford, and no doubt their very opposite temperaments had a happy effect upon each other, Addison being as shy, studious, and quiet, as Steele was lazy, reckless, and uproarious. After two years of hard study, Addison gained a scholarship in Magdalen, from the superiority of his Latin verses. I have nothing to tell you of his life there, but that he was very nervous, that he kept late hours, and that most of his studies were after dinner, a circumstance which, as Miss Aiken observes, is pretty conclusive of the sobriety of his habits at this period. A grove at Magdalen still retains the name of " Addison's Walk," and some of its trees are said to have been planted by him.

At the age of twenty-two he published his first poem, some verses addressed to Dryden, which won for him the friendship of that poet at the outset of his career. Dryden, now a poor old man, whose life was imbittered with keen disappointments and vain regret, was pleased by the extravagant flattery, which congratulated him on having "heightened the majesty of Virgil, given new charms to Horace, lent to Persius smoother numbers and a clearer style, and set a new edge on the satire of Juvenal." But the veteran poet fully reciprocated this fulsome praise in a postscript to the translation of " The Æneid," where he " affected to be afraid that his own performance would not sustain a comparison with the version of the fourth Georgic by the most ingenious Mr. Addison, of Oxford. . . . . After his bees," said Dryden, " my latter swarm is scarcely worth the hiving."

Addison's father wished him to be a clergyman, and he would have entered the clerical profession if Lords Somers and Montagu had not used their powerful influence in another direction. They decided that talent and principle were sadly needed in the service of the country, too often disgraced by their diplomatists, and that the State could not spare such a young man to the Church. He was therefore given by his friends to the service of the crown. His second poem was on the king, and addressed to Lord Somers. His majesty and the keeper of the seals seemed gratified by this attention, and he soon received the solid reward of a pension of three hundred pounds, which enabled him to travel in Italy and France, and gain a knowledge of the French language, which was indispensable in the position for which he was destined. He made this foreign experience very useful to himself and pleasant to others by his notes of travel, and his habit of observing manners, society, scenery, etc., which made him so apt and attractive a critic at home. He travelled, as all should do, with eyes wide open, his mind ready to receive new impressions, and, pen in hand, to jot down all facts worthy of comment. He also became acquainted with many persons of rank and learning while on the Continent, and really gained a very high reputation abroad before he was known or talked of in his own country. Such men as Boileau and Malebranche received him with distinguished favor, and he formed a delightful friendship with Mr. Edward Wortley Montagu, who afterward married the witty and accomplished Lady Mary, whose letters you have no doubt enjoyed. But the Muses were the only ladies whose acquaintance he cultivated just then, and he devoted himself earnestly to study, feeling, as he said in his letter to his patron, that the only return he could make his lordship would be to apply himself entirely to his business, which was acquiring the French language. He ex-

presses the difficulties he has met with in one of his letters
home: "I should have went to Italy before now had not
yᵉ French tongue stopt me, which has bin a Rub in my
way harder to get over than yᵉ Alps; but I hope yᵉ next
time I have yᵉ honor to wait on you I shall be able to talk
with you in yᵉ language of yᵉ place." He published an
account of his tour, and his poetical epistle to his good
friend Montagu, now Lord Halifax, is considered his best
effort in verse. I will give you a few lines from this:

> "Poetic fields encompass me around,
> And still I seem to tread on classic ground;
> For here the Muse so oft her harp has strung,
> That not a mountain rears its head unsung;
> Renowned in verse, each shady thicket grows,
> And every stream in heavenly numbers flows."

I believe the phrase "classic ground" made its *début*
in this poem, and it is by no means the only happy expression which Addison has given us. Listen to the long sigh
which follows his glowing description of Italy:

> "How has kind Heaven adorned the happy land,
> And scattered blessings with a wasteful hand!
> But what avails her unexhausted stores,
> Her blooming mountains and her sunny shores,
> With all the gifts that heaven and earth impart,
> The smiles of Nature and the charms of art;
> While proud Oppression in her valleys reigns,
> And Tyranny usurps her happy plains?
> The poor inhabitants behold in vain
> The redd'ning orange and the swelling grain;
> Joyless he sees the growing oils and wines,
> And in the myrtle's fragrant shade repines;
> Starves, in the midst of Nature's bounty curst,
> And in the loaded vineyard dies for thirst."

With William's death Addison's patron lost his office,
and he lost his pension. Thrown upon his own resources, he

determined to continue his travels as tutor to some young gentleman on the grand tour, and very soon the pompous Duke of Somerset proposed that he should accompany his son in that capacity. This was a pleasant plan, but his grace seemed to consider the honor of such association sufficient remuneration, or at any rate offered a very small salary, which Mr. Addison declined, and the affair ended. The state of things at home was not encouraging—his promised position gone, his party unpopular, his pension taken away, and old debts still unpaid at Oxford. So our philosophic scholar did not hasten his return, and enjoyed a long and circuitous homeward route with a merry party of friends.

He writes from Holland to Mr. Wyche, an accomplished gentleman and diplomatist of some note, to thank him for some wine, the excellence of which he seemed to have fully tested:

"DEAR SIR: My hand at present begins to grow steady enough for a letter; so that y⁰ properest use I can put it to is to thank y⁰ honest gentleman that set it a shaking. I have had this morning a desperate design in my head to attack you in verse, which I should certainly have done could I have found out a Rhime to Rummer. But tho' you have escaped for y⁰ present, you are not yet out of danger, if I can a little recover my talent at Crambo. I am sure, in whatever way I write to you, it will be impossible for me to express y⁰ deep sense I have of y⁰ many favours you have lately shown me. I shall only tell you that Hambourg has bin the pleasantest stage I have met with in my Travails. If any of my friends wonder at me for living so long in that place, I dare say it will be thought a very good excuse when I tell 'em Mr. Wyche was there. As your company made our stay at Hambourg agreeable, your wine has given us all y⁰ satisfaction that we have found in our journey through Westphalia.

If drinking your health will do you any good, you may expect to be as long-lived as Methuselah, or, to use a more familiar instance, as y⁰ oldest Hoc in y⁰ cellar;" and so forth. You see there is too much of the air of the "morning after" in this grateful and complimentary note.

Lack of funds at last drove him home, and he reached England in the summer of 1703. He was most cordially received on his return, and introduced at once to the famous "Kit-Cat Club," of which he soon became the pride and ornament. This club, a distinguished assemblage of the brightest stars of the Whig party, nobles, diplomatists, and men of letters, originated in 1700, in rather an humble way. Mr. Jacob Tonson, a celebrated bookseller of London, was remarkably fond of certain nice dishes, prepared by a pastry cook in Gray's Inn's Lane—particularly of his *mutton-pies*. He induced him to move to the Fountain Tavern, in the Strand, with promises of better patronage. Tonson knew the authors of the day, and one day invited some of them to an entertainment at the pastry cook's. They, too, were charmed with the mutton-pies, and the bookseller offered to repeat the collation each week, if he might publish their productions. The cook's name was Christopher; his sign, "The Cat and Fiddle," hence the quaint name of the club. Horace Walpole says that "its members included not only the wits of the time, but the patriots that saved Britain." There Addison was happy and at home. Reticent and reserved, he never appeared to such advantage as when "thawed by wine," and surrounded by a group of admiring friends. Coleridge says: "You know that some men are like musical glasses; to produce their finest tones, you must keep them *wet*." This bad habit of using wine to conquer his natural timidity, led him to excess in drinking, a fault all the more noticeable, because his character in every other respect was so pure and spotless. Macaulay says, in regard to this failing, that "the smallest speck is seen on a white ground, and of any other statesman or writer of Queen Anne's reign, we should no more think of saying that he sometimes took too much wine, than that he wore a long wig and sword."

I will not go into particulars of the many public offices held by Addison, which never agreed with his literary tastes, and for which he was not especially suited; his fame being chiefly due to his charming essays, which were published in the *Spectator*, a little paper devoted to good-humored criticisms on the manners and morals of the day. In the spring of 1709, Addison's old school-fellow, the generous, genial, good-for-nothing Steele, had started a little sheet, called *The Tatler*, which, for one penny, gave a short article, and some scraps of news. Three times a week this paper appeared, something entirely new in England; and Addison, who was then in Ireland, would occasionally write for it. But the *Spectator* soon took its place, a larger and more ambitious sheet. Here Steele and Addison worked together, determined to do something to refine and correct the habits of the times. And, indeed, a reform was needed, for the state of society was very corrupt. Gambling, drunkenness, swearing, and indecency of language, were indulged in by too many of the so-called "fine gentlemen" of that reign. Bull-rings and cockpits were more attractive than books; and a reader must needs be a pedant, while *any* knowledge among *women*, excepting on the topics of dress and flirtation, was ridiculed and censured. The plan of these friends succeeded wonderfully, and their paper, which came out two or three times a week, was eagerly looked for, and read by thousands—circulating through every part of the kingdom, the delight of the learned, the busy, the idle. It did not fail to reach those for whom it was especially intended. "On the tray, beside the delicate porcelain cups, from which beauty and beau sipped their fragrant chocolate or tea, by the toilet-table in the late noonday, lay the welcome little sheet of sparkling wit, or elegant criticism, giving a new zest to the morning meal, and suggesting fresh topics for the afternoon chat in the toyshop or on the mall." These witty papers, overflowing with good-natured satire, produced more effect than any amount of dull moral lectures. Ridicule is often better than a sermon, when reproof is needed. Although we owe the origin of this style of periodical literature to Steele, who wrote delightfully himself, yet Addison was the soul and life of the *Spectator*, and his style is still considered a model of pure, elegant English. Steele appreciated his friend, and was always grateful — never jealous. "I fared," he says, "like a distressed prince, who calls in a powerful neighbor to his aid; I was undone by my auxiliary; when I had once called him in, I could not subsist without dependence on him." And again: "I rejoiced in being excelled; and made those little talents, whatever they are, which I have, give way and be subservient to the superior qualities of a friend whom I loved, and whose modesty would never have admitted them to come into daylight, but under such a shelter."

Addison's papers are marked with one of the four letters, C. L. I. O., taken either from the Muse's name, or from the initial letters of Chelsea, London, Islington, and the Office where they were written. Among the articles most quoted to illustrate his delicate yet genuine humor, are those on "The Use of a Fan," "The Dissection of a Beau's Head," and a "Coquette's Heart." You will find them very amusing. I give you the first-mentioned, to tempt you to look up the others:

"MR. SPECTATOR:

"Women are armed with fans as men with swords, and sometimes do more execution with them. To the end, therefore, that ladies may be entire mistresses of the weapon which they bear, I have erected an academy for the training up of young women in the exercise of the fan, according to the most fashionable airs and motions that are now practised at court. The ladies who carry fans under me are drawn up twice a day in my great hall, where they are instructed in the use of their arms, and exercised by the following words of command: Handle your fans, Unfurl your fans, Discharge your fans, Ground your fans, Recover your fans, Flutter your fans. By the right observation of these few plain words of command, a woman of a tolerable genius, who will apply herself diligently to her exercise for the space of but one half-year, shall be able to give her fan all the graces that can possibly enter into that little modish machine.

"But to the end that my readers may form to themselves a right notion of this exercise, I beg leave to explain it to them in all its parts. When my female regiment is drawn up in array, with every one her weapon in her hand, upon my giving the word to Handle their fans, each of them shakes her fan at me with a smile, then gives her right-hand woman a tap upon the shoulder, then presses her lips with the extremity of her fan, then lets her arms fall in easy motion, and stands in readiness to receive the next word of command. All this is done with a close fan, and is generally learned in the first week.

"The next motion is that of unfurling the fan, in which are comprehended several little flirts and vibrations, as also gradual and deliberate openings, with many voluntary fallings asunder in the fan itself, that are seldom learned under a month's practice. This part of the exercise pleases the spectators more than any other, as it discovers, on a sudden, an infinite number of cupids, garlands, altars, birds, beasts, rainbows, and the like agreeable figures, that display themselves to view, whilst every one in the regiment holds a picture in her hand.

" Upon my giving the word to Discharge their fans, they give one general crack, that may be heard at a considerable distance, when the wind sits fair. This is one of the most difficult parts of the exercise, but I have several ladies with me, who at their first entrance could not give a pop loud enough to be heard at the farther end of the room, who can now discharge a fan in such a manner that it shall make a report like a pocket-pistol. I have likewise taken care (in order to hinder young women from letting off their fans in wrong places, or on unsuitable occasions) to show upon what subject the crack of a fan may come in properly: I have likewise invented a fan, with which a girl of sixteen, by the help of a little wind, which is enclosed about one of the largest sticks, can make as loud a crack as a woman of fifty with an ordinary fan.

" When the fans are thus discharged, the word of command, in course, is to Ground their fans. This teaches a lady to quit her fan gracefully when she throws it aside in order to take up a pack of cards, adjust a curl of hair, replace a falling pin, or apply herself to any other matter of importance. This part of the exercise, as it only consists in tossing a fan with an air upon a long table (which stands by for that purpose), may be learned in two days' time as well as in a twelvemonth.

" When my female regiment is thus disarmed, I generally let them walk about the room for some time; when, on a sudden (like ladies that look upon their watches after a long visit), they all of them hasten to their arms, catch them up in a hurry, and place themselves in their proper stations upon my calling out, Recover your fans. This part of the exercise is not difficult, provided a woman applies her thoughts to it.

" The fluttering of the fan is the last, and indeed the

master-piece of the whole exercise; but if a lady does not mis-spend her time, she may make herself mistress of it in three months. I generally lay aside the dog-days and the hot time of the summer for the teaching this part of the exercise; for as soon as ever I pronounce, Flutter your fans, the place is filled with so many zephyrs and gentle breezes as are very refreshing in that season of the year, though they might be dangerous to ladies of a tender constitution in any other.

"There is an infinite variety of motions to be made use of in the flutter of a fan. There is the angry flutter, the modest flutter, the timorous flutter, the confused flutter, the merry flutter, and the amorous flutter. Not to be tedious, there is scarce any emotion in the mind which does not produce a suitable agitation in the fan; insomuch that, if I only see the fan of a disciplined lady, I know very well whether she laughs, frowns, or blushes. I have seen a fan so very angry, that it would have been dangerous for the absent lover who provoked it to have come within the wind of it; and at other times so very languishing, that I have been glad, for the lady's sake, the lover was at a sufficient distance from it. I need not add that a fan is either a prude or a coquette, according to the nature of the person who bears it. To conclude my letter, I must acquaint you that I have from my own observations compiled a little treatise for the use of my scholars, entitled, 'The Passions of the Fan,' which I will communicate to you if you think it may be of use to the public. I shall have a general review on Thursday next, to which you shall be very welcome if you will honor it with your presence. I am, etc.

"P. S. I teach young gentlemen the whole art of gallanting a fan.

"N. B. I have several little plain fans made for this use, to avoid expense."

But better than all is the character of " Sir Roger de Coverley"—a fine specimen of the old English gentleman, simple-hearted, generous, and eccentric. He was really attached to this creation of his own genius, saying, "We are born for each other," and, fearful that some other hand might treat the foibles of the worthy knight with less love and tenderness than his own, gently hurried him from the world. He deserves our praise for not only discerning Milton's genius in that age when pinchbeck was more valued than gold, but for compelling the public to agree with him. He says: "Milton's chief talent, and, indeed, his distinguishing excellence, lies in the sublimity of his thoughts. There are others of the modern who rival him in every other part of poetry ; but in the greatness of his sentiments he triumphs over all the poets, both modern and ancient, Homer alone excepted. It is impossible, for the imagination of man to disturb itself with greater ideas than those which he has laid together in his first, second, and sixth books."

In the spring of 1713, the play of " Cato," which had been lying in his desk since his return from Italy, because he shrank from the disgrace of a possible failure, was brought out at Drury Lane, with immense success, played without interruption for thirty-five nights, and only stopped then because one of the principal actors was ill. This tragedy was translated into most of the modern languages, but is not read now, being too stately and formal for popularity. The celebrated Booth, then a young man, made his fortune by his skilful rendition of the part of Cato.

Though this play, as a whole, is forgotten, yet some of its lines are often quoted. For instance :

" 'Tis not in mortals to command success,
But we'll do more, Sempronius, we'll *deserve* it."

" A day, an hour of virtuous liberty,
  Is worth a whole eternity of bondage."

" The woman that deliberates is lost."

" 'Tis the divinity that stirs within us.
  'Tis Heaven itself that points out an hereafter,
  And intimates eternity to man."

In his forty-fifth year Addison married the Countess of
Warwick, a gay, dashing, worldly, and thoroughly selfish
woman, to whose son he had once been tutor. But they
did not live happily, and he was often glad to escape from
his magnificent home to his club, or some tavern, where
he could have a pleasant talk with, or rather, at his
friends, for he was a little too fond of monologues, drinking
the healths of the absent ones to such an unnecessary extent, that he soon lost his own. When in the mood, and
with a few choice spirits, he would throw off all reserve
and entertain them most delightfully. That brilliant
woman, Lady Mary Montagu, said she had known all the
wits, and that Addison was the best company in the world.
Pope, the sharp, envious little critic, owned there was a
charm in his talk which could be found nowhere else.
Swift also said he had never known any talker so agreeable. Steele said : " He was above all men in that talent
we call *humor*, and enjoyed it in such perfection, that I
have often reflected, after a night spent with him apart
from all the world, that I had had the pleasure of convers-
ing with an intimate acquaintance of Terence and Catul-
lus, who had all their wit and nature, heightened with
humor more exquisite and delightful than any other man
ever possessed." He afterward speaks of that smiling
mirth, that delicate satire, and genteel raillery, which appeared in Mr. Addison when he was free among intimates ;
free from that remarkable bashfulness which is a cloak
that hides and muffles merit ; and his abilities were cov-

ered only by modesty which doubles the beauties which are seen, and gives credit and esteem to all that are concealed."

But these rare gifts were not exhibited to crowds, and to strangers he often appeared silent, if not stupid. He used to say there was no such thing as *conversation* but between *two persons*.

In the first number of the *Spectator*, he writes of his timidity and gravity in his own quaint and charming style. He tells us that he threw away his rattle before he was two months old, and would not make use of his coral till the *bells* were taken from it. At the university, he distinguished himself by a most profound silence. To quote his own words: "During the space of eight years, excepting in the public exercises of the college, I scarce uttered the quantity of a hundred words; and, indeed, I do not remember that I ever spoke three sentences together in my whole life." His last days were saddened by suffering, the venomous criticisms of his rivals, and political vexations, but he endured all these trials with cheerfulness and fortitude, and his peaceful death was a fitting close to a life in which there was so little to regret. Calling his wild and thoughtless son-in-law to his bedside, he grasped his hand, saying softly, "See how a *Christian* can die!" and soon after breathed his last, on the 17th day of June, 1719. His body was borne, at dead of night, to the Abbey. Sweet music floated on the air, and torches shed their glimmering light over dark arches and silent graves as the accomplished scholar was laid to rest in the chapel of Henry IV. His integrity is without a stain, and, with all his power of ridicule and satire, he has not left a word that could be called ungenerous or unkind:

> " Whose humor, as gay as the fire-fly's light,
>   Played round every subject, and shone as it played;

> Whose wit, in the combat as gentle as bright,
> Ne'er carried a heart-stain away on its blade."

His favorite psalm. was the twenty-third, which he paraphrased in verse, and many of his hymns are well known. Thackeray says: "When this man looks from the world, whose weaknesses he describes so benevolently, up to the heaven which shines over us all, I can hardly fancy a human face lighted up with a more serene rapture; a human intellect, thrilling with a purer love and adoration than Joseph Addison's. Listen to him; from your childhood you have known the verses; but who can hear their sacred music without love and awe?

> 'Soon as the evening shades prevail,
> The moon takes up the wondrous tale,
> And nightly to the listening earth
> Repeats the story of her birth;
> And all the stars that round her burn,
> And all the planets in their turn,
> Confirm the tidings as they roll,
> And spread the truth from pole to pole.

> 'What though in solemn silence all
> Move round this dark terrestrial ball,
> What though no real voice nor sound
> Among their radiant orbs be found?
> In reason's ear they all rejoice,
> And utter forth a glorious voice;
> Forever singing as they shine,
> The hand that made us is divine.'

It seems to me those verses shine like the stars. When he turns to heaven, a Sabbath comes over that man's mind; and his face lights up from it with a glory of thanks and prayer. His sense of religion stirs through his whole being. In the fields, in the town; looking at the birds in the trees, at the children in the streets; in the morning or in the moonlight; over his books in his own room; in a happy party at a country merry - making, or a town

6

assembly, good-will and peace to God's creatures, and love and awe of Him who made them, fill his pure heart and shine from his kind face. If Swift's life was the most wretched, I think Addison's was one of the most enviable —a life prosperous and beautiful—a calm death—an immense fame and affection afterward for his happy and spotless name."

HOLLAND HOUSE.

Jonat: Swift.

SWIFT.

"I was an odd sort of man."

I HAVE now to tell you of another satirist, one of the wittiest men that ever lived, but who was unhappy all his days, and succeeded in making his best friends miserable, when he did not kill them with outright cruelty—a man so different from the good and gentle Addison, that one cannot turn to him with any pleasure.

JONATHAN SWIFT was born in Dublin, on the 30th of November, 1667. But his parents were English, and he had nothing of the Irish character. His mother, being left a widow in very embarrassed circumstances, her little boy was given to the care of an uncle, with whom he lived until he was twenty-one. Lack of means, and the want of a home and a father's protection and love, with a galling sense of constant dependence, may have saddened and imbittered his life; but he had the additional misfortune to be born without a *heart*, or, if he did possess that rather necessary organ, it was so cold, selfish, and unloving, as hardly to deserve the name.

Speaking one day in a contemptuous way of his uncle, to whom he owed so much, a gentleman dared to rebuke him as he deserved.

"Did he not give you an education?" he asked.

"Yes," said Swift, gruffly, "the education of a dog."

"Then, sir, you have not the gratitude of a dog!" and, indeed, he had not.

He must have been very lazy at school and academy, for, when he claimed the usual degree of Bachelor of Arts, he was considered too deficient for admission, and only gained it at last by "special favor," which meant special lack of merit. But this shamed him, and, determined to reform, he resolved to turn over a new leaf, and study eight hours a day. Some one says quaintly that good resolutions are like fainting ladies—they want to be carried out!—and Swift, who had an iron will, did carry out this plan, and worked hard and steadily for several years. He was educated at Trinity College, through the kindness of his relatives. After his Uncle Goodwin's death, he was helped by another uncle, who bestowed his benefactions in a more agreeable way, as Swift really acknowledged his kindness, and called him "the best of his relations."

Scott tells us of a friendly cousin, who remembered him in these days: "Sitting one day in his chamber, absolutely penniless, he saw a seaman in the court below, who seemed inquiring for the apartment of one of the students. It occurred to Swift that this man might bring a message from his Cousin Willoughby, then settled as a

Lisbon merchant, and the thought had scarcely crossed his mind, when the door opened, and the stranger, approaching him, produced a large leathern purse of silver coin, and poured the contents before him as a present from his cousin. Swift, in his ecstasy, offered the bearer a part of his treasure, which the honest sailor generously declined. And from that moment Swift, who had so deeply experienced the miseries of indigence, resolved so to manage his scanty income as never again to be reduced to extremity."

His mother advised him, after leaving college, to seek the patronage of Sir William Temple, a friend of his uncle's, and a distant relative. This gentleman consented to give him a home, and make him his private secretary, but the position was distasteful and humiliating. He was, to be sure, in an elegant house, with books all about him, but he was treated as an upper servant, while always expected to fawn, and cringe, and flatter, or else lose the favor of a man decidedly his inferior. Here he became known to King William, who used sometimes to visit Moor Park, when its owner was laid up with the gout, and his majesty, walking round the fine garden, took considerable notice of the swarthy secretary, teaching him to cut asparagus in the Dutch fashion, and eat it with Dutch economy. The latter lesson Swift remembered and made use of.

There is a funny story about an alderman whom the dean once invited to dinner: "Amongst other vegetables, asparagus formed one of the dishes. The dean helped his guest, who shortly again called upon his host to be helped a second time, when the dean, pointing to the alderman's plate, said, 'Sir, first finish what you have upon your plate.' 'What, sir, eat my stalks?' 'Ay, sir, King William always ate the stalks!'

"'And, George,' said one of his friends, after hearing

the story, 'were you blockhead enough to obey him?'
'Yes, doctor, and if you had dined with Dean Swift, *tête-à-tête*—faith, you would have been obliged to eat your stalks, too!'"

The king also offered to make Swift a captain of horse, which, as his òwn notions were all military, was intended as an honor; but, of course, the great genius inwardly scorned this proposition, while refusing with mock humility, and went on in the life so irksome and galling to his proud nature, "feeling like a caged tiger, submitting to the keeper who brings him food."

In the words of Collier: "Standing midway between the elegantly selfish Sir William, who wrote, and gardened, and quoted the classics, and the liveried sneerers of the servants' hall, poor Swift gnawed at his own heart in disdainful silence, writhing helplessly under the lofty chidings of his honor and the vulgar insolence of his honor's own man."

Once, in a desperate mood, he rebelled, and went away, but, finding a recommendation from his patron was needed to gain him any other position, he asked pardon, and returned, to remain until the death of Sir William, in 1698.

Thackeray says: "I don't know any thing more melancholy than the letter to Temple, in which, after having broke from his bondage, the poor wretch crouches piteously toward his cage again, and deprecates his master's anger. He asks for testimonials for orders:

"'The particulars required of me are what relate to morals and learning, and the reasons of quitting your honor's family—that is, whether the last was occasioned by any ill action. They are left entirely to your honor's mercy, though, in the first, I think I cannot reproach myself for any thing further than for infirmities. This is all I dare at present beg from your honor, under circumstances of life not worth your regard. What is left me to

wish, next to the health and prosperity of your honor and
family, is that Heaven would one day allow me the opportunity of leaving my acknowledgments at your feet. I
beg my most humble duty and service be presented to my
ladies, your honor's lady and sister.' Can prostration fall
deeper? Could a slave bow lower?"

During these years of servile dependence and suffering, he read almost constantly, wrote his famous treatise,
"The Battle of the Books," and won the undying love of
Esther Johnson, the daughter of Temple's steward; a
pretty, black-eyed girl, who recited to him, and learned to
think him a hero, almost a god.

This acquaintance proved a blessing to Swift, the
brightest thing in his dark life; but to her it brought lifelong sorrow. As apparent trifles often influence our whole
lives, I shall have to add reality to romance, and say
that he nearly killed himself one day by eating too many
apples, and was troubled ever after, at times, with a dizzi-
ness and deafness, which pursued him through life, and at
last sent him to his grave. When I think of his oddity
and cruelty, I try to believe that his brain was always
diseased, which would be some excuse for his strange life.
But I can tell you one good thing about him; he loved
and respected his *mother*, and went to see her every year.
Queer in this, as in every thing else, he would travel on
foot, sleeping at night at some second-rate tavern, where
he could get lodged for a penny and have clean sheets for
sixpence. I don't really know whether he did this because he wanted to see that sort of life—or to save a
shilling. "Economy was with him the handmaid of
Charity. He would save a sixpence by walking instead of
riding, and send it at once to a poor neighbor. He always
carried small coins in his pocket for charity, in his daily
walks, never giving more than one at a time." He
always kept an exact account of every penny that he

spent or received, and there seemed to be a constant struggle in his mind between *economy* and *justice.* His attempts to adjust these accurately led to very ridiculous results. If he happened to dine with a friend poorer than himself, he would insist upon paying for his dinner, as if at a public house, and give his own guest money in advance, to choose their own entertainment. On one occasion, when Pope and Gay visited him after supper, he calculated narrowly what they would have cost him, and gave each half a crown. Pope, in describing this, said: "Doctor Swift has an odd, blunt way, that is mistaken by strangers for ill-nature. It is so odd, that there's no describing it but by facts. I will tell you one that first comes into my head. One evening Gay and I went to see him; you know how intimately we were all acquainted. On our coming in, 'Heyday, gentlemen,' says the doctor, 'what's the meaning of this visit? How came you to leave all the great lords you are so fond of, to come hither to see a poor dean?'

"'Because we would rather see you than any of them.'

"'Ay, any one, that did not know you as well as I do, might believe you. But since you are come, I must get some supper for you, I suppose.'

"'No, doctor, we have supped already.'

"'Supped already? that's impossible; why, it is not eight o'clock yet. That's very strange! but if you had not supped, I must have got something for you. Let me see, 'what should I have had? a couple of lobsters; ay, that would have done very well; two shillings; tarts a shilling. But you will drink a glass of wine with me, though you supped so much before your usual time only to spare my pocket.'

"'No, we had rather talk with you than drink with you.'

"'But if you had supped with me, as in all reason you

ought to have done, you must then have drunk with me. A bottle of wine, two shillings—two and two is four, and one is five; just two and sixpence apiece. There, Pope, there's half a crown for you, and there's another for you, sir; for I won't save any thing by you, I am determined.'

"This was all said and done with his usual seriousness on such occasions; and, in spite of every thing we could say to the contrary, he actually obliged us to take the money!"

He began early to think he was a poet, and published some "Pindaric odes," but they made little impression. Dryden, who was a connection, told him plainly—"Coz, you will never make a poet," which caused Swift to hate him ever after. An irreligious divine, a heartless politician, could not well be a true poet, but he could write verses in a very easy, natural way, and, as he said himself, in a poem on his own death:

> " The dean was famous in his time,
> And had a kind of knack at rhyme."

He excelled in humorous satire, though destitute of refinement and originality. But his power lay in his *prose;* clear, concise, and strong, though, too often, coarse and unreasonably severe. After his patron's death, who left him a legacy and his papers, he went to Ireland.as chaplain and private secretary to the Earl of Berkeley, and, after many disappointments, obtained the living of Laracor, some years later. Here he seems to have been faithful to his duties, however unfitted for them, and preached regularly, for six years, to an audience of fifteen persons, reading prayers every Wednesday and Saturday; the first time to his clerk alone, to whom he addressed the service thus: "Dearly-beloved Roger, the Scripture moveth you and me in sundry places."

Here, in his thirty-fifth year, he began his career as a

6*

political writer, by a pamphlet on the side of the Whigs;
and three years later (1704) appeared his famous satiric
allegory, "The Tale of a Tub." This extraordinary
name was suggested by the fact that sailors are wont to
fling out a tub in order to turn aside a whale from his
threatened dash on the ship. So he threw out this satire,
to prevent his opponents from injuring the ship of State.
It ridicules the disputes between the different religious
sects, and, although it established his fame as a brilliant
satirist, yet it led good people to look on him with dis-
trust.

Here is the story, briefly told: "Three brothers—
Peter, Martin, and Jack—receive from their dying father
coats, which, if carefully kept clean, will last them all their
lives. As the fashions change, they add to the simple
coat shoulder-knots, gold lace, silver fringes, embroidery
of Indian figures, twisting the meaning of their father's
will so as to give a seeming sanction to these innovations.
Peter" (evidently the apostle of that name, here taken to
represent the Roman Catholic Church) "locks up the will,
assumes the style of a lord, and wears his coat proudly, as
it is. His brothers, stealing a copy of the document,
leave the great house, and begin to reform their coats.
Martin" (Luther) "goes to work cautiously in stripping off
the adornments, and leaves some of the embroidery alone,
lest he may·injure the cloth. But Jack" (Calvin), "in his
hot zeal, plucks off all at once, and in so doing splits the
seams, and tears away great pieces of the coat. Thus does
Swift depict the corruptions of early Christianity and the
results of the Reformation, in a satire of uncommon power
and strange, mad drollery. His sympathies are all with
Martin, and Peter gets off better than Jack."

He soon deserted the Whigs, failing to gain from them
the preferment he desired, and several years were devoted
to writing on political subjects in a fierce and bitter style,

attacking his old party in the most savage, caustic way. His great ambition was a bishopric in England; but his new allies did not quite dare to put the sneering, cavilling author of the "Tale of a Tub" in that position.

Hannay says, however, that the piety of that period was so extreme as to be odious and sickening cant. "The real reason was, that he had satirized a favorite—for this was the age of favorites and back-stairs influence—and Swift had scattered some of his terrible Greek fire over the sycophants of St. James."

They did at last reward him with the deanery of St. Patrick's, in Dublin; but, unfortunately for his prospects, the queen's death soon after brought the Whigs again into power, and he was forced to remain in Ireland, which was little better than exile.

He became immensely popular in Ireland by a political pamphlet, urging the use of home manufactures, and by a series of letters, signed "M. B. Drapier," warning the people not to exchange their gold and silver for the bad money of a certain William Wood, who had obtained a patent for coining half-pence for the use of Ireland, to an immense extent. Swift proved that it was a gross fraud, certain to ruin the nation, and the patent was annulled. For this he had such a popularity with the rabble as to gain the title of "The King of the Mob." His influence over the people was unbounded. The eyes of the kingdom were now turned with one consent on the man by whose unbending fortitude and preëminent talents this triumph was achieved. The Drapier's Head became a sign, his portrait was engraved, woven upon handkerchiefs, stuck upon medals, and displayed in every possible manner as the liberator of Ireland. And, like true Irishmen, they were all ready to fight for him. "If," said he to an archbishop who blamed him for kindling a riotous flame, "if I had lifted up my finger, they would have torn you to pieces." When Walpole meditated his arrest, his proposal was checked by a prudent friend, who inquired if he could spare ten thousand soldiers to guard the messenger who should execute so perilous a commission. It is said that his grateful admirers even begged for locks of his hair, until he feared he should have none left. All this gratitude and glory would have been a bright spot in his dark life, which was a tragedy from beginning to end, if he had been a true patriot. But the good work sprang from hatred of England, rather than honest devotion to Green Erin. Still it may not be best to analyze too closely the motives of our greatest men, and, to be impartial, I will quote a few words from an Irish author: " On this gloom one luminary rose, and Ireland worshipped it with Persian idolatry; her true patriot—her first—almost her last. Sagacious and intrepid, he saw, he dared; above suspicion, he was trusted; above envy, he was beloved; above rivalry, he was obeyed. His wisdom was practical and prophetic— remedial for the present, warning for the future. He first taught Ireland that she might cease to be a despot. But he was a churchman. His gown impeded his course and entangled his efforts—guiding a senate, or heading an army, he had been more than Cromwell, and Ireland not less than England. As it was, he saved her by his courage, improved her by his authority, adorned her by his talents, and exalted her by his fame. His mission was but of ten years; and for ten years only did his personal power mitigate the government. But, though no longer feared by the great, he was not forgotten by the wise; his influence, like his writings, has survived a century, and the foundations of whatever prosperity we have since erected are laid in the disinterested and magnanimous patriotism of Swift."

In 1726 he published his most perfect satire, "Gulliver's Travels," in which he describes the wonderful and amusing adventures of a commonplace and well-meaning surgeon, Lemuel Gulliver, who, after being shipwrecked, finds himself in the country of Liliput, where the inhabitants are about six inches high, and every other object in exact proportion. Afterward he visits the land of the gigantic Brobdingnagians, where the smallest dwarf is at least thirty feet high. The object of the allegory is to show how contemptible and foolish are the vices and passions of mankind, and how contemptible human nature appears to him. Every child is charmed with this story, and it never fails to entertain those who do not see, or do not care to see, the undercurrent of almost fiendish satire that runs through the whole. Here is a pleasant specimen of his grave irony, describing Gulliver's boating experiences in Brobdingnag:

"The queen, who often used to hear me talk of my sea-voyages, and took all occasions to divert me when I was melancholy, asked me whether I understood how to handle a sail or an oar, and whether a little exercise of rowing might not be convenient for my health. I answered, that I understood both very well; for, although my proper employment had been to be surgeon or doctor to the ship, yet often upon a pinch I was forced to work like a common mariner. But I could not see how this could be done in their country, where the smallest wherry was equal to a first-rate man-of-war among us, and such a boat as I could manage would never live in any of their rivers. Her majesty said, if I would contrive a boat, her own joiner should make it, and she would provide a place for me to sail in. The fellow was an ingenious workman, and, by my instructions, in ten days finished a pleasure-boat, with all its tackling, able conveniently to hold eight Europeans. When it was finished, the queen was so delighted, that she ran with it in her lap to the king, who ordered it to be put in a cistern full of water, with me in it

by way of trial; where I could not manage my two sculls,
or little oars, for want of room.   But the queen had before
contrived another project.   She ordered the joiner to
make a wooden trough of three hundred feet long, fifty
broad, and eight deep, which, being well pitched, to prevent leaking, was placed on the floor along the wall in an
outer room of the palace.   It had a cock near the bottom
to let out the water, when it began to grow stale; and
two servants could easily fill it in half an hour.   Here I
often used to row for my own diversion, as well as that of
the queen and her ladies, who thought themselves well entertained with my skill and agility.   Sometimes I would
put up my sail, and then my business was only to steer,
while the ladies gave me a gale with their fans; and when
they were weary, some of the pages would blow my sail
forward with their breath, while I showed my art by
steering starboard or larboard, as I pleased.   When I had
done, Glumdalclitch always carried back my boat into
her closet, and hung it on a nail to dry."

I do not know but that his coolest irony is seen in his
satire on the misgovernment of Ireland, in a pamphlet entitled, " A Modest Proposal to the Public, for Preventing
the Children of Poor People in Ireland from being a Burden to their country, and for making them Beneficial to
the Public."   He suggests that these superfluous children
be used for *food*, as they then might be changed from
a public grievance into a source of pecuniary benefit.
"I have been assured," says he, "by a very knowing
American of my acquaintance in London, "that a young
healthy child, well-nursed, is, at a year old, a most delicious,
nourishing, and wholesome food, whether stewed, roasted,
baked, or boiled; and, I make no doubt, it will equally
serve in a *ragout*."   He goes on to argue in this way with
such earnestness and gravity, that the pamphlet was

quoted by a French writer of the time, to illustrate the hopeless barbarity of the English.

But do not imagine that the author of these burlesques was a happy man, for I cannot picture a more miserable being. He wrote to his friend Bolingbroke at this time: " It is time for me to have done with the world, and so I would if I could get into a better before I was called into the best—and not have to die here, like a poisoned rat, in a hole."

His only consolation seemed to be his intimate acquaintance with the unfortunate Miss Johnson, who, at his request, had followed him to Dublin, and lived near him. All these years he had written her almost daily letters, full of love and tenderness; told her he loved her better than his life, a thousand million times—but neither married her nor allowed her to marry any one else. At the same time he was keeping up a correspondence with another beautiful girl, who had also recited to him, and whose affections he ·trifled with in the most unprincipled way, permitting her to love him with all the power of a very intense nature. And the unfortunate *dénouement*, he tells us, was so unlooked for! When he came one day to say adieu in a *fatherly* way, as was natural and proper, he was distressed to hear the maiden confess—her love! In his own words:

> " Cadenus felt within him rise
> Shame, disappointment, and surprise,
> He knew not how to reconcile
> Such language with her usual style;
> And yet her thoughts were so expressed,
> He could not hope she spoke in jest.
> His thoughts had wholly been confined
> To form and cultivate her mind;
> He hardly knew, till he was told,
> Whether the nymph were young or old;
> Had met her in a public place,
> Without distinguishing her face.

> Much less could his declining age
> Vannessa's earliest thoughts engage
> And if her youth indifference met,
> His person must contempt beget.
> Or grant her passion be sincere,
> How shall his innocence be clear;
> Appearances were all so strong,
> The world must think him in the wrong."

Those last two lines have certainly the appearance of truth, and the world's verdict is not very far from his supposition. When the poor girl heard of Stella, she was wildly jealous, then almost crazy with grief, and at last died of a broken heart. It is said her death shocked the dean; it did not make him more human in his treatment of Stella. She always lived in another house, but near enough to come when he was ill or suffering, and nurse him with untiring devotion. She arranged his table when he gave a dinner, but never took her proper place there. It is affirmed that he was at last privately married to her in the deanery garden, but this made no difference in their peculiar relations. She still remained in her own home. Crushed by this cruel, unnatural treatment, Stella sank into her grave in her forty-fourth year; and Swift really mourned then, because he wanted her care, and missed her unselfish affection. He never mentioned her without a sigh. He preserved one of those dark, glossy curls in a paper, on which was written " *Only a woman's hair.*"

Scott interprets this cynical indifference as an attempt to hide his deep feeling. If that was his aim, his success was admirable.

It is extraordinary that a man who was neither young, nor handsome, nor rich, nor even amiable, should have inspired such love. His countenance was sour and severe, and his complexion muddy. Johnson says, in his stately way, that, although he washed his face with " *Oriental scrupulosity,*" it would never look clean. Perhaps he

conquered with his *eyes*, which Pope said were "azure as
the heavens, with a charming archness in them."

After Stella's death he became crabbed, and stingy,
and deaf, and cross, and miserable. His birthday, which
was always celebrated with bonfires and great rejoicings,
was to him the saddest day of the year. He had made a
foolish vow not to wear glasses, so he could not read. He
thus describes his own condition:

> "Deaf, giddy, helpless, left alone,
> To all my friends a burden grown;
> No more I hear my church's bell
> Than if it rang out for my knell;
> At thunder now no more I start
> Than at the rumbling of a cart;
> Nay, what's incredible, alack!
> I hardly hear a woman's clack."

He lost reason and memory, and died a solitary idiot
in the hands of servants, on the 19th of October, 1745.
He bequeathed most of his property to an hospital for
lunatics and idiots—

> "To show, by one satiric touch,
> No nation wanted it so much."

Let us turn from this sad picture to some specimens
of his wit:

A pert young man once said to him, "Do you know,
Mr. Dean, that I set up for a wit?" "Do you so?" answered Mr. Swift; "take my advice and—sit down again."

In travelling, he called at a hospitable house, where
the good but garrulous lady asked him with great eagerness what he would have for dinner. "Will you have an
apple-pie, sir, or a cherry-pie, sir, or a plum-pie, sir?"
"Any pie, madam, but a mag-pie."

He disliked profuse apology, and, when a farmer's wife
spoiled his dinner by saying "It is not good enough for

his worship to sit down to," he exclaimed: "Then why didn't you get a better? You knew I was coming. I've a great mind to go away and dine on a red herring."

A gentleman, trying to persuade him to dine at his house, said, "I will send the bill of fare." Swift replied, "Send me your bill of company."

The taxes were very severe in Ireland. Lady Carteret, wife of the lord-lieutenant, said to him: "The air of Ireland is very excellent and healthy." "For goodness' sake," said Swift, "don't say so in England, madam, for if you do, they will certainly *tax* it."

His favorite barber, having decided to take a public house and yet keep up his old business, begged the dean to give him "a smart little touch of poetry, to clap under his sign." So he wrote this couplet, which remained for many years:

> "Rove not from pole to pole, but step in here,
> Where naught excels the shaving, but the beer."

He was fond of making *extempore* proverbs, to suit the circumstances. Walking with some friends in a gentleman's garden, who did not invite them to enjoy his tempting fruit, Swift observed that it was a saying of his dear grandmother:

> "Always pull a peach,
> When it is within your reach!"

and at once helped himself, followed by the whole company.

His servants were truly attached to him, and would never leave him; yet his method of discipline was peculiar. One of them annoyed him by her carelessness—leaving doors open. She had once obtained permission to attend her sister's wedding, and had been gone some fifteen minutes, when she was sent for to return. Back she came, post-haste, to the dean's study, to know what he wanted. "Shut the door!" was the laconic answer, with a long moral understood.

He sometimes loved to impose upon the credulity of the Irish, especially their faith in him. When a large crowd had gathered one morning to see an *eclipse*, he gave a crier a shilling to announce, "that it was the pleasure of the dean that the eclipse should not come off till nine o'clock the next day." Whereupon they all quietly dispersed.

There is a witty epigram, reporting a little sharp-shooting between the caustic dean and some unknown fair one, in which the lady certainly had the best of it:

> " Cries Sylvia to a reverend dean,
>   ' What reason can be given,
> Since marriage is a holy thing,
>   That there are none in heaven ? '
>
> ' There are no *women*,' he replied ;
>   She quick returned the jest:
> ' Women there are, but I'm afraid
>   They cannot find a *priest.*' "

In judging the character and conduct of this unhappy man, we should remember his peculiar temperament and his disordered brain. He was loved and sincerely lamented by his friends, by the poor, by the whole Irish nation whom he helped so powerfully. He wanted a proper position in life, and was no more selfish than other men in his efforts to obtain it. He did much for England, and expected England to do something for him. His faults were so prominent, that his virtues are apt to be forgotten; and, no doubt, his memory has been treated with too much harshness. A man could not have been wholly bad whom Addison spoke of " as the most agree-able companion, the truest friend, the greatest genius of his times."

Sir James Mackintosh said of him: "The distinguishing feature of his moral character was a strong sense of *justice,* which disposed him to exact with rigor, as well as in general scrupulously to observe, the duties of society. These powerful feelings, exasperated probably by some circumstances of his own life, were gradually formed into an habitual and painful indignation against triumphant wrong, which became the ruling principle of his character and writings. His hatred of hypocrisy sometimes drove him to a parade of harshness, which made his character appear less amiable than it really was. His friendships were faithful, if not tender, and his beneficence was active, though it rather sprang from principle than feeling. No stain could be discoverable in his private conduct, if we could forget his intercourse with one unfortunate and with one admirable woman."

LARACOR CHURCH.

A. Pope

POPE.

"His whole nature was small, thin, and fine, rather than large or broad. Like . a tongue of flame, however, thin and small as it was, it was high-aspiring."

AMONG the brilliant wits of Queen Anne's reign, none stands higher than ALEXANDER POPE, born in the memorable year of the revolution, May 22, 1688. But sadness mingled with joy in his mother's heart, for her child was both sickly and deformed. His *face*, in childhood, however, was remarkably pleasant, his temper mild and gentle, and his voice so sweet that he was called "the little nightingale." When this pretty, delicate boy became a famous poet, he used his powers of sarcasm so often and so freely, that he was feared and hated as well as admired; and gruff old Dr. Johnson said of him, that "the

weakness of his body continued through his life, but the
mildness of his mind ended with his childhood." Playing in the yard one day, when not more than three years
old, he came very near being killed by a mad cow, which
had not the slighest respect for youthful genius.   He
was loading a little cart with stones and dirt, when the
animal struck at him, wounded him in the throat, tossing
off his hat and feather with her horns, and flung the poor
little fellow down on the heap of stones he had been
playing with.   A kind aunt taught him to read, and he
learned to write by carefully copying the printed characters in books, diverting himself in that way as other
children do with scrawling pictures.

He began to compose poetry almost as soon as he
could talk, and says of himself :

> " While yet a child and all unknown to fame,
>   I lisped in numbers, for the numbers came."

Among his poems you will find an " Ode on Solitude,"
written before he was twelve, which is a wonderful production for a boy-poet—a true poem and perfect in its
way.   As it is short, I will give you the whole of it :

> " Happy the man whose wish and care
>   A few paternal acres bound ;
>   Content to breathe his native air,
>   In his own ground.
>
> " Whose herds with milk, whose field with bread,
>   Whose flocks supply him with attire,
>   Whose trees in summer yield him shade,
>   In winter fire.
>
> " Blessed who can unconcern'dly find
>   Hours, days, and years slide soft away,
>   In health of body, peace of mind,
>   Quiet by day.

" Sound sleep by night: study and ease
Together mixed, sweet recreation ;
And innocence, which most does please
With meditation.

" Thus let me live, unseen, unknown,
Thus unlamented let me die,
Steal from the world, and not a stone
Tell where I lie."

This is a quiet, unambitious picture, but you can judge but little of one's true feelings by his writings. This slender, sweet-faced boy had already built many a glowing air-castle for the future, and had revelled in wild dreams of coming fame. He was fond of copying the style of other authors, and in one of his early effusions imitated Cowley, Milton, Spenser, Homer, and Virgil; but Dryden was the poet whom he most admired, and he induced some friends to take him to Will's Coffee-house, that he might look at the great man, whose style he proposed to follow. How the heart of the ambitious, intellectual little hero-worshipper would have bounded and thrilled with joy could he have foreseen his future triumphs, and realized that he was not to be compared with, but considered superior to, this literary lion whom he was gazing at with such curiosity, admiration, and reverence! About this time, his father, a Catholic, and wealthy linen-draper, gave up business in disgust at the shadow which the revolution had flung upon his church, and retired to Binfield, near Windsor Forest, where he owned a farm of twenty acres, and a small, cosy house, with a row of graceful elms before the door. Here for several summers the young dreamer gave himself up to the study of books and Nature, becoming familiar with a great number of the English, French, Italian, Latin, and Greek poets. "This I did," he says, "without any design except to amuse myself; and got the languages by hunting after the stories in the several poets I read, rather than read the books to get the languages, and was like a boy gathering flowers in the fields and woods, just as they fell in my way. These five or six years I look upon as the happiest in my life."

Thackeray speaks of this as "a beautiful holiday picture. The forest and the fairy story-book—the boy spelling Ariosto or Virgil under the trees, battling with the Cid for the love of Chimene, or dreaming of Armida's garden—peace and sunshine round about—the kindest love and tenderness waiting for him at his quiet home yonder, and Genius throbbing in his young heart, and whispering to him: 'You shall be great—you shall be famous—you, too, shall love and sing—you will sing her so nobly, that some kind heart shall forget you are weak and ill-formed.'"

Pope never knew the toils and pleasures of college-life, and was decidedly a self-educated man. His father used to encourage his poetical tastes, carefully correcting whatever he wrote, while his dear, simple-hearted mother and loving sister almost worshipped him. The latter says: "I think no man was ever so little fond of money;" and again, "I think my brother, when he was young, read more books than any man in the world."

Some people thought him half crazy in those days—were doubtful whether he would make a madman or a poet. But he kept on reading and writing, translating from the classic poets, paraphrasing Chaucer's tales, etc., and in 1711 appeared his "Essay on Criticism," finished before he was twenty-one, which was received with universal admiration, and compelled all to own his power. In it you will find many true thoughts, dressed in language sparkling, pointed, elegant, and its pithy, witty couplets are often quoted. No other poet, always excepting Shakespeare, has furnished more brief quotations, full of truth, yet tinged with worldly wisdom. Let me run through this Essay, giving some of the most familiar lines :

> " 'Tis with our judgments, as with our watches, none
> Go just alike, yet each believes his own."

> " A little learning is a dangerous thing ;
> Drink deep, or taste not the Pierian spring."

> " True wit is nature, to advantage dressed,
> What oft was thought, but ne'er so well expressed."

> " Words are like leaves, and where they most abound,
> Much fruit of sense beneath is rarely found." ·

> " To err is human—to forgive, divine."

> " For fools rush in where angels fear to tread."

And those lines to illustrate his idea that " sound must seem an echo to the sense : "

> " When Ajax strives some rock's vast weight to throw,
> The line too labors, and the words move slow ;
> Not so when swift Camilla scours the plain,
> Flies o'er the unbending corn and skims along the main."

In the next year he published " The Rape of the Lock," which tells the story of a silken curl cut from a fair maiden's head by a gay and daring young nobleman. The affair caused a violent quarrel between the two families, and Pope wrote this miniature epic—airy, fanciful, exquisite—to laugh them together again. Besides being the most brilliant specimen of the mock-heroic style ever attempted in English verse, it gives a more faithful and vivid idea of fashionable life in the reign of Queen Anne than we could gain from any sober history of the time. Listen to the description of Belinda's artificial charms :

> " And now, unveiled, the toilet stands displayed,
> Each silver vase in mystic order laid :
> First robed in white, the nymph intent adores,
> With head uncovered, the cosmetic powers ;

7

A heavenly image in the glass appears,
To that she bends, to that her eyes she rears ;
The inferior priestess at her altar's side,
Trembling, begins the sacred rites of pride ;
Unnumbered treasures ope at once, and here
The various offerings of the world appear ;
From each she nicely culls with curious toil,
And decks the goddess with the glittering spoil.
This casket India's glowing gems unlocks,
And all Arabia breathes from yonder box ;
The tortoise here and elephant unite,
Transformed to combs, the speckled and the white.
Here files of pins extend their shining rows,
Puffs, powders, patches, Bibles, billet-doux.
Now awful Beauty puts on all its arms ;
The fair each moment rises in her charms,
Repairs her smiles, awakens every grace,
And calls forth all the wonders of her face ;
Sees by degrees a purer blush arise,
And keener lightnings quicken in her eyes.
The busy Sylphs surround their darling care,
These set the head, and those divide the hair ;
Some fold the sleeve, whilst others plait the gown,
And Betty's praised for labors not her own."

The machinery of the poem, as critics call the intro-
duction of supernatural beings into the action of the plot,
was taken from the Rosicrucian doctrine that the four
elements are filled with sylphs, gnomes, nymphs, and sala-
manders. These tiny, invisible sprites, which give half
the charm to the story, were added after it was finished.
Belinda was surrounded by a body-guard of these aërial
visitors—

"Some, orb in orb, around the nymph extend ;
Some thrid the mazy ringlets of her hair,
Some hang upon the pendants of her ear."

And yet all their care was in vain—her "favorite lock"
was stolen in spite of them all. I must give you the story
of that daring theft :

" For lo ! the board with cups and spoons is crowned,
The berries crackle, and the mill turns round :
On shining altars of Japan they raise
The silver lamp ; the fiery spirits blaze :
From silver spouts the grateful liquors glide,
While China's earth receives the smoking tide ;
At once they gratify their scent and taste,
And frequent cups prolong the rich repast.
Straight hover round the fair her airy band ;
Some, as she sipped, the fuming liquor fanned ;
Some o'er her lap their careful plumes displayed,
Trembling and conscious of the rich brocade.
Coffee (which makes the politician wise,
And see through all things with his half-shut eyes)
Sent up in vapors to the baron's brain
New stratagems the radiant lock to gain.
Ah ! cease, rash youth ; desist ere 'tis too late ;
Fear the just gods, and think of Scylla's fate !
Changed to a bird, and sent to flit in air,
She dearly paid for Nisus' injured hair !

 But when to mischief mortals bend their will,
How soon they find fit instruments of ill !
Just then, Clarissa drew, with tempting grace,
A two-edged weapon from her shining case ;
So ladies, in romance, assist their knight,
Present the spear, and arm him for the fight.
He takes the gift with reverence, and extends
The little engine on his fingers' ends ;
This just behind Belinda's neck he spread,
As o'er the fragrant steams she bent her head.
Swift to the lock a thousand sprites repair,
A thousand wings, by turns, blow back the hair !
And thrice they twitched the diamond in her ear ;
Thrice she looked back, and thrice the foe drew near.
Just in that instant, anxious Ariel sought
The close recesses of the virgin's thought :
As on the nosegay in her breast reclined,
He watched the ideas rising in her mind.
Sudden he viewed, in spite of all her art,
An earthly lover lurking at her heart.
Amazed, confused, he found his power expired,
Resigned to fate, and with a sigh retired.

The peer now spreads the glittering forfex wide
To enclose the lock ; now joins it, to divide.
E'en then, before the fatal engine closed,
A wretched Sylph too fondly interposed ;
Fate urged the shears, and cut the Sylph in twain
(But airy substance soon unites again),
The meeting points the sacred hair dissever
From the fair head, forever, and forever ! "

Soon after the appearance of this enchanting little poem, Pope published "The Temple of Fame," a revival of Chaucer's "House of Fame," and his descriptive poem of "Windsor Forest;" but he had no real love for nature, excelling in satiric sketching of the absurdities and affectations of artificial society. These poems, though so clever and charming, did not help very much to fill his purse; and poets, like ordinary mortals, find money a very necessary thing. So he went to work in earnest, and the next dozen years were spent in translating Homer's great epics, "The Iliad" and "The Odyssey," and from these he gained a comfortable fortune. But it was hard, uncongenial work. He said to a friend : "In the beginning of my translating Homer, I wished anybody would hang me, a hundred times. It sat so heavily on my mind at first, that I often used to dream of it, and even do, sometimes, still to this day. My dream usually was, that I had set out on a very long journey, puzzled which way to take, and full of fears that I should never get to the end of it. My time and eyes have been wholly employed upon Homer, whom I almost fear I shall find but one way of imitating, which is in his *blindness*." As translations, they are very praiseworthy, but must not be compared with the original. "A pretty poem, Mr. Pope, but you must not call it Homer," was the criticism of the great scholar, Bentley.

"Like Dryden translating Virgil, Pope did little more than reproduce the sense of Homer's verse in smooth

and neatly-balanced English couplets, leaving the spirit
behind in the glorious rough old Greek, that tumbles on
the ear like the roar of a winter sea."

'A large part of the money thus gained he spent very
wisely in buying a house and garden at Twickenham, one
of the most beautiful spots on the banks of the Thames.
He made his home a little paradise, and the grounds,
adorned with grottoes and fountains, were a miracle of
beauty. Here he brought his parents, who lived with him
till their death, and here he entertained the greatest, wittiest, and wisest men of his time, all of whom were proud
to call themselves his friends. Like Swift, he loved and
reverenced his mother, and it is touching to notice how all
these famous wits and philosophers and divines have a
kind word or thoughtful remembrance for that dear old
lady. Swift mentioned him as one

> ———— " whose filial piety excels
> Whatever Grecian story tells."

He has himself written beautifully on this subject :

> " Me, let the tender office long engage,
> To rock the cradle of reposing age,
> With lenient arts extend a mother's breath,
> Make languor smile, and smooth the bed of death ;
> Explore the thought, explain the asking eye,
> And keep awhile one parent from the sky."

Perhaps the life of this dutiful son, in such a beautiful
home, may seem to you a happy one; but deformed,
sensitive, dreading ridicule, and exasperated by cruel
taunts, he suffered much more than he enjoyed. Every
morning he had to be dressed like a child. His distorted
figure was encased in stays of stiff canvas, and three
pairs of stockings were needed to make his slender legs
respectable. His stature was so low, that he was obliged

to use a high chair at table, and could neither go to bed nor rise without help. Do you wonder that he was often irritable, exacting, childish? It is said that, though sometimes merry in company, he was never seen to laugh. His health was improved by his retirement from city life. He was not strong enough to endure the excitements there.

Addison and his friends used often to sit until two o'clock in the morning with their pipes and punch, and, unlike Pope, laughed and grew fat.

Swift, Addison, Steele, Gay, and Thomson, were all corpulent. As Thackeray puts it: "All that fuddling and punch-drinking, that club and coffee-house boozing, shortened the lives and enlarged the waistcoats of the men of that age." Once in a while he would invite these jovial friends to Twickenham for a handsome dinner, but his general habits were a little stingy. He once placed a pint of wine on his table, and, after drinking a glass himself, left the room, saying to his guests: "Gentlemen, I leave you to your wine." This is almost worse than Swift's way of paying his friends for the food they had not eaten! He was very economical in regard to paper, and most of his translations were written on the backs of envelopes and such odd scraps. He was rather a disagreeable visitor, keeping the servants in a constant state of impatience by his numerous calls. His best thoughts would often come at night, and then Betty was rung for, and a cup of coffee must be brought to aid the eccentric invalid in jotting them down. He was a great epicure, and would lie in bed for days together, unless told of some especial delicacy, when he would get up at once to enjoy it.

His friendships with men were delightful, until some reason came for a quarrel; but he had no honest regard for women, whom he always wrote of in the most spiteful, ungenerous way. Failing to gain their love, his stilted admiration changed to earnest hating. For instance, look at his acquaintance with Lady Mary Montagu, whom, at first, he praised excessively, and told her so in set phrases in many fine letters. Whenever he thought one particularly good, he would copy it, and send it to some other lady, to produce effect. In one of these letters, so full of sham sentiment, addressed to Lady Mary, he says: "I think I love you as well as King Herod could Herodias (though I never had so much as one dance with you), and would as freely give you my head in a dish, as he did another's head." But Lady Mary was once so amused by his extravagant professions of regard as to laugh outright in her adorer's face, and from that time he pursued her not with honey, but gall, until she gave him the *sobriquet* of "The Wasp of Twickenham," and said that he assumed the mask of a moralist in order to decry human nature, and to give vent to his hatred of man and woman kind.

Gay, a brother poet, once sent him a touching story, very simply and sweetly told, of two country lovers, killed by a lightning-flash during a summer shower. Pope thought it extremely well done—and at once sent it to Lady Montagu—*as his own.* His great and increasing fame caused him to be hated and attacked by a host of inferior writers. Some one says that "a poet should have the hide of a hippopotamus to be happy," and Pope was very thin skinned. They stung and exasperated him, until at length, like Dryden, he revenged himself by a bitter poem, "The Dunciad," in which he lashed his envious critics most unmercifully, giving many a fame they could have gained in no other way. These scribblers have gained immortality, though not exactly in the way they desired, preserved like straws in amber—"the trash of literature vitrified by the lightning of indignant genius."

His life was really in danger after this fierce attack

upon his enemies, but he still took his daily walk alone, and, though so feeble, would allow no one to go with him. "I had rather die at once," said he, "than live in fear of those rascals." Indeed, he felt a keen delight in seeing how deeply his "scorn-winged arrows" had pierced the hearts of the "dunces," exclaiming:

> "I know I'm proud—I must be proud to see
> Men, not afraid of God, afraid of me."

It is curious to trace this word "dunce" to its source, the great teacher of the Franciscan order, *Duns* Scotus, whom his followers called the "subtle doctor." But those who did not accept his theology would say to his disciples: "Oh, you are a Dunsman," or, more briefly, "You are a Duns," and, as his teaching and theories lost ground, the word became in time a synonyme for stupidity. In his "Essay on Man," Pope attempts to vindicate Providence, and to show the necessity of evil in the world, and that our finite capacities fail to see the wisdom of God's perfect plan. In short:

> "All nature is but art, unknown to thee;
> All chance, direction, which thou canst not see;
> All discord, harmony not understood;
> All partial evil, universal good;
> And spite of pride, in erring reason's spite,
> One truth is clear, whatever is, is right."

His own idea of this poem is well expressed in these lines:

> "Eye Nature's walks, shoot folly as it flies,
> And catch the manners living as they rise;
> Laugh where we must, be candid where we can,
> But vindicate the ways of God to man."

Pope has been accused of being a fatalist, but he positively asserts man's free agency and responsibility: and though he did not look at life and life's realities from the noblest stand-point, he certainly intended to write in favor of morality and Christianity. The "Essay" is full of beautiful lines, but I will only make one extract:

> "All are but parts of one stupendous whole,
> Whose body Nature is, and God the soul;
> That, changed through all, and yet in all the same,
> Great in the earth, as in th' ethereal frame,
> Warms in the sun, refreshes in the breeze,
> Glows in the stars, and blossoms in the trees;
> Lives through all life, extends through all extent,
> Spreads undivided, operates unspent;
> Breathes in our soul, informs our mortal part,
> As full, as perfect, in a hair as heart;
> As full as perfect, in vile man that mourns,
> As the rapt seraph that adores and burns;
> To Him no high, no low, no great, no small;
> He fills, He bounds, connects, and equals all."

His style is pointed, precise, polished. Unlike his model, Dryden, he wrote with great care, and elaborated and pruned with untiring hand. He knew

> "The last and greatest art, the art to blot."

Yet, with all his care, some of his lines are rather silly when criticised separately. For instance:

> "Why has not man a microscopic eye?
> For this plain reason—man is not a fly."

Sydney Smith, the witty English divine, has given us a parody of this:

> "Why has not man a collar and a log?
> For this plain reason—man is not a dog."

> "Why is not man served up with sauce in dish?
> For this plain reason—man is not a fish."

Swift and Pope were good friends, and always corresponded. Both were morbid and misanthropic. Swift despised mankind, but liked individuals. Pope tolerated

7 *

the masses, but hated particular men and women. Their
letters are sad to read, because there they showed their
jealousies, and prejudices, and hates. "As good friends
exchange jam, or turkeys, or oysters, these potentates
occasionally sent each other little pots of gall, or prepara-
tions of poison, as friendly gifts."

Pope, when he first met Addison, was his warm admirer and humble servant. It was he who wrote the pro-
logue for " Cato," and he even went so far as to lampoon
Addison's enemies, in a coarse way, which offended rather
than pleased his patron. There were other reasons why they
could not be friends. Addison did like to have all the atten-
tions and all the praise, and was naturally jealous of the
rising genius. Then, too, Tickell, his bosom friend, published a translation of " The Iliad " at the same time with
Pope, which was thought by some to be more scholarly and
exact, as Pope had never studied at a university. Pope
accused Addison of helping Tickell in his work, which was
not true; but of course there could be no friendship in the
future. Pope was too indignant to be silent, and the
verses which he sent to Addison are known to all:

> " And were there one whose fires
> True genius kindles, and fair fame inspires—
> Blest with each talent and each art to please,
> And born to write, converse, and live with ease ?
> Should such a man, too fond to rule alone,
> Bear, like the Turk, no brother near the throne ?
> View him with scornful yet with jealous eyes,
> And hate for arts that caused himself to rise ;
> Damn with faint praise, assent with civil leer,
> And, without sneering, teach the rest to sneer ;
> Willing to wound, and yet afraid to strike,
> Just hint a fault and hesitate dislike ;
> Alike reserved to blame as to commend,
> A timorous foe, and a suspicious friend ;
> Dreading even fools, by flatteries besieged,
> And so obliging that he ne'er obliged ;

> Like Cato, gives his little senate laws,
> And sits attentive to his own applause;
> While wits and templars every sentence raise,
> And wonder with a foolish face of praise;
> Who but must laugh, if such a man there be?
> Who would not weep if Atticus were he?"

There is *venom* in this description, and just enough truth to make the libel more effective. How much better and happier a man he might have been if he had carried out in his life the beautiful sentiment found in his "Universal Prayer:"

> "Teach me to feel another's woe,
> To hide the fault I see;
> That mercy I to others show,
> That mercy show to me."

TWICKENHAM.

You observe the difference between the authors last described and Shakespeare? He wrote for all men, all countries, and all time. Swift, Addison, Pope, wrote for their own time alone, to suit the artificial state of society; and you will find little *true* pathos, humanity, or humor. Pope was witty, ingenious, acute, sparkling, sarcastic; but he was not a *natural* poet, and never forgot himself. Through all his life he delighted in artifice, and hardly drank tea without a stratagem. But his misfortune leads us to overlook many faults. He died at Twickenham, on the 30th of May, 1744, after a life of incessant ill-health and incessant industry, adorned with a greater share of fame and honor than often falls to the lot of poets.

YOUNG.

———"Whom dismal scenes delight,
Frequent at tombs and in the realms of night."

EDWARD YOUNG, whose fame is chiefly due to his
"Night Thoughts," now little read, but often quoted, was
a very different man from either the "vitriolic Swift" or
the sparkling poet we last spoke of. His father was an
eloquent dean, and preached so well that he was appointed
chaplain to King William and Queen Mary, and the little
Edward, who was born in 1681, was honored by having
the princess royal (afterward Queen Anne) for his god-
mother. He was educated at All Souls College, Oxford,
and, though he did not gain a scholarship, Oxford was
certainly proud of him; for, only two years after his
graduation, he was appointed to speak a Latin oration at
the founding of a library there.

Pope says that Young had much of a sublime genius, but lacked *common-sense*, and genius without that sturdy guide is apt to become mere bombast. So he was thought a little weak by his friends, who laughed at his foibles, while they acknowledged his talent. It is said that he was dissipated in his early days, and led a gay, worldly life, under the patronage of a notoriously bad man—the Duke of Wharton. He may have been badly influenced by his profligate friend, but it is also true that he was remarkably well read in the Bible, and powerful in answering and refuting the arguments of his skeptical friends.

Tindal, a noted atheist of those days, used to spend much of his time at All Souls, and enjoyed discussing points of religious controversy with the young men, and this is his testimony: "The other boys I can always answer, because I know where they have their arguments, which I have read a hundred times; but that fellow, Young, is continually pestering me with something of his own."

Even if Young did try that wicked life, he left it in disgust, and, to his praise of virtue, adds a personal experience, which taught him to abhor all forms of vice. It makes him, perhaps, a better teacher of morality, for, as some one says, with great beauty of expression, "Experience, like the stern-lights of a ship, only illumines the path over which we have passed." Young's great mistake in life was his desire to gain the patronage and friendship of royalty and the nobility by fawning flattery; and this miserable ambition caused his whole life—and it was a long one—to be a series of disappointments and mortifications. Thinking, perhaps, that Addison gained his good fortune by a complimentary poem addressed to the king, "he hoped to soar to wealth and honor on wings of the same kind." So his first poem was addressed to Queen Anne, praising her in the most extravagant and absurd

manner, and his next poem, " On the Last Day," was also
dedicated to her. I believe he gained nothing by this
fulsome flattery but a pension from her majesty, as these
lines seem to prove in speaking of the court :

> " Whence Gay was banished in disgrace,
> Where Pope could never show his face ;
> Where Young must torture his invention
> To flatter knaves, or lose his pension."

In 1717 he went to Ireland with his patron, the dissolute Wharton, who was then really kind to him, giving
him much material aid, but afterward deserted him most
meanly. The greater part of Young's life was spent in
an unsuccessful struggle for fame as a courtier and poet.
At last he retired, disgusted and misanthropic.

At the age of fifty, he took clerical orders, and passed
the rest of his days in uneasy retirement, satirizing those
things he had failed to gain, and to which he ever looked
back with regret, still making an occasional effort to
satisfy his darling ambition. These feelings he tried to
hide in his poems by a veil of dignity and sublime indifference, which fails to deceive the careful reader. His
first important work was a satire on the " Love of Fame,"
which he styles the " universal passion," as he might well
do, if he judged the world by his own longings. This
satire, divided into seven epistles, is often strong and
vigorous, with many keen and happy hits ; but he was
not sufficiently gay, playful, or good-natured, to make it
quite satisfactory. As Swift remarked, " They should
have either been more angry or more merry." But they
were widely circulated, and brought the author more than
three thousand pounds. Of course, the reign of the new
monarch was ushered in by Young—ever waiting for a
favorable moment to advance his own claims—by a complimentary poem which he styled " Ocean ; an Ode."

King George, in his speech when he ascended the throne, had recommended the encouragement of the seamen; and the anxious poet and would-be favorite took his cue from this circumstance.

This ode concludes with a "wish," of which I will give you a specimen, quoting three of the thirteen stanzas, just to show how little we can know of an author's real feelings from what he gives to the world as such. The rhymes are very bad:

> " O may I steal
>   Along the vale
> Of humble life, secure from foes ;
>   My friend sincere,
>   My judgment clear,
> And gentle business my repose.
>
> " Prophetic schemes,
>   And golden dreams,
> May I, unsanguine, cast away !
>   Have what I *have*,
>   And *live*, not *leave*,
> Enamoured of the present day !
>
> " My hours my own,
>   My faults unknown !
> My chief revenue in content !
>   Then leave one beam
>   Of honest fame,
> And scorn the labored monument !"

He *hoped* to be rewarded by a bishopric, but this was withheld on the ground of the poet's extreme devotion to *retirement*, which he had so often expressed ! Rather hard, wasn't it, for the disappointed man ? Nothing was left him, after all his efforts, but to ponder in *solitude* over the folly of writing romantic stuff in which was neither sincerity nor heart. Honesty seems the best policy, after all, with poets as well as common people.

Whipple says : " A man of letters is often a man with

two natures—one a book nature, the other a human nature. These often clash sadly. Seneca wrote in praise of poverty, on a table formed of solid gold, with two millions of pounds let out at usury. Sterne was a very selfish man, according to Warburton, an irreclaimable rascal, yet a writer unexcelled for pathos and charity. Sir Richard Steele wrote excellently well on temperance, when he was sober. Dr. Johnson's essays on politeness are admirable; yet his 'You lie, sir,' and 'You don't understand the question, sir,' were too common characteristics of his colloquies. He and Dr. Shebbeare were both pensioned at the same time. The report immediately flew that the king had pensioned two bears—a he-bear and a she-bear. Young, whose gloomy fancy cast such sombre tinges on life, was in society a brisk, lively man, continually pelting his hearers with puerile puns. Mrs. Carter, fresh from the stern, dark grandeur of the 'Night Thoughts,' expressed her amazement at his flippancy. 'Madam,' said he, 'there is much difference between talking and writing.' The same poet's favorite theme was the nothingness of worldly things; his favorite pursuit was rank and riches. Had Mrs. Carter noticed this incongruity, he might have added, 'Madam, there is much difference between writing didactic poems and *living* didactic poems.'"

In 1730 his college gave him the rectory of Welwyn, in Hertfordshire, the only substantial favor he ever received, and that came *unasked;* and in May of the next year he married a widow, Lady Elizabeth Lee, to whom and her two children the poet was tenderly attached. This beautiful and lovely lady inspired one of the happiest and most elegant impromptus ever uttered.

Dr. Young (we must give him the only title he ever gained) was walking in his garden with two ladies, one of them Lady Lee. On being called away by a servant to speak to a parishioner on some important business, he was very unwilling to leave the ladies, and, on being almost driven into the house by their gentle violence, he thus addressed them:

> " Thus Adam once at God's command was driven
> From Paradise by angels sent from heaven;
> Like him I go, and yet to go am loath;
> Like him I go, for angels drove us both.
> Hard was his fate, but mine still more unkind,
> His Eve went with him, but mine stays behind."

His wife died in 1741, and this, with other domestic grief, induced him to write the "Night Thoughts," which have been so justly celebrated. In them you will find much to admire, and no doubt you have quoted from them without being aware of it; but his style is so solemn, with a would-be sublimity that too often approaches bombastic unmeaningness, and there is such a lack of connection, and sometimes of common-sense, that you will never be likely to read it continuously. He has given us many proverbs and quotable lines, which are familiar to all. For instance:

> " Tired nature's sweet restorer, balmy sleep."
>
> " Procrastination is the thief of time."
>
> " All men think all men mortal but themselves."
>
> " How blessings brighten as they take their flight!"
>
> " That life is long which answers life's great end."
>
> " Death loves a shining mark—a signal blow."

His last days, like those of too many of our great men, were sad and solitary. He is said to have been tyrannized over by a virago of a housekeeper, who drove his only son from his door, and kept him constantly unhappy.

He died in 1765, at the age of eighty-four.

His life was a curious contrast of worldliness and piety, luxury and devotion. His affections seemed always divided between God and Mammon. His book would hardly make us happier or better; his morality is often little better than prudence, and his gloomy truisms often sadden without improving. It is not advisable to give full expression to morbid feelings in prose or verse.

When Young, whose very name seems incongruous, was composing his "Thoughts," he would either ramble alone among the tombs, or sit in a darkened room, dimly lighted by candles.

Give me the author who loves to write in the sunshine among the flowers; whose object is to soothe and cheer, as well as instruct. One of our own poets has spoken in a higher and more blessed strain, making us feel that there are "Voices of the Night" which elevate and console:

> "O holy Night! from thee I learn to bear
> What man has borne before.
> Thou layest thy finger on the lips of Care,
> And they complain no more."

Yet we should not be too severe, for we cannot fail to find much in the character and writings of Young worthy of our admiration, and will close this sketch with the words of his biographer, Johnson, who says: "In spite of all his defects, he was a genius and a poet."

THOMSON.

" To him, who in the love of Nature holds
  Communion with her visible forms, she speaks
  A various language."

AFTER Young, comes the fat, lazy Scotchman, JAMES
THOMSON, whom we always think of as author of "The
Seasons."

His father was a good minister of Ednam, in Rox-
burghshire, and there, in 1700, James was born. The
good man's family being rather large, nine children in all,
he found it as much as he could do to feed and clothe
them, without thinking much of education, and another
minister, who lived near (perhaps not blessed with so
many olive-branches), finding James a clever boy, offered
to take him home, and provide him with all the books he

needed. At school, he was not thought a prodigy, excelling in no one study. But in those early days, he used to scribble poetry to amuse his kind friend and his playfellows; yet never was quite satisfied with his rhymes, looking them over every New-Year's-Day, only to throw them all into the fire. His friends wanted him to be a minister, and he was fitting for this profession at Edinburgh, with no other prospect for the future than the laborious life of a country parson, when he one day astonished his grave professor and charmed the class with a remarkably beautiful paraphrase of a psalm. His teacher blamed him for using language so fine as not to be understood by common people, but he cared more for the applause of his young friends than the censure of the grave doctor, and, coming to the conclusion that he was, by nature, more of a poet than preacher, gave up his studies, and soon went to London to seek his fortune. This was rather a bold step for a green, awkward youth, with neither money nor friends, and success did not smile on him at first, as you shall see.

He had secured several letters of recommendation to persons who could have helped him greatly, and had tied them carefully in the corner of his handkerchief, but London streets and London sights so dazzled and dazed the young Scotchman, that they were quietly taken from his pocket, with every thing else of value there, while he was gaping along, quite forgetting what had sent him to so wonderful a place. He was so poor, that he was not able to buy a pair of shoes, which he really needed. "But, never mind," thought our raw countryman, "I have something in my head worth more than all the shoes in the city." But light did not come at once to the young adventurer. He offered the manuscript of "Winter" to several publishers, but no one cared to take it; at last he found one, who bought it at a ridiculously low price—and then regretted that he had not refused it. It appeared in print in 1726. All that Thomson now needed was a patron. In those days it was not only politic, but absolutely necessary, for success, that the poets should cram some rich or powerful man with graceful, high-flown compliments, until (with very much the same effect as the flattery of the wily fox in Æsop's "Fables" had upon the silly crow, who soon drops the coveted bit of cheese), they open the purse-strings of the delighted magnate, and climb rapidly into favor. Thomson received, in this easy way, twenty guineas for a dedication to Sir Spencer Compton, of the poem, for which his publisher had thought three guineas a good recompense.

The appearance of "Winter" was a new sensation in the literary world. Dame Nature had been comparatively neglected for a long time. All the great poets, from Chaucer to Milton, had loved to commune with her, but, as Hare says, "When Milton lost his eyes, Poetry lost hers," and soon came the artificial school, where mountain and meadow and moonlight, and "all the forest music of an English landscape," were forgotten, and man and the town, the drawing-room and candle-light, usurped their place.

Poets looked at Nature through the spectacles of books. "It was as though a number of eyes had been set in a row, like boys playing at leap-frog, each hinder one having to look through all that stood before it, and, hence seeing Nature, not as it is in itself, but refracted and distorted by a number of more or less turbid media. Ever and anon, too, some one would be seized with the ambition of surpassing his predecessors, and would try by a feat at leap-eye, to get before them; in so doing, however, from ignorance of the ground, he mostly stumbled and fell. Making an impotent effort after originality, he would attempt to vary the combination of words in which

former writers had spoken of the same objects; but as
one is ever liable to trip and to violate idiom at least,
if not grammar, when speaking a foreign language, so by
these aliens to Nature, and sojourners in the land of
Poetry, images and expressions which belonged to particular circumstances, or to particular phases of feeling,
were often misapplied to circumstances and feelings with
which they were wholly incongruous. 'When the jay
spread out his peacock's tail, many of the quills were
sticking up in the air.'"

But those whose opinions were contagious liked "Winter;" amateurs sounded the praises of the new poet, who
now, happy as well as hopeful, soon completed his pano-
rama of the "varied year." It adds to the charm of these
poems to know that their author was sincere in his praise
of Nature, whom he really loved for her own sake. He
was in earnest when he wrote this noble stanza:

> "I care not, Fortune, what you me deny;
> You cannot rob me of free Nature's grace,
> You cannot shut the windows of the sky,
> Through which Aurora shows her brightening face;
> You cannot bar my constant feet to trace
> The woods and lawns, by living stream, at eve:
> Let health my nerves and finer fibres brace,
> And I their toys to the great children leave;
> Of fancy, reason, virtue, naught can me bereave."

How well he sings the loves of the birds in spring:

> "When first the soul of love is sent abroad,
> Warm through the vital air, and on the heart
> Harmonious seizes, the gay troops begin
> In gallant thought to plume the painted wing,
> And try again the long-forgotten strain,
> At first faint-warbled. But no sooner grows
> The soft infusion prevalent and wide,
> Than, all alive, at once their joy o'erflows
> In music unconfined. Up springs the lark,

Shrilled-voiced and loud, the messenger of morn;
Ere yet the shadows fly, he mounted sings
Amid the dawning clouds, and from their haunts
Calls up the tuneful nations.   Every copse
Deep-tangled, tree irregular, and bush
Bending with dewy moisture, o'er the heads
Of the coy quiristers that lodge within,
Are prodigal of harmony.   The thrush
And wood-lark, o'er the kind-contending throng
Superior heard, run through the sweetest length
Of notes; when listening Philomela deigns
To let them joy, and purposes, in thought
Elate, to make her night excel their day.
The blackbird whistles from the thorny brake;
The mellow bullfinch answers from the grove:
Nor are the linnets, o'er the flowering furze
Poured out profusely, silent.   Joined to these
Innumerous songsters, in the freshening shade
Of new-sprung leaves, their modulations mix
Mellifluous.   The jay, the rook, the daw,
And each harsh pipe, discordant heard alone,
Aid the full concert: while the stock-dove breathes
A melancholy murmur through the whole.
    'Tis love creates their melody, and all
This waste of music is the voice of love;
That e'en to birds, and beasts, the tender arts
Of pleasing teaches.   Hence the glossy kind
Try every winning way inventive love
Can dictate, and in courtship to their mates
Pour forth their little souls."

His description also of a man freezing in the winter snows is very graphic and pathetic:

" As thus the snows arise, and foul and fierce
All Winter drives along the darkened air;
In his own loose-revolving fields, the swain
Disastered stands; sees other hills ascend,
Of unknown joyless brow; and other scenes,
Of horrid prospect, shag the trackless plain;
Nor finds the river, nor the forest, hid

Beneath the formless wild; but wanders on
From hill to dale, still more and more astray;
Impatient flouncing through the drifted heaps,
Stung with the thoughts of home; the thoughts of home
Rush on his nerves, and call their vigor forth
In many a vain attempt. How sinks his soul!
What black despair, what horror fills his heart!
When for the dusky spot, which fancy feigned
His tufted cottage rising through the snow,
He meets the roughness of the middle waste,
Far from the track, and blest abode of man:
While round him night resistless closes fast,
And every tempest, howling o'er his head,
Renders the savage wilderness more wild.
Then throng the busy shapes into his mind,
Of covered pits, unfathomably deep,
A dire descent! beyond the power of frost;
Of faithless bogs; of precipices huge,
Smoothed up with snow; and, what is land unknown,
What water of the still unfrozen spring,
In the loose marsh or solitary lake,
Where the fresh fountain from the bottom boils.
These check his fearful steps; and down he sinks
Beneath the shelter of the shapeless drift,
Thinking o'er all the bitterness of death,
Mixed with the tender anguish nature shoots
Through the wrung bosom of the dying man—
His wife, his children, and his friends unseen.
In vain for him th' officious wife prepares .
The fire fair-blazing, and the vestment warm;
In vain his little children, peeping out
Into the mingling storm, demand their sire,
With tears of artless innocence. Alas!
Nor wife, nor children, more shall he behold,
Nor friends, nor sacred home. On every nerve
The deadly Winter seizes; shuts up sense;
And, o'er his inmost vitals creeping cold,
Lays him along the snow, a stiffened corse—
Stretched out, and bleaching in the northern blast."

Thomson next tried his pen upon tragedy, but never pleased the public. One silly line in his first play—

8

"O Sophonisba! Sophonisba O!"

was parodied by some wicked wag, and

"O Jemmy Thomson! Jemmy Thomson O!"

was sung, and whistled, and echoed, till, from laughing at this one blunder, the town ridiculed the whole. This was particularly hard on Thomson, who was so intensely anxious and excited, whenever one of his dramas was put on the stage, that he could be heard in an upper gallery; reciting word for word with the players, and he said his wig actually became *uncurled*, from "the sweat of his distress!"

Not long after this, in 1731, he travelled over the Continent, as tutor to the son of the distinguished lawyer, Chancellor Talbot, living in luxury, without any expense, enjoying, as few have the power to enjoy, all the delights and privileges of such a tour. After his return to England, he published a very long poem, in five parts, on "Liberty," upon which he had spent two years, which he thought his noblest work. But no one agreed with him; few read it then; it is hardly known now. So little can authors judge of the merits of their own works.

In 1738, being obliged, by the death of his patron, to resume work, he wrote two more tragedies, which also proved failures. But the Prince of Wales gave him a yearly pension of one hundred pounds, and, through the influence of a friend, he gained the office of Surveyor-General of the Leeward Islands, which yielded him three hundred pounds each year—after he had paid some one else for doing the work! He was the very "high-priest of indolence," and now, with an abundance of means, he spent the last years of his life in a thoroughly lazy way, in his pretty cottage at Richmond. "So intensely indolent was he, that he is said to have been in the habit, when lounging in his dressing-gown, along the sunny walks of his garden, of biting a mouthful out of the peaches ripening on his wall, too lazy to lift his hand to pluck them."

In this quiet home, with nothing in the world to do, he spent several years on his "Castle of Indolence," a dreamy, drowsy allegory, written in the style of Spenser, the very words of which seem to lull you to repose.

> " A pleasing land of drowsy head it was,
>   Of dreams that wave before the half-shut eye,
>   And of gay castles in the clouds that pass,
>   Forever flushing round a summer sky;
>   There eke the soft delights, that witchingly
>   Instil a wanton sweetness through the breast,
>   And the calm pleasures, always hovered nigh;
>   And whate'er smacked of 'noyance or unrest
> Was far, far off expelled from that delicious nest."

"The good knight Industry breaks the magician's spell; but (alas for the moral teaching of the allegory!) we have grown so delighted with the still and cushioned life, whose hours glide slumberously by, that we feel almost angry with the restless being who dissolves the delicious charm." I will give a few verses from the opening of the poem:

> " O mortal man, who livest here by toil,
>   Do not complain of this thy hard estate;
>   That like an emmet thou must ever moil,
>   Is a sad sentence of an ancient date;
>   And, certes, there is for it reason great;
>   For, though sometimes it makes thee weep and wail,
>   And curse thy star, an early drudge and late,
>   Withouten that would come a heavier bale,
> Loose life, unruly passions, and diseases pale.

> " In lowly dale, fast by a river's side,
>   With woody hill o'er hill encompass'd round,
>   A most enchanting wizard did abide,
>   Than whom a fiend more fell is nowhere found.
>   It was, I ween, a lovely spot of ground;

And there, a season atween June and May,
Half-pranked with spring, with summer half-imbrowned,
A listless climate made, where, sooth to say,
No living wight could work, ne cared e'en for play.

"Was naught around but images of rest;
Sleep-soothing groves, and quiet lawns between;
And flowery beds that slumberous influence kest,
From poppies breathed; and beds of pleasant green,
Where never yet was creeping creature seen.
Meantime unnumbered glittering streamlets played,
And hurled everywhere their waters sheen;
That, as they bickered through the sunny glade,
Though restless still themselves, a lulling murmur made.

"Joined to the prattle of the purling rills,
Were heard the lowing herds along the vale,
And flocks loud bleating from the distant hills,
And vacant shepherds piping in the dale:
And now and then sweet Philomel would wail,
Or stock-doves 'plain amid the forest deep,
That drowsy rustled to the sighing gale;
And still a coil the grasshopper did keep;
Yet all these sounds yblent inclined all to sleep.

"Thither continual pilgrims crowded still,
From all the roads of earth that pass thereby;
For, as they chanced to breathe on neighboring hill,
The freshness of this valley smote their eye,
And drew them ever and anon more nigh;
Till clustering round th' enchanter false they hung,
Ymolten with his siren melody;
While o'er th' enfeebling lute his hand he flung,
And to the trembling chords these tempting verses sung:

"'Behold! ye pilgrims of this earth, behold!
See all but man with unearned pleasure gay:
See her bright robes the butterfly unfold,
Broke from her wintry tomb in prime of May!
What youthful bride can equal her array?
Who can with her for easy pleasure vie?
From mead to mead with gentle wing to stray,
From flower to flower on balmy gales to fly,
Is all she has to do beneath the radiant sky.

" ' Behold the merry minstrels of the morn,
   The swarming songsters of the careless grove,
   Ten thousand throats! that from the flowering thorn,
   Hymn their good God, and carol sweet of love,
   Such grateful kindly raptures them emove:
   They neither plough, nor sow, ne, fit for flail,
   E'er to the barn the nodding sheaves they drove;
   Yet theirs each harvest dancing in the gale,
Whatever crowns the hill, or smiles along the vale.

" ' Come, ye who still the cumbrous load of life
   Push hard up hill; but as the farthest steep
   You trust to gain, and put an end to strife,
   Down thunders back the stone with mighty sweep,
   And hurls your labors to the valley deep,
   Forever vain; come, and, withouten fee,
   I in oblivion will your sorrows steep,
   Your cares, your toils, will steep you in a sea
Of full delight; oh come, ye weary wights, to me!

" ' With me you need not rise at early dawn,
   To pass the joyous day in various stounds;
   Or, louting low, on upstart fortune fawn,
   And sell fair honor for some paltry pounds;
   Or through the city take your dirty rounds,
   To cheat, and dun, and lie, and visit pay,
   Now flattering base, now giving secret wounds:
   Or prowl in courts of law for human prey,
In venal senate thieve, or rob on broad highway.

" ' No cocks, with me, to rustic labor call,
   From village on to village sounding clear:
   To tardy swain no shrill-voiced matron's squall;
   No dogs, no babes, no wives, to stun your ear;
   No hammers thump; no horrid blacksmith fear;
   No noisy tradesman your sweet slumbers start,
   With sounds that are a misery to hear:
   But all is calm, as would delight the heart
Of Sybarite of old, all nature, and all art.

" ' What, what is virtue, but repose of mind,
   A pure ethereal calm, that knows no storm:
   Above the reach of wild ambition's wind,

Above the passions that this world deform,
And torture man, a proud malignant worm ?
But here, instead, soft gales of passion play,
And gently stir the heart, thereby to form
A quicker sense of joy ; as breezes stray
Across th' enlivened skies, and make them still more gay.

" ' The best of men have ever loved repose ;
They hate to mingle in the filthy fray ;
Where the soul sours, and gradual rancor grows,
Imbittered more from peevish day to day.
E'en those whom Fame has lent her fairest ray,
The most renowned of worthy wights of yore,
From a base world at last have stolen away :
So Scipio, to the soft Cumæan shore
Retiring, tasted joy he never knew before.

" ' Oh, grievous folly ! to heap up estate,
Losing the days you see beneath the sun ;
When, sudden, comes blind unrelenting fate,
And gives th' untasted portion you have won,
With ruthless toil, and many a wretch undone,
To those who mock you gone to Pluto's reign,
There with sad ghosts to pine, and shadows dun :
But sure it is of vanities most vain,
To toil for what you here untoiling may obtain.' "

Thomson's friend Lyttleton contributed one stanza to
this poem, containing a portrait of its author :

" A bard here dwelt, more fat than bard beseems,
Who, void of envy, guile, and lust of gain,
On virtue still, and nature's pleasing themes,
Poured forth his unpremeditated strain ;
The world forsaking with a calm disdain,
Here laughed he careless in his easy seat;
Here quaffed, encircled with the joyous train,
Oft moralizing sage ; his ditty sweet,
He loathed much to write, ne cared to repeat."

Thomson wrote in various styles, but *excelled* in *description.* He has given us many noble thoughts, beautifully

and vigorously expressed. In regard to the true end of
life, he says:

> " Who, who would like, my Narva, just to breathe
> This idle air, and indolently run,
> Day after day, the still returning round
> Of life's mean offices and sickly joys ?
> But in the service of mankind to be
> A guardian god below; still to employ
> The mind's brave ardor, in heroic arms,
> Such as may raise us o'er the grovelling herd,
> And make us shine forever—that is life ! "

Of Providence :—

> " There is a power
> Unseen that rules the illimitable world,
> That guides its motions, from the brightest star
> To the least dust of this sin-tainted mould ;
> While man, who madly deems himself the lord
> Of all, is naught but weakness and dependence.
> This sacred truth, by sure experience taught,
> Thou must have learned when wandering all alone ;
> Each bird, each insect, flitting through the sky,
> Was more sufficient for itself than thou."

He had at least one romance in life, being at one time
deeply in love with a Miss Amanda Somebody, whose
mother did not fancy him as a husband for her daughter,
as he was "nothing but a poet ; " and he told his sorrows
in several very sentimental songs:

> " For once, O Fortune, hear my prayer,
> And I absolve thy future care ;
> All other blessings I resign,
> *Make but the dear Amanda mine !* "

But cruel Fortune and Amanda's mother paid no attention to his sighs and sentiment. It is said that the young
lady fainted when told of his death ; but, as she soon after
married a gallant admiral, I presume she was not so sadly
in earnest as the poor poet.

I find one humorous poem, "The Barber's Nuptials,"
quite in the vein of Thomas Hood and the witty rhymers
of our own day:

"THE BARBER'S NUPTIALS.

" In Liquor-pond Street, as is well known to many,
 An artist resided, who shaved for a penny;
 Cut hair for three-halfpence; for three pence he bled,
 And would draw for a groat every tooth in your head.

" What annoyed other folks never spoiled his repose,
 'Twas the same thing to him whether stocks fell or rose;
 For blast and for mildew he cared not a pin,
 His crops never failed, for they grew on the chin!

" Unvexed by the cares that ambition and state has,
 Contented he dined on his daily potatoes;
 And the pence that he earned by excision of bristle,
 Were nightly devoted to wetting his whistle.

" When copper ran low he made light of the matter,
 Drank his purl upon tick at the old Pewter Platter;
 Read the news, and as deep in the secret appeared
 As if he had lathered the minister's beard.

" But Cupid, who trims men of every station,
 And 'twixt barbers and beaux makes no discrimination,
 Would not let this superlative shaver alone,
 Till he tried if his heart was as hard as his hone.

" The fair one whose charms did the barber inthrall,
 At the end of Fleet-market, of fish kept a stall;
 As red as her cheek was no lobster e'er seen,
 Not an eel that she sold was so soft as her skin.

" By love strange effects have been wrought, we are told,
 In all countries and climates, hot, temperate, or cold;
 Thus the heart of our barber love scorched like a coal,
 Though 'tis very well known he lived under the *pole*.

" First, he courted his charmer in sorrowful fashion,
 And lied like a lawyer to move her compassion;

He should perish, he swore, did his suit not succeed,
And a barber to slay was a barbarous deed.

" Then he altered his tone, and was heard to declare,
If valor deserved the regard of the fair,
That his courage was tried, though he scorned to disclose
How many brave fellows he'd took by the nose.

" For his politics, too, they were thoroughly known,
A patriot he was to the very backbone ;
Wilkes he gratis had shaved for the good of the nation,
And he held the *Whig* club in profound veneration.

"—For his tenets religious—he could well expound
Emanuel Swedenborg's myst'ries profound,
And new doctrines could broach with the best of 'em all,
For a periwig-maker ne'er wanted a *caul*.

" Indignant she answered: ' No chin-scraping sot
Shall be fastened to me by the conjugal knot ;
No! to Tyburn repair, if a noose you must tie,
Other fish I have got, Mr. Tonsor, to fry :

" ' Holborn-bridge and Blackfriars my triumphs can tell,
From Billingsgate beauties I've long borne the bell ;
Nay, tripemen and fishmongers vie for my favor :
Then d'ye think I'll take up with a two-penny shaver ?

" ' Let dory, or turbot the sov'reign of fish,
Cheek by jowl with red-herring be served in one dish ;
Let sturgeon and sprats in one pickle unite,
When I angle for husbands, and barbers shall bite.'

" But the barber persisted (ah, could I relate 'em !)
To ply her with compliments soft as pomatum ;
And took every occasion to flatter and praise her,
Till she fancied his wit was as keen as his razor.

" He protested, besides, if she'd grant his petition,
She should live like a lady of rank and condition ;
And to Billingsgate market no longer repair,
But himself all her business would do to a hair.

8*

" Her smiles, he asserted, would melt even rocks,
    Nay, the fire of her eyes would consume barbers' blocks;
    On insensible objects bestow animation,
    And give to old periwigs regeneration.

" With fair speeches cajoled, as you'd tickle a trout,
    'Gainst the barber the fish-wife no more could hold out;
    He applied the right bait, and with flattery he caught her,
    Without flattery a female's a fish out of water.

" The state of her heart, when the barber once guessed,
    Love's siege with redoubled exertion he pressed,
    And as briskly bestirred him, the charmer embracing,
    As the wash-ball that dances and froths in his basin. .

" The flame to allay that their bosoms did so burn,
    They set out for the church of St. Andrew in Holborn,
    Where tonsors and trulls, country Dicks and their cousins,
    In the halter of wedlock are tied up by dozens.

" The nuptials to grace, came from every quarter,
    The worthies at Rag-fair, old caxons who barter,
    Who the coverings of judges' and counsellors' nobs
    Cut down into majors, queues, scratches, and bobs.

.   .   .   .

" From their voices united such melody flowed,
    As the Abbey ne'er witnessed, nor Tott'nham Court-road;
    While St. Andrew's brave bells did so loud and so clear ring,
    You'd have given ten pounds to 've been out of their hearing.

" For his fee, when the parson this couple had joined,
    As no cash was forthcoming, he took it in kind:
    So the bridegroom dismantled his rev'rence's chin,
    And the bride entertained him with pilchards and gin."

Thomson was a wonderfully good-natured man, and so
patient that, even when his friends bribed his servants to
annoy him, he was never known to lose his temper. He
did not live long to enjoy his peaceful home, for, taking
cold from a boat-ride after a long walk one August after-

noon, a fever ensued, which proved fatal. The year of his death was 1748. It was of him that Lord Lyttleton said, he left

"No line which, dying, he could wish to blot."

THOMSON'S COTTAGE.

Gray

GRAY.

"A heart, within whose sacred cell,
The peaceful virtues loved to dwell."

THOMAS GRAY, of all English poets perhaps the most finished artist, was born in that noisy part of London, Cornhill, on a December's day, in 1716.

His father, like Milton's, was a scrivener, but, unlike that good man, failed to make his home happy—in fact, drove his wife away from it by his harshness and ill-temper. She was a noble, energetic woman, as are almost all the mothers of the good and great, and, when forced to separate from her husband, at once opened a millinery store, with her sister for a partner, supporting herself and her children. She had a large family, twelve in all, but all except Thomas died in infancy from suffocation, caused by a fullness of blood. He, too, was attacked in the same terrible way, and was only saved by his mother's courage and devotion, for she opened a vein in his neck with her own hand, thus bringing him back from the very grasp of death.

"Her brother being a master at Eaton, the lad went there, and soon found among his school-fellows young Horace Walpole, with whom he soon struck up a close friendship. Many a time no doubt Walpole, Gray, and West, another chum of the scrivener's son, did their Latin verses together, and many a golden summer evening they passed merrily with bat and ball in the meadows of the smoothly-flowing Thames."

In his nineteenth year Gray was admitted pensioner at Cambridge, maintained both at school and college by the industry of his mother. But he did not enjoy the three years he spent at Cambridge, and complained, in a serio-comic way, of the course of study there: "Must I pore into metaphysics? Alas! I cannot see in the dark. Nature has not furnished me with the optics of a cat. Must I pore into mathematics? Alas! I cannot see in too much light. I am no eagle. It is very possible that two and two make four, but I would not give four farthings to demonstrate this ever so clearly, and if these be the profits of life, give me the amusements of it." He gave almost all his time to the languages, ancient and modern, writing a little poetry now and then.

Walpole was with him also at college, and when Gray left, in 1739, his friend proposed that they should visit the Continent in company. They did travel together through

France and Italy, but soon had a serious quarrel, which led to their separation. Two men so utterly unlike could hardly be intimate for any length of time. Walpole was an elegant lounger, a dilettante in arts and letters; clever, but conceited and haughty—"the most eccentric, the most artificial, the most fastidious, the most capricious of men." These four rather uncomplimentary superlatives are borrowed from Macaulay, the brilliant essayist, who also gives a very graphic account of his character and life. He says: "The conformation of his mind was such, that whatever was little seemed to him great, and whatever was great seemed to him little; serious business was a trifle to him, and trifles were his serious business. To chat with blue-stockings; to write little complimentary verses on little occasions; to superintend a private press; to record divorces and bets; to decorate a grotesque house with pie-crust battlements; to procure rare engravings and antique chimney-boards; to match odd gauntlets; to lay out a maze of walk within five acres of ground— these were the grave employments of his long life. From these he turned to politics, as an amusement. After the labors of the print-shop and the auction-room, he unbent his mind in the House of Commons; and, after having indulged in the recreation of making laws and voting millions, he returned to more important pursuits — to researches after Queen Mary's comb, Wolsey's red hat, the pipe which Van Tromp smoked during his last sea-fight, and the spur which King William struck in the flank of Sorrel."

Of course, there could be no real sympathy between these men. The poet was a studious traveller deeply interested in architecture, painting, sculpture, and music; comparing carefully, as Addison had done, the state of the countries through which he passed, with the descriptions given of them by ancient authors; writing a minute account of every thing.

Walpole had no wish to change his pleasure-trip into a season of severe mental labor, and says: "The quarrel between Gray and me arose from his being too serious a companion. I had just broke loose from the restraints of the university, with as much money as I could spend, and was willing to indulge myself. Gray was for antiquities, whilst I was for perpetual balls and plays. The fault was mine."

Walpole was a great talker, frivolous and vivacious, and alive to the merest whiff of gossip, which he knew well how to adorn and magnify, and he declared Gray to be the worst company in the world, measuring and choosing all his words.

After Gray returned from his solitary tour, he went back to Cambridge, where he passed a most quiet, uneventful life. He liked much better to read than compose, and was attracted there by the valuable libraries. Of course the day's routine was very monotonous: "Reading here, reading there, nothing but books with different sauces." He said in one of his charming letters, about this time, "that his life was like Harry the Fourth's supper of hens, roast chicken, chicken-ragout, chicken boiled, and chicken fricassée."

In a letter to his old classmate and constant friend, Mr. West, he says: "When you have seen one of my days, you have seen a whole year of my life; they go round and round like the blind horse in the mill, only he has the satisfaction of fancying he makes a progress, and gets over some ground. My eyes are open enough to see the same dull prospect, and to know that, having made four-and-twenty steps more, I shall be just where I was; I may, better than most people, say my life is but a span, were I not afraid lest you should not believe that a person so short-lived could write even so short a letter as this."

It was necessary for him to economize, and his expenses were smaller here than elsewhere. Here is one of his philosophical reflections on that point: "It is a foolish thing that, without money, one cannot either live as one pleases, or when and with whom one pleases. Swift somewhere says, that 'money is liberty,' and I fear that money is friendship too and society, and almost every external blessing. It is a great though an ill-natured comfort, to see most of those who have it in plenty, without pleasure, without liberty, and without friends."

In 1742, he wrote with unusual zeal, delighting his special friends with an "Ode on Spring," another on a "Distant Prospect of Eton College," and a "Hymn to Adversity," but these were not published until some years later. The second of these I give you:

"ON A DISTANT PROSPECT OF ETON COLLEGE.

> " Ye distant spires, ye antique towers,
>   That crown the watery glade,
>   Where grateful Science still adores
>   Her Henry's holy shade;
> And ye, that from the stately brow
> Of Windsor's heights th' expanse below
>   Of grove, of lawn, of mead, survey,
> Whose turf, whose shade, whose flowers among
> Wanders the hoary Thames along
>   His silver-winding way.
>
> " Ah, happy hills! ah, pleasing shade!
>   Ah, fields beloved in vain!
> Where once my careless childhood strayed,
>   A stranger yet to pain!
> I feel the gales that from ye blow
> A momentary bliss bestow,
>   As waving fresh their gladsome wing;
> My weary soul they seem to soothe,
> And, redolent of joy and youth,
>   To breathe a second spring.

"Say, Father Thames, for thou hast seen
   Full many a sprightly race,
Disporting on thy margent green,
   The paths of pleasure trace;
Who foremost now delight to cleave,
With pliant arm, thy glassy wave?
   The captive linnet which inthrall?
What idle progeny succeed
To chase the rolling circle's speed,
   Or urge the flying ball?

" While some, on earnest business bent,
   Their murmuring labors ply
'Gainst graver hours that bring constraint
   To sweeten liberty:
Some bold adventurers disdain
The limits of their little reign,
   And unknown regions dare descry:
Still as they run they look behind,
They hear a voice in every wind,
   And snatch a fearful joy.

" Gay hope is theirs by fancy fed,
   Less pleasing when possest;
The tear forgot as soon as shed,
   The sunshine of the breast:
Theirs buxom health, of rosy hue,
Wild wit, invention ever new,
   And lively cheer, of vigor born;
The thoughtless day, the easy night,
The spirits pure, the slumbers light,
   That fly the approach of morn.

" Alas! regardless of their doom,
   The little victims play;
No sense have they of ills to come,
   Nor care beyond to-day:
Yet see how all around them wait
The ministers of human fate,
   And black Misfortune's baleful train!
Ah, show them where in ambush stand,
To seize their prey, the murtherous band!
   Ah, tell them they are men!

"These shall the fury Passions tear,
　　The vultures of the mind,
Disdainful Anger, pallid Fear,
　　And Shame that skulks behind;
Or pining Love shall waste their youth,
Or Jealousy, with rankling tooth,
　　That inly gnaws the secret heart;
And Envy wan, and faded Care,
Grim-visaged, comfortless Despair,
　　And Sorrow's piercing dart.

"Ambition this shall tempt to rise,
　　Then whirl the wretch from high
To bitter Scorn a sacrifice,
　　And grinning Infamy.
The stings of Falsehood those shall try,
And hard Unkindness' altered eye,
　　That mocks the tear it forced to flow;
And keen Remorse with blood defiled,
And moody Madness laughing wild
　　Amid severest woe.

"Lo! in the vale of years beneath
　　A griesly troop are seen,
The painful family of Death,
　　More hideous than their queen:
This racks the joints, this fires the veins,
That every laboring sinew strains,
　　Those in the deeper vitals rage:
Lo! Poverty, to fill the band,
That numbs the soul with icy hand,
　　And slow-consuming Age.

"To each his sufferings: all are men,
　　Condemned-alike to groan;
The tender for another's pain,
　　Th' unfeeling for his own.
Yet, ah! why should they know their fate,
Since sorrow never comes too late,
　　And happiness too swiftly flies?
Thought would destroy their paradise.
No more;—where ignorance is bliss,
　　'Tis folly to be wise."

We have nothing from his pen again until 1747, when he immortalized Mr. Walpole's favorite cat in an ode. Poor Selima fell into a tub, from which she had intended to take out a few gold fishes, and, sad to tell, found a watery grave. You will like to read the story:

   " 'Twas on a lofty vase's side,
     Where China's gayest art had dyed
       The azure flowers that blow.
     Demurest of the tabby kind,
     The pensive Selima reclined,
       Gazed on the lake below.

   " Her conscious tail her joy declared,
     The fair round face, the snowy beard,
       The velvet of her paws:
     Her coat that with the tortoise vies,
     Her ears of jet, and emerald eyes,
       She saw, and purred applause.

   " Still had she gazed ; but midst the tide
     Two angel forms were seen to glide,
       The Genii of the stream.
     Their scaly armour's Tyrian hue,
     Through richest purple to the view,
       Betrayed a golden gleam.

   " The hapless nymph with wonder saw ;
     A whisker first, and then a claw,
       With many an ardent wish,
     She stretched in vain to reach the prize :
     What female heart can gold despise,
       What cat's averse to fish?

   " Presumptuous maid ! with books intent,
     Again she stretched ; again she bent,
       Nor knew the gulf between :
     (Malignant Fate sat by and smiled),
     The slippery verge her feet beguiled,
       She tumbled headlong in.

   " Eight times emerging from the flood,
     She mewed to every watery god

Some speedy aid to send.
No dolphin came, no nereid stirred,
A fav'rite has ho friend.

" From hence, ye beauties undeceived,
Know one false step is ne'er retrieved,
And be with caution bold.
Not all that tempts your wandering eyes,
And heedless hearts, is lawful prize,
Nor all that glisters gold."

After Gray's death, Walpole placed the china vase on a pedestal at Strawberry Hill, with a few lines of the ode for an inscription.

The "Elegy in a Country Churchyard" was given to the world in 1750, and was at once admired and appreciated, running through eleven editions. This perfect poem needs no praise of mine. Words seem miserable interpreters of the hold that elegy has upon the world. There have been more than fifty translations of the poem: into French, fifteen; into Italian, thirteen; into German, six; into Latin, twelve; into Greek, eight; into Hebrew, one; into Portuguese, one. At least eight years were spent by Gray in elaborating it.

Dr. Adam Smith says: "Gray joins to the sublimity of Milton the elegance and harmony of Pope, and nothing is wanting to render him, perhaps, the first poet of England, but to have written a little more."

I cannot do better than give you the first nine verses, hoping you may be tempted to read the rest, if you have not already done it, and then commit the whole to memory. Look at the third line of the first verse, and see how many different ways you can arrange the words, and yet keep the same idea:

" The curfew tolls the knell of parting day,
The lowing herd wind slowly o'er the lea,
The ploughman homeward plods his weary way,
And leaves the world to darkness and to me.

" Now fades the glimmering landscape on the sight,
    And all the air a solemn stillness holds, .
Save where the beetle wheels his droning flight,
    And drowsy tinklings lull the distant folds ;

" Save that, from yonder ivy-mantled tower,
    The moping owl does to the moon complain
Of such as, wandering near her secret bower,
    Molest her ancient solitary reign.

" Beneath those rugged elms, that yew-tree's shade,
    Where heaves the turf in many a mouldering heap,
Each in his narrow cell forever laid,
    The rude forefathers of the hamlet sleep.

" The breezy call of incense-breathing Morn,
    The swallow twittering from the straw-built shed,
The cock's shrill clarion, or the echoing horn,
    No more shall rouse them from their lowly bed.

" For them no more the blazing hearth shall burn,
    Or busy housewife ply her evening care :
No children run to lisp their sire's return,
    Or climb his knees the envied kiss to share.

" Oft did the harvest to their sickle yield,
    Their furrow oft the stubborn glebe has broke ;
How jocund did they drive their team afield !
    How bowed the woods beneath their sturdy stroke !

" Let not Ambition mock their useful toil,
    Their homely joys, and destiny obscure ;
Nor Grandeur hear with a disdainful smile
    The short and simple annals of the poor.

" The boast of Heraldry, the pomp of Power,
    And all that Beauty, all that Wealth e'er gave,
Await alike the inevitable hour.
    The paths of glory lead but to the grave."

Three years after the publication of this poem, to
which he owes his fame, he lost the dear mother whom
he had so long, so tenderly loved. She was an old lady,
almost seventy-three, but Gray never failed to treat her

with the sincerest reverence and affection. Her epitaph, written by himself, is too formal to show his deep sorrow at his loss :

> "Beside her Friend and Sister,
> Here sleep the Remains
> of
> DOROTHY GRAY, .
> Widow; the careful, tender Mother
> Of many Children : one of whom alone
> Had the misfortune to survive her."

His life was now very solitary. He had been accustomed to spend a part at least of each summer with his mother, and he often wrote to her. Now he was alone, and you can see his mood by the tone of his letters : "I cannot boast at present either of my spirits or my situation —my employments or fertility. The days and the nights pass, and I am never the nearer to any thing but that one to which we all are hastening;.yet I love people that leave some traces of their journey behind them, and have strength enough to advise you to do so while you can."

He would doubtless have remained in his quiet chambers all his life, if some gay young men in adjoining rooms had not fairly driven him away with their frequent revels and noisy demonstrations. They amused themselves at last by playing a practical joke on the sensitive recluse, and this was more than he could endure. He was remarkably timid in regard to fire, and always kept a rope-ladder in his bedroom. These mischievous fellows, knowing this weakness, roused him one dark night with the cry of fire ! shouting that the staircase was all in flames ! Up went the window, down went the ladder, out scrambled the poor, frightened poet, only to jump into a tub of cold water, carefully placed on the ground to receive him. He never forgave the insult, and soon removed to Pembroke Hall. This he describes as "an era" in a life so barren of events.

In 1757 appeared two more odes, "The Progress of Poesy" and "The Bard," considered by some critics the triumphs of his genius. But they are not so generally popular as "The Elegy," and were considered too fine to be intelligible by the common reader when they came out. It was in this year, too, that he did an almost unheard-of thing—refused the laureateship—giving his reason in these words: "The office has always humbled the possessor; if he was a poor writer, by making him more conspicuous; if he were a good one, by setting him at war with the little fry of his own profession."

Perhaps he thought of Swift's rough rhyme, which contains the same idea:

> " If on Parnassus' top you sit,
> You rarely bite, are always bit;
> Each poet of inferior size
> On you shall rail and criticise,
> And strive to tear you limb from limb,
> While others do the same for him."

He had been so long in a monkish twilight among his books, and music, and valued relics, that he dreaded the full sunlight of a prominent position.

In 1768 he was appointed to the Professorship of Modern History at Cambridge, a place he had tried in vain to gain several years before. But he never gave any lectures, although always resolving to do his duty, and always mourning over his inefficiency. Ill-health was, no doubt, the cause of this failure.

Immediately after his appointment he went on a tour to the lakes of Cumberland and Westmoreland, keeping, as usual, an elegant and lively journal to amuse his friends. But he was at heart very solitary. He says: "Happy they that can create a rose-tree, or plant a honeysuckle: that can watch the brood of a hen, or see a fleet of their own ducklings launch into the water; it is with a sentiment of envy I speak it, who never shall have even a thatched roof of my own, nor gather a strawberry but in Covent Garden."

His spirits became more and more depressed, full of regrets that he had not accomplished more as a poet.

Long a sufferer from the gout, he died at last from that painful disease, after six days of intense suffering, at the age of fifty-five.

By his own request he was buried near his mother, to whom he was so tenderly attached; and, by a wish expressed in his will, the sum of ten pounds was given to the poor in his parish on the day of his funeral.

He was a profound scholar, perhaps the most learned man in Europe; indeed, his fund of knowledge seemed inexhaustible. He was well read in every branch of history; in metaphysics, morals, criticism, politics, and natural history; was ardently devoted to painting, music, architecture, and yet found time to devote to heraldry and antiquities. He was even an expert in the science of cookery.

Mackintosh says, "He was the first discoverer of the beauties of nature in England, and has marked out the course of every picturesque journey that can be made in it."

Mason declares that, "excepting the pure mathematics, and the studies dependent on that science, there was hardly any part of human learning in which he had not acquired a competent skill; in most of them a consummate mastery."

He was a perfect master of the English language in prose as well as poetry.

Cowper said: "I have been reading Gray's works, and think him sublime. I once thought Swift's letters the best that could be written; but I like Gray's better. His humor or wit, or whatever it is to be called, is never ill-natured or offensive, and yet, I think, equally poignant with the dean's."

He certainly deserves a most distinguished position, and, after Milton and Shakespeare, Chaucer and Spenser, there is perhaps no one with a better claim to the fifth place among our English poets than Thomas Gray.

GRAY'S HOUSE AT STOKE

9

JOHNSON.

"Johnson, to be sure, has a roughness in his manner; but no man alive has a more tender heart."

NEARLY a hundred years ago, in a retired court in Fleet Street, London, might be found a little family composed of individuals so odd, grotesque, and unique, that it would be impossible to find their parallel in the history of civilized society.

Let us look in upon them at breakfast, about ten o'clock in the forenoon. The central figure possesses a colossal frame, long, shambling legs, a repulsive face, scarred with scrofula, one eye sightless and disfigured, the other feeble and blinking; his clothes seem to have been hung upon him as rags are wrapped about a scarecrow, his shirt-collar loose, the linen of which originally white— but here imagination must come to our aid;—the little

black wig all askew, his knee-buckles and shoeties fluttering as he moves, his whole appearance showing utter indifference to the elegancies of life. He gulps down his
tea as though his throat were the race-way of an ordinary
mill. All his motions are clumsy, heavy, and awkward.
No stranger could begin to guess correctly who or what
he was. Nothing about his person showed that the
greatest intellect of his age dwelt in that unsightly body.
His household are equally unattractive. An humble doctor, poor in purse, slight in skill, threadbare in dress, but
of spotless character, served as cup-bearer to the lord of
the mansion, who has thus characterized him in a poetic
tribute of surpassing beauty :

> "In misery's darkest caverns known,
>   His useful care was ever nigh,
> Where hopeless anguish poured its groan,
> And lonely want retired to die.
>
> .   .   .   .
>
> "His virtues walked their narrow round,
>   Nor made a pause, nor left a word ;
> And sure th' Eternal Maker found
>   The single talent well employed."

The other inmates of this singular abode were a poor,
blind woman, entirely dependent upon the charity of the
owner, yet peevish, querulous, and impudent; another
decayed gentlewoman, also old and friendless, sharing the
bounty of the householder, and a single negro-servant, who
was "Jack-of-all-trades."

About four o'clock in the afternoon, you might have
seen the same ungainly figure pacing the streets of the
city, in quest of a dinner at the "Mitre." He moves with
an absent, melancholy air, with a heavy tread and rolling
gait, jostling the porters and market-women as he passes,
muttering strange thoughts, like a madman, touching
every post as he goes, and, on arriving at his place of

destination, stopping a moment to decide which foot to place first on the threshold, in order to secure a good omen and cordial welcome. Seated at table, with two or three admirers, he devotes himself to the wants of the inner man, giving no heed to what those around him say or think. He swallows his food with the ravenous eagerness of a famished wolf. After his repast, he gives himself to the entertainment of his friends. They hang upon his lips, every word is treasured in memory, or written down upon the spot. If at midnight, of the same day, you were to look into the most brilliant literary club which ever met within the precincts of the first city in the world, you would find the same singular personage in the foreground of a group of eager and excited listeners, discoursing in tones of authority, like Jove uttering his unalterable decrees to a "council of gods on Olympus." If any one fails to see the force or application of one of these dicta, and ventures to say so, you hear a gruff growl, followed by a thunderous "Sir, it is my business to give you arguments, not to give you *brains !*"—and the questioner is knocked down with the butt-end of the pistol. Such was SAMUEL JOHNSON, the greatest genius, 'the most original man of his age. Thanks to his most devoted admirer, Boswell, we now know almost as much of his life as did he himself, and can follow him from his cradle to his grave.

His father was a poor bookseller in the provincial town of Lichfield; a man of apparent good health, yet constitutionally "blue," who used to read every book displayed on his stall, but never made much by selling them. He must have been punctual, for little Samuel was baptized on the very day of his birth. He was an awkward, clumsy child, with features originally good, but distorted by disease. There was a silly superstition in those days, that if a person so afflicted could be touched by the hand of royalty he would be instantly cured—hence the name " King's Evil." So his distressed mother, full of faith and hope, carried him to London, and Queen Anne did really try her power of healing by " laying on of hands;" but of course it was all in vain. When asked in after-years if he could remember the event, he said he had a " confused but somehow solemn recollection of a lady in diamonds and a long black hood."

His mother did something much more sensible than this—she used to talk and pray with her boy in a way that he never forgot; and her simple definition of " heaven as a place where good people go, and hell a place where bad people go," never faded from his mind. He was always an independent, impetuous, spunky little fellow; and when but three years old, was seen perched on his father's shoulder in a crowded cathedral, listening to a famous preacher of that day. "He would not stay at home," and seemed perfectly happy in his exalted position, looking at the great divine.

His disease made him almost blind in one eye, and he was often led to and from school by a servant. Happening one evening to return alone, he got down on his hands and knees to ascertain the width of the kennel before daring to cross it. His teacher, seeing his trouble, followed at a little distance to be sure of his safety. Finding that he was thus watched, he felt so insulted that he ran back in high rage, and beat her as hard as he could.

There is a story that when a mere child he chanced to tread upon a duckling, the *eleventh* of a brood, and killed it; upon which he dictated to his mother the following epitaph:

> " Hete lies good master duck,
> Whom Samuel Johnson trod on ;
> If it had lived, it had been *good luck*,
> For then we'd had an *odd one !* "

But Boswell disputes this on Johnson's authority, who told him that his father made the verses, and wished to pass them for his. He said: "My father was a foolish old man; that is to say, foolish in talking of his children."

He studied Latin first at a Lichfield school, with a Mr. Hunter, who whipped his pupils not only when they did not know their lessons, but when they failed to answer every question he might choose to ask. He would say to Tom or Dick, "What is the Latin for *candlestick?*" If the boy could not answer, then came the flogging. In after-life, Johnson actually expressed gratitude for this rather severe way of giving instruction. "My master whipped me very well: without that, sir, I should have done nothing." He was a great favorite at school; always far ahead of the others; rather noisy and fond of talking, but ever ready to help those who could not learn their lessons by looking them over once or twice, as he did, for his memory was wonderful. His school-mates used to treat him with great respect—partly because he was so clever, and partly in hope of his aid in future. They would often carry him in their arms and on their backs all the way to school. He was unable to enter into their sports, and liked much better to saunter in the fields, or sit quietly and read, than to play with ball or marbles.

For several years after leaving school he devoted himself to reading—any thing, every thing that came in his way, so that when he went to Oxford in his nineteenth year, he was better fitted for the university than if he had gone through a regular drill. At the age of fifty-four he said: "Sir, in my early years I read very hard. It is a sad reflection, but a true one, that I knew almost as much at eighteen as I now do; my judgment, to be sure, was not so good, but I had all the facts." This shows how intense must have been his application to books in early life, and how wonderful his success in acquiring knowledge. He had no regular plan for study ; it was never the same for two days together. He believed that a young man should read what he liked to read, but as much as five hours each day.

During his first year in college, he translated Pope's "Messiah" into Latin verse, in a manner that gained him great praise, and raised him in the estimation of all. He now began to feel the misery of that depression which had constantly clouded his father's life, and was to dog his own steps till death, giving him a fear of coming insanity hard to endure. He speaks of this as a "vile melancholy, which kept him mad half his life, or at least not sober."

He was rather unruly when in college, treating no one with respect, considered gay and frolicsome by his classmates, a ringleader in every riot. But his poverty and pride had much to do with this. He said, of that time: "Ah, sir, I was mad and violent; it was bitterness which they mistook for frolic. I was miserably poor, and I thought to fight my way by my literature and wit, so I disregarded all power and authority." He is but another instance of that pithy remark of an old writer, that "no great work, or worthy of praise, or memory, but came out of poor cradles."

But, although embarrassed by debts, he was independent as ever, and scorned to accept charity. A pair of new shoes were once set at his door, but, although needing them sadly, he threw them away in anger. Pity was as hard to endure as ridicule.

His father was so unfortunate, in 1731, as to lose the little property he possessed by some speculation, and Johnson was obliged to leave college in the autumn without his degree, having been there a little more than three years. The old man died in the following December, leaving his son almost penniless. A prayer in his diary, about this time, contains a petition that "his poverty may not lead him into crime." In this forlorn condition he became usher in a school in a neighboring town, walking there to save his coach-fare. The routine and drudgery of a teacher's life were irksome to him, proving as "unvaried as the notes of a cuckoo." Leaving in disgust, he went soon after to Birmingham, to try to earn a few guineas by translating for a bookseller.

While thus vagrant and lonely, he fell in love in the strangest way (the only sign I ever saw of that insanity which he so much dreaded), wooing and winning, without the least difficulty, a coarse, fat woman, who painted her cheeks, dressed in shocking taste, and talked in the most affected way, the dowdy widow of a Mr. Porter, one of Johnson's early friends. He could not be accused of marrying for money, for she was as poor as himself. There is no doubt that he really loved her, and thought her a beauty, petting her in his own clumsy, elephantine manner, with all the ardor and sincerity of a more graceful lover. The daughter of this lady says, that, when Johnson first called upon her mother, his appearance was very forbidding. "He was then lean and lank, so that his immense structure of bones was hideously striking to the eye, and the scars of scrofula were deeply visible. He also wore his hair stiff and straight, and parted behind, and he often had seemingly convulsive starts and odd gesticulations, which tended at once to excite surprise and ridicule." But the red-faced widow had good sense after all, for she never cared for these external disadvantages, and thought him the most agreeable man she had ever seen in her life. They must have been a queer couple—

> " He like a mile in length,
> And she like a mile-stone."

She was nearly double his age, yet had not lost her coquetry. Her young husband determined to conquer this at once, as you will see from his own comical account of their ride to church on the wedding-day : " Sir, she had read the old romances, and had got into her head the fantastical notion that a woman of spirit should use her lover like a dog. So, sir, at first she told me that I rode too fast, and she could not keep up with me, and when I rode a little slower she passed me and complained that I lagged behind. I was not to be made the slave of caprice, and I resolved to begin as I meant to end. I therefore pushed on briskly till I was fairly out of her sight. The road lay between two hedges, and I was sure she could not miss it, and I contrived that she should soon come up with me. When she did, I observed her to be in tears."

Money was now essential. All the petting and caressing in the world would never feed and clothe his tawdry, buxom " Tetsey," and he opened an academy near his native town. In the *Gentleman's Magazine,* for 1736, there is the following advertisement : " At Edial, in Staffordshire, near Lichfield, young gentlemen are boarded and taught the Latin and Greek languages by Samuel Johnson." But this proved a failure. " Samuel Johnson " was a young man, almost unknown, with no special gift for teaching. Eighteen months passed away, and the academy could boast of only three pupils, one of whom was David Garrick, afterward one of the most celebrated actors ever known, famous both in tragedy and comedy. With a keen eye for the ludicrous, and possessed of wonderful powers of mimicry, you may be sure that " Davy " saw and heard much to amuse him during those school-days at Lichfield. Tired of drilling three roguish boys, Johnson now resolved to go to London, as so many others with full brains and empty pockets had done before him, some to starve, a few to succeed. Garrick accompanied him, and these two men, so utterly unlike in talents and appearance, were ever after good friends.

But these were hard times for authors, and Johnson suffered with the rest. The days of patrons were over. Literature was at its lowest ebb, and writers were held in little repute. Booksellers had such limited sales that they could afford to pay but small sums for the best manuscripts. Politics opened a more certain road to fame than learning, and noblemen were more eager to grasp the prizes of office than to aid the cause of letters. Pope, by his unmerciful assault upon the scribblers of his day, had cast contempt upon the name of "poet," and what he maliciously ascribed to the authors of his time became the actual inheritance of those who came after. With the very name were associated poverty, duns, and the sponging-house. Some poets of real genius lodged in garrets, and thought themselves lucky to dine in a cellar. Eminent scholars sold their talents to the periodical press for a mere song, or bargained away manuscripts which had cost them years of toil for a few pounds, to save them from starvation or the jail. When success came, they knew not how to enjoy it prudently. After being dogged by bailiffs, and half starved for months, the receipt of gold made them greedy, and the wages of a year's hard work were squandered in a week. Intense enjoyment succeeded intense suffering, and they had no idea of economy. Johnson had a bitter experience of this wretched life. It was more than a year before he could get any permanent employment, often walking the streets all night for want of shelter, and only seeking society on " clean-shirt " day.

He at last became a regular contributor to the *Gentleman's Magazine*, from which he obtained a tolerable support for clever writing on the Tory side. He sent for his wife, for whom he found decent lodgings in Woodstock Street, near Hanover Square. A few weeks later his

famous poem on "London" appeared, anonymously, and
created great excitement amongst the critics, little and
big. All agreed that this unknown poet was a genius,
and could not be long concealed. Pope treated him most
generously, praised his poem, and tried to help him in
various ways. But their circumstances were very unlike.
Pope was successful; his fame was made—not a distant
prize to be fought for, through all sorts of rebuff and disappointment. He had an elegant home, plenty of money,
and troops of titled friends, while Johnson was far behind,
among the reckless, half-starved unfortunates, who were
either hungry or drunk most of the time—men of genius,
but too often profligate and dissolute. He felt the difference keenly, and in one pathetic passage in his satire,
which was written in imitation of Juvenal, tells his own
story, very sad because so true:

"THE FATE OF POVERTY.

" By numbers here from shame or censure free,
All crimes are safe but hated poverty.
This, only this, the rigid law pursues,
This, only this, provokes the snarling muse.
The sober trader at a tattered cloak
Wakes from his dream, and labors for a joke ;
With brisker air the silken courtiers gaze,
And turn the varied taunt a thousand ways.
Of all the griefs that harass the distressed,
Sure the most bitter is a scornful jest ;
Fate never wounds more deep the generous heart,
Than when a blockhead's insult points the dart.
Has Heaven reserved, in pity to the poor,
No pathless waste, or undiscovered shore ?
No secret island in the boundless main ?
No peaceful desert yet unclaimed by Spain ?
Quick let us rise, the happy seats explore,
And bear Oppression's insolence no more.
This mournful truth is everywhere confessed,
SLOW RISES WORTH, BY POVERTY DEPRESSED."

His tragedy of "Irene," which was brought out by the influence of his friend Garrick, was a failure. It was full of noble sentiments, but too stately to be popular on the stage. In 1744 he published the life of Richard Savage, his intimate companion during those first dreary years of London life. It is one of the best biographies ever written. Sir Joshua Reynolds read it through, not at one *sitting*, but at one *standing*, never moving from the first page to the last. But Savage was a poor friend for Johnson in those dark, despondent days of want and despair, leading him into many scenes which afterward he would gladly have ignored.

The year 1747 should be remembered as the one in which he gave to the world the "Plan of a Dictionary of the English Language," the great work of his life. This was dedicated to the Earl of Chesterfield, a man of infinite manner and infinitesimal morals. Blessed with brilliant wit and irresistible address, he was considered the first speaker in the House of Lords, and was one of the king's secretaries. He received Johnson's homage with his never-failing blandness, bestowed a few guineas in a graceful way, hoped for the success of the project, but was at heart (that is, if he possessed any,) disgusted with this uncouth specimen of a literary man, and resolved to be troubled with no more visits. "He was by no means desirous of seeing his carpets blackened with London mud, and his soups and wines thrown to right and left over the gowns of fine ladies, and waistcoats of fine gentlemen, by an absent, awkward scholar, who gave strange starts and uttered strange growls, who dressed like a scarecrow and ate like a cormorant."

During some years Johnson continued to call on his patron, but, after being repeatedly told by his footman that his lordship was "not at home," took the hint, and ceased to present himself at the inhospitable door. But our author was in earnest, and could exist without the assistance of this wily courtier. For seven years he toiled on, employing six assistants as copyists, securing from his bookseller the sum of fifteen hundred pounds for his support during that time. Thinking of this dictionary as the work of an unaided scholar, without friends, or funds, or books, it is perhaps the greatest monument of learning, energy, and perseverance, which the literary annals of the world present. "The Dictionary of the French Language," which by good judges is considered inferior to Johnson's great work, employed forty scholars many years, under the patronage of the French Academy, with royal libraries and royal treasures at their command. Garrick wrote the following lines on the publication of the dictionary :

> "Talk of war with a Briton, he'll boldly advance,
> That one English soldier can beat ten of France.
> Would we alter the boast, from the sword to the pen,
> Our odds are still greater, still greater our men.
> In the deep mines of Science our Frenchmen may toil,
> Can their strength be compared to Locke, Newton, or Boyle?
> Let them rally their heroes, send forth all their powers,
> Their versemen, their prosemen, then match them with ours.
> First Shakespeare and Milton, like gods in the fight ;
> Have put their whole Drama and Epic to flight,
> In satires, epistles, and odes, would they cope?
> Their number retreats before Dryden and Pope;
> And Johnson, well armed, like a hero of yore,
> Has beat forty French, and will beat forty more."

Johnson despised monosyllables, and his fondness for high-sounding words is often seen in his dictionary. "Net-work is defined to be any thing reticulated or decussated, with interstices between the intersections." If any one should look up these definitions with an honest desire to find their meanings, he would hardly feel satisfied with the result, and, combining the secondary meaning in one, the simple word "net-work" will be thus defined: "Any thing formed with interstitial vacuities, or intersected at acute angles, with spaces between one thing and another, between the points where lines cross each other." Often a simple word was defined by one more complex; a short by a long one, as "burial" by "sepulture," "dry" by "dessicative," "fit" by "paroxysm," showing too his preference for words of Latin origin. He carried his private prejudices into the Dictionary. He hated Whigs and Scotchmen, and never failed to show his dislike to them by a definition when opportunity offered. There is something in, his definition of a lexicographer, as "a harmless, literary drudge," which is quite touching. The slight blemishes which may be found do not hide the excellence and value of the work, which will be consulted as long as the language is spoken.

It is time to speak again of the Earl of Chesterfield, who, discovering that the penniless author whom he had sent from his door was something more than a "respectable Hottentot," and that his work would reflect honor on its patron, wrote two essays in his choicest style, for the paper of the day, in high commendation of the coming Dictionary. Johnson, with lofty indignation, declined his aid at that late day. The letter in which he rebuked his dilatory and selfish patron is one of the grandest specimens of literary censure ever written.

He says to the Right Honorable the Earl of Chesterfield—"MY LORD: I have been lately informed by the proprietor of *The World*, that two papers, in which my Dictionary is recommended to the public, were written by your lordship. To be so distinguished, is an honor, which, being very little accustomed to favors from the great, I know not well how to receive, or in what terms to acknowledge.

"When, upon some slight encouragement, I first visited your lordship, I was overpowered, like the rest of mankind, by the enchantment of your address; and could not forbear to wish that I might boast myself *Le vainqueur du vainqueur de la terre ;*—that I might obtain that regard for which I saw the world contending; but I found my attendance so little encouraged, that neither pride nor modesty would suffer me to continue it. When I had once addressed your lordship in public, I had exhausted all the art of pleasing which a retired and uncourtly scholar can possess. I had done all that I could; and no man is well pleased to have his all neglected, be it ever so little.

"Seven years, my lord, have now passed since I waited in your outward rooms,. or was repulsed from your door; during which time I have been pushing on my work through difficulties, of which it is useless to complain, and have brought it, at last, to the verge of publication, without one act of assistance, one word of encouragement, or one smile of favor. Such treatment I did not expect, for I never had a patron before.

"The shepherd in Virgil grew at last acquainted with Love, and found him a native of the rocks.

"Is not a patron, my lord, one who looks with unconcern on a man struggling for life in the water, and, when he has reached the ground, encumbers him with help? The notice which you have been pleased to take of my labors, had it been early, had been kind; but it has been delayed till I am indifferent, and cannot enjoy it; till I am solitary, and cannot impart it; till I am known, and do not want it. I hope it is no very cynical asperity not to confess obligations where no benefit has been received, or to be unwilling that the public should consider me as owing that to a patron, which Providence has enabled me to do for myself.

"Having carried on my work thus far with so little obligation to any favorer of learning, I shall not be disappointed though I should conclude it, if less be possible, with less; for I have been long wakened from that dream of hope, in which I once boasted myself with so much exultation, my lord,

"Your lordship's most humble, most obedient servant,
"Samuel Johnson."

The book appeared without a dedication, and, when some friend expressed surprise, Johnson said: "I confess no obligation. I feel my own dignity, sir. I have made a voyage round the world of the English language, and while I am coming into port, with a fair wind, on a sunshiny day, my Lord Chesterfield sends out two little cockboats to tow me into port."

So has the peerless genius of the lexicographer fastened to the page of history this heartless libertine, as the naturalist sometimes impales a gilded butterfly or loathsome bug, and places it upon the walls of his cabinet, as an object of interest to students in other years. While tugging at his oar in this long but successful voyage, his great mind was busy in other directions. In 1749 he brought out another "Satire," on the "Vanity of Human Wishes," rather too profound and philosophical for general admiration. His friend Garrick was discouraged. He said that "London" was very readable, the second "Satire" was hard as Greek, and he supposed the third would be Hebrew. Yet, although the style is ponderous, it has a vigor and power equal to Juvenal himself. Walter Scott said, he "enjoyed these satires more than other poetry." He also started, and carried on, almost without help, a paper called *The Rambler*, which he modelled after *The Spectator*, but there was little resemblance to that sprightly sheet; *The Idler*, which followed, was more readable, but not at all tempting for a leisure hour, the long sermons and labored language being rather fatiguing to a common mind.

Here is a fair sample of the style from a *Rambler*, of April, 1750: "If the most active and industrious of mankind was able, at the close of life, to recollect distinctly his past moments, and distribute them in a regular account, according to the manner in which they have been spent, it is scarcely to be imagined how few would be marked out to the mind by any permanent or visible effects, how small a proportion his real action would bear to his seeming possibilities of action, how many chasms he would find of wide and continued vacuity, and how many interstitial spaces unfilled, even in the most tumultuous hurries of business, and in the most eager vehemence of pursuit."

Johnson thought and talked like an ordinary person, but wrote in "Johnsonese." If he ever forgot himself and wrote simply, a correction would be sure to follow. His letters to Mrs. Thrale from the Hebrides are often easy and entertaining; but he translated them into "Johnsonese" as soon as he returned. He tells her, when he went up-stairs, "a dirty fellow bounced out of the bed on which one of us was to lie." But in the "Journal" you find the incident transformed thus: "Out of one of the beds on which we were to repose started up at our entrance a man black as a Cyclops from the forge." Goldsmith said very truly, "If you were to write a fable about little fishes, doctor, you would make them talk like whales.

The death of his wife in 1752 put an end to his writing for some time. He mourned for her as if she had been all that he fancied her. On her monument he placed a Latin epitaph, describing her as beautiful, cultivated, witty, and religious; and when speaking of her in after-years would exclaim, "Pretty creature!" as if recalling a dream of loveliness. The old proverb that "love is blind" was certainly verified in his case. Six years later, in 1758, he lost his good mother, who died in her ninety-first year, at the old home in Lichfield. He was then just fifty; but in his last letter he forgets his stately style, and writes like a child. He says:

"Dear Honored Mother:

"Neither your condition nor your character make it fit for me to say much. You have been the best mother, and are, I believe, the best woman in the world. I thank you for your indulgence to me, and beg forgiveness for all that I have done ill, and all I have omitted to do well. God grant you His Holy Spirit, and admit you to everlasting happiness, for Jesus Christ's sake! Amen. Lord Jesus, receive your Spirit! Amen.

"I am, dear, dear mother, your dutiful son,

"Sam Johnson."

To pay the expenses of her funeral, he wrote diligently for a week, and the result was "Rasselas," a story of Abyssinia—in fact, a series of moral essays, full of beautiful thoughts on his old theme, the "vanity of human wishes," very slightly covered by an imaginary tale of Eastern life. The book had a great success, being translated into almost all the languages of Europe.

The world at last began to discover Johnson's worth. The king even heard of him as the man who compiled the dictionary—a poor scribbler, who needed money—and he conferred on him a yearly pension of three hundred pounds. The following year he met in Mr. Davies's back parlor a person who had been longing for such an interview—to whom, vain, disagreeable, and garrulous though he may have been, both Johnson and his friends owe much.

I beg leave to introduce to my readers Johnson's shadow, James Boswell, Esq., of Scotland. Ever after that memorable evening, Boswell seemed to have but one idea in his head (some severe critics have suggested that *one* was an improvement on the previous emptiness), and that was Dr. Johnson! To follow his every step, to catch every word that fell from his lips and record it, was the ambition of his life. Every thing was ennobled that his new hero had touched or worn. His brown coat, his little scorched wig, his cocked hat, his heavy shoes, and huge cane, were all sacred in his eyes. He not only described his favorite dishes, but noted down just how much he ate of the fish-sauce, or the veal-pie with plums; nor did he forget what was more important.

Much of Johnson's remarkable talk would have been lost had Boswell been less of a slave and toady. He seemed proud of any notice from his master, and would note it down, though it were but an insult. He would usually call out the great moralist by asking a question, or contradicting a statement. Sometimes he got nothing but a rebuke, which would have silenced most persons forever. On one occasion he had been teasing Johnson with many direct questions, as, "What did you do, sir?" "What did you say, sir?" until he became enraged, and thundered, "I will not be put to the question, sir! Don't you consider, sir, that these are not the manners of a gentleman? I will not be baited with 'what' and 'why;' 'What is this?' 'What's that?' 'Why is a cow's tail long?' 'Why is a fox's tail bushy?'" "Why, sir," replied the humbled yet persistent questioner, "you are so *good* that I ventured to trouble you!" "Sir," growled Johnson, "my being so *good* is no reason that you should be so ill. You have but two topics—*yourself* and *me*—and I am sick of both!" So did this literary lion treat this spaniel that forever fawned upon him. Miss Burney, one of the popular writers of that day, describes Boswell as perfectly regardless of every thing and everybody, except Johnson—not even answering questions put to him, lest he might lose the smallest word from the doctor's lips. His father, the old laird of Auchinlech, was annoyed and mortified by his son's extravagant hero-worship. "There's nae hope for Jamie, mon; Jamie is gone clean gyte. What do you think, mon? he's done with Paoli; he's off wi' the land-louping scoundrel of a Corsican; and who do you think he has pinned himself to now, mon? a dominie, mon; an auld dominie: he keeped a schule, and cau'd it an acaadamy."

Yet why should poor "Bozzy" be always ridiculed and abused? We are certainly greatly indebted to him, and should be grateful for the truthful portrait he has given of his "teacher, guide, and friend," in the very best biography ever written.

We will give a few extracts, to illustrate the singular habits, and rough, though brilliant style of conversation, belonging to the great Cham of Literature. Boswell says:

"While talking or even musing, as he sat in his chair, Johnson commonly held his head to one side, toward his right shoulder, and shook it in a tremulous manner, moving his body backward and forward, and rubbing his left knee in the same direction, with the palm of his hand. In the intervals of articulating, he made various sounds with his mouth, sometimes as if ruminating, or what is called chewing the cud, sometimes giving a half whistle, sometimes making his tongue play backward from the roof of his mouth, as if clucking like a hen, and sometimes protruding it against his upper gums in front, as if pronouncing quickly under his breath 'too, too, too,' all this accompanied sometimes with a thoughtful look, but more frequently with a smile. Generally when he had concluded a period in the course of a dispute, by which time he was a good deal exhausted by violence and vociferation, he used to blow out his breath like a whale. This, I suppose, was a relief to his lungs, and seemed in him to be a contemptuous mode of expression, as if he had made the arguments of his opponent fly like chaff before the wind.

"One instance of his absence and particularity, as it is characteristic of the man, may be worth relating: When he and I took a journey together into the west, he visited the late Mr. Banks, of Dorsetshire; the conversation turning upon pictures, which Johnson could not well see, he retired to a corner of the room, stretching out his right leg as far as he could reach before him, then bringing up his left leg and stretching the right still farther on. The old gentleman, observing him, went up to him, and in a very courteous manner assured him that, though it was not a new house, the flooring was perfectly safe. The doctor started from his reverie, like a person waked out of sleep, but spoke not a word.

"When he walked the streets, what with the constant roll of his head and the concomitant motion of his body, he appeared to make his way by that motion, independent of his feet. That he was often much stared at while he advanced in this manner may easily be believed; but it was not safe to make sport of any one so robust as he was. Mr. Langton saw him once in a fit of absence, by a sudden start, drive the load off a porter's back, and walk forward briskly without being conscious of what he had done. The porter was very angry, but stood still and eyed the huge figure with much earnestness, till he was satisfied that his wisest course was to be quiet and take up his burden again."

We know from this faithful record how he sometimes gorged himself at table, till the veins swelled into knots on his forehead, and the perspiration streamed from his face; how he often swallowed nineteen cups of tea, and if in the right mood would gulp down twenty-five; how he laughed like a rhinoceros, and went scuffling and rolling about with dirty linen and unbuckled shoes, biting his nails to the quick, and hoarding every scrap of orange-peel he could find; a tremendous companion in social life; never enduring contradiction, and denouncing all who failed to agree with him as dunces and fools. But we are also told of his generous nature, his warm heart, his giant mind. He was ever ready to defend the unfortunate and protect the friendless; and, however severe in his own judgment, he would never allow any one to speak ill of his friends in his presence.

We have many pleasant pictures of him helping "poor Goldy" out of his perplexities, with the tenderness of a father; weeping at Garrick's new-made grave; carrying home on his broad shoulders a poor woman who had fainted and fallen in the streets; writing loving letters to his little godchild when sick and suffering; petting his homely old cat Hodge, for whom he used to go out and buy oysters. All this proves that "there was nothing of the bear but the skin."

He said to Boswell, "Sir, I consider myself a very polite man." In one sense this was thoroughly ludicrous; in another, thoroughly true.

In conversation he was very variable, sometimes saying nothing when all were longing for his opinion, again monopolizing the conversation, especially if there were other good talkers present. He would never allow Burke to outdo him, grunting and snorting savagely when he thought it time for him to stop. He acknowledges that he found Burke a powerful rival, and said once, when sick, "Don't let Burke in; he would kill me now!"

I will now give you a few sentences, that you may judge of his conversation and style:

On the speculations of some one as to our condition before this life, possibly in a lower order of being, he said: "Sir, it is all conjecture about a thing useless, even were it known to be true; knowledge of all kinds is good, but conjecture as to what it would be useless to know, such as whether men went upon all-fours, is idle."

A lady-friend complained that men had much more

liberty than women. "Why, madam," said Johnson, "women have all the liberty they should wish to have. We have all the labor and the danger, and women all the advantage. We go to sea, we build houses, we do every thing, in short, to pay our court to the women." But she persisted that a superiority was allowed to men to which they were not entitled. "It is plain, madam, one or other must have the superiority. As Shakespeare says, 'If two men ride on a horse, one must ride behind.' Then, madam," said Johnson, "the horse would throw them both."

He was fond of fast driving, and admired pretty women, however poor a judge he proved himself of female charms, and said one day: "If I had no duties, and no reference to futurity, I would spend my life in driving briskly in a post-chaise with a pretty woman; but she should be one who would understand me, and would add something to the conversation."

Hannah More was a special favorite, and could always put him in good-humor with her bright sallies and quick retorts. He honored her with several pet names, such as "child," "dearest," and—"little fool," the latter phrase having more real tenderness in it than all the others. She used to be placed next him at dinners, where he was expected to talk. It was quite important that some one should be able to flatter or draw him into a loquacious mood on these occasions, otherwise he might not "begin" at all, but sit as silent and abstracted as one dumb. Once when invited to a large dinner-party, where every one was waiting for an eloquent discussion, or, still better, one of his characteristic monologues, when ears, and memory, and note-books, were all ready, his only remark was "Pretty baby!" to a little child playing on the floor. But when with Hannah More his great mind was never sluggish. Her sister Sally has given a pleasant, sprightly account of their first visit to his house:

"We have paid another visit to Miss Reynolds. She had sent to engage Dr. Percy (Percy's collection—now you know him), quite a sprightly modern, instead of a rusty antique, as I expected. He was no sooner gone than the most amiable and obliging of women (Miss Reynolds) ordered the coach, to take us to Dr. Johnson's *very own house ;* yes, Abyssinia's Johnson! Dictionary Johnson! Rambler's, Idler's, and Irene's Johnson! Can you picture to yourselves the palpitation of our hearts as we approached his mansion ? The conversation turned upon a new work of his, just going to press (' The Tour to the Hebrides '), and his old friend Richardson. Mrs. Williams, the blind poetess, who lives with him, was introduced to us. She is engaging in her manners, her conversation lively and entertaining. Miss Reynolds told the doctor of all our rapturous exclamations on the road. He shook his scientific head at Hannah, and said ' she was a *silly thing.*' When our visit was ended, he called for his hat (as it rained) to attend us down a very long entry to our coach, and not Rasselas could have acquitted himself more *en cavalier.* We are engaged with him at Sir Joshua's, Wednesday evening. What do you think of us ? I forgot to mention that, not finding Johnson in his little parlor when we came in, Hannah seated herself in his great chair, hoping to catch a little ray of his genius ; when he heard it he laughed heartily, and told her it was a chair on which he never sat. He said it reminded him of Boswell and himself when they stopped a night at the spot (as they imagined) where the weird sisters appeared to Macbeth ; the idea so worked upon their enthusiasm that it quite deprived them of rest. However, they learned the next morning, to their mortification, that they had been deceived, and were quite in another part of the country."

He knew how to compliment a lady with great grace and

delicacy. Mrs. Siddons, the celebrated actress, once paid him a visit. When she entered the room there happened to be no chair ready for her, which observing, he said with a smile: "Madam, you who so often occasion a want of seats to other people, will the more easily excuse the want of one yourself." But he also knew well how to repel by brusqueness. To a lady asking his advice about her manuscript, saying, "I have other irons in the fire, but what would you do with this article?" he replied, with more severity than politeness, "Put it with your other irons." I never heard of but one lady who had the courage to retort when thus answered. When in Scotland, eating their national dish of hodgepodge, the lady at whose table he was sitting inquired if it was good. "Good for hogs, madam." "Then, pray," said she, "let me help you to some more!"

One of his rough repartees has been put in rhyme by Peter Pindar:

> " In Lincolnshire, a lady showed our friend
> A grotto, that she wished him to commend;
> Quoth she, ' How cool in summer this abode !'
> ' Yes, madam ' (answered Johnson), '*for a toad.*' "

He lived for several years in the family of Mr. Thrale, a wealthy brewer, who was also in the House of Commons, a man of uncommon kindness and good sense. His death was a terrible affliction to Johnson, who was now very solitary. Mrs. Thrale was a pretty, chatty woman, cultivated, and a good talker, whose flighty, volatile nature had been restrained and controlled by her dignified and noble husband. But after his death all was changed. She had petted and praised "the Doctor," and had been proud of him as an inmate of her house, but now she treated him so coolly that he soon left, not without a blessing on the house and her who had caused his departure. When she disgraced herself a few years after by marrying an Italian

10

music-teacher, Piozzi, and was preparing to leave England
to escape the scorn and censure of her old friends, Johnson
sent after her a letter, which shows his noble nature:

"DEAR MADAM: What you have done, however I
may lament it, I have no pretence to resent, as it has not
been injurious to · me. I therefore breathe out one sigh
more of tenderness, perhaps useless, but at least sincere.

"I wish that God may grant you every blessing, that
you may be happy in this world for its short continuance,
and eternally happy in a better state; and whatever I can
contribute to your happiness I am very ready to repay for
that kindness which soothed twenty years of a life radi-
cally wretched. Do not think slightly of the advice which
I now presume to offer. Prevail upon Mr. Piozzi to settle
in England; you may live here with more dignity than in
Italy, and with more security; your rank will be higher,
and your fortune more under your own eye. I desire not to
detail all my reasons, but every argument of prudence and
interest is for England, and only some phantoms of imagination seduce you to Italy. I am afraid, however,
that my counsel is vain, yet I have eased my heart by
doing it.

"When Queen Mary took the resolution of sheltering
herself in England, the Archbishop of St. Andrews, attempting to dissuade her, attended on her journey, and,
when they came to the irremeable stream that separated
the two kingdoms, walked by her side into the water, in
the middle of which he seized her bridle, and, with earnestness proportioned to her danger and his own affection,
pressed her to return. The queen went forward. If the
parallel reaches thus far, may it go no farther! The tears
stand in my eyes."

A few years before his death he wrote "The Lives of
the Poets," perhaps his best work, certainly the best intro-
duction we have to the poets, from Cowley to Gray. Every

sketch is tinged with his own prejudices, yet they are invaluable to the lover of literature.

Johnson's last days were full of sadness and suffering. He longed for life, not because he enjoyed it, but because he had such a peculiar horror of death. He felt that no one could or should be sure of salvation and future happiness, and dreaded, like a little child, to go out alone into the dark. It is pleasant to know that he died very easily, in apparent peace. His last words were, " God bless you!" to a young lady who came in at the last to inquire for him. He was laid in Westminster Abbey, on a December day in 1784, among those eminent men of whom he had been the historian.

> " No need of Latin or of Greek to trace
> Our Johnson's memory, or inscribe his grave ;
> His native language claims this mournful space,
> To pay the immortality he gave."

LICHFIELD, THE BIRTHPLACE OF JOHNSON.

Oliver Goldsmith.

GOLDSMITH.

"And e'en his failings leaned to virtue's side."

W<small>E</small> come next to G<small>OLDSMITH</small>, the blundering, artless, good-natured, whimsical genius, whom every one laughs at and every one loves.

His character, an odd compound of the good and the bad, the ridiculous and the sublime, was his only inheritance from his good, simple-hearted, generous, impulsive, improvident father, who, marrying very young, with little to live on but faith and hope, struggled for a dozen years with poverty and real want, as curate of the hamlet of Pallas, Longford County, in Ireland.

There, in an old, half-rustic mansion, looking down on the river Inny, Oliver Goldsmith first saw the light, on the 10th of November, 1728, the fifth child in a family of eight. Both father and child should be rather pitied than blamed for their unworldliness and incompetency, for it was just like the race. They were always, according to their own account, a strange family; their hearts were in the right place, but their heads seemed to be doing any thing but what they ought—of no cleverness in the ways of the world.

Two years after Oliver's birth, better times came to the honest curate, who, by the death of his wife's uncle, succeeded to a living, and moved from the old homestead at Pallas to the rectory of Lissoy, in the county of Westmeath—a comfortable place, with seventy acres of land, just outside the pretty little village. Here the good man kept open house, "with a crowd in the kitchen and a crowd round the parlor-table; profusion, confusion, kindness, and poverty."

We have two pictures of his father from Goldsmith's own pen. "My father, the younger son of a good family, was possessed of a small living in a church. His education was above his fortune, and his generosity greater than his education. Poor as he was he had his flatterers, poorer than himself; for every dinner he gave them they returned him an equivalent in praise; and that was all he wanted. The same ambition that actuates a monarch at the head of his army, influenced my father at the head of his table. He told the story of the ivy-tree, and that was laughed at; he repeated the jest of the two scholars with one pair of breeches, and the company laughed at that; but the story of Taffy in the sedan-chair was sure to set the table in a roar. Thus his pleasure increased in proportion to the pleasure he gave; he loved all the world, and he fancied all the world loved him."

Another sentence perhaps contains the key to Goldsmith's after-charities, often so extravagant and unjust to himself:

"He wound us up to be mere machines of pity, and rendered incapable of withstanding the slightest impulse made either by real or fictitious distress. In a word, we were perfectly instructed in the art of giving away thousands before we were taught the necessary qualifications of getting a farthing."

In "The Deserted Village" we have a poetical version of the same story:

"THE VILLAGE PREACHER.

"Near yonder copse, where once the garden smiled,
And still where many a garden flower grows wild;
There, where a few torn shrubs the place disclose,
The village preacher's modest mansion rose.
A man he was to all the country dear,
And passing rich with forty pounds a year;
Remote from towns, he ran his godly race,
Nor e'er had changed, nor wished to change his place;
Unskilful he to fawn, or seek for power
By doctrines fashioned to the varying hour;
Far other aims his heart had learned to prize,
More bent to raise the wretched than to rise.
His house was known to all the vagrant train,
He chid their wanderings, but relieved their pain;
The long-remembered beggar was his guest,
Whose beard descending swept his aged breast;
The ruined spendthrift, now no longer proud,
Claimed kindred there, and had his claims allowed:
The broken soldier, kindly bade to stay,
Sat by his fire, and talked the night away;
Wept over his wounds, or, tales of sorrow done,
Shouldered his crutch, and showed how fields were won.
Pleased with his guests, the good man learned to glow,
And quite forgot their vices in their woe;

Careless their merits or their faults to scan,
His pity gave ere charity began.
  "Thus to relieve the wretched was his pride,
And e'en his failings leaned to virtue's side;
But in his duty prompt at every call,
He watched and wept, he prayed and felt for all.
And, as a bird each fond endearment tries,
To tempt its new-fledged offspring to the skies;
He tried each art, reproved each dull delay,
Allured to brighter worlds, and led the way.
  "Beside the bed where parting life was laid,
And sorrow, guilt, and pain, by turns dismayed,
The reverend champion stood.   At his control,
Despair and anguish fled the struggling soul;
Comfort came down the trembling wretch to raise,
And his last faltering accents whispered praise.
  "At church, with meek and unaffected grace,
His looks adorned the venerable place;
Truth from his lips prevailed with double sway,
And fools, who came to scoff, remained to pray.
The service past, around the pious man,
With ready zeal, each honest rustic ran;
E'en children followed with endearing wile,
And plucked his gown, to share the good man's smile.
His ready smile a parent's warmth expressed,
Their welfare pleased him, and their cares distressed;
To them his heart, his love, his griefs were given,
But all his serious thoughts had rest in heaven:
As some tall cliff that lifts its awful form,
Swells from the vale, and midway leaves the storm,
Though round its breast the rolling clouds are spread,
Eternal sunshine settles on its head."

Oliver's education began when he was about three
years old, under the care of Mistress Elizabeth Delap, who
thought him a dunce, of whom nothing could be made;
but who was, in after-years, very proud of boasting that
she was the first to put a book into his hands.

Thomas, or "Paddy" Byrne, as he was called, the
village schoolmaster, next tried to give the careless boy

some love of study.   But Byrne had been a traveller and
soldier as well as teacher, and would often charm his
scholars with accounts of his marvellous adventures, of
robbers, pirates, and smugglers, and of the fairy super-
stitions of Ireland, when he should have been drilling
them in their lessons.   One of his listeners, enthusiastic
and full of imagination, gained in this way a crazy longing to travel and see those wonders for himself.

His style, in a severer mood, is described in a picture,
which shows him to have been master of the *ferule* as well
as the sword:

> " Beside yon straggling fence that skirts the way,
>   With blossomed furze unprofitably gay,
>   There, in his noisy mansion, skilled to rule,
>   The village master taught his little school;
>   A man severe he was, and stern to view,
>   I knew him well, and every truant knew:
>   Well had the boding tremblers learned to trace
>   The day's disasters in his morning face;
>   Full well they laughed with counterfeited glee
>   At all his jokes, for many a joke had he;
>   Full well the busy whisper circling round,
>   Conveyed the dismal tidings when he frowned:
>   Yet he was kind, or, if severe in aught,
>   The love he bore to learning was in fault;
>   The village all declared how much he knew,
>   'Twas certain he could write and cipher too;
>   Lands he could measure, terms and tides presage,
>   And e'en the story ran that he could gauge:
>   In arguing, too, the parson owned his skill,
>   For, e'en though vanquished, he could argue still;
>   While words of learned length and thundering sound
>   Amazed the gazing rustics ranged around—
>   And still they gazed, and still the wonder grew,
>   That one small head could carry all he knew."

Without doubt, the four or five years that Goldsmith
spent with this stern yet garrulous pedagogue, gave

direction to his whole life. In addition to his various accomplishments, Byrne wrote a little poetry now and then, and his admiring pupil, either from his example or a natural fancy for rhyming, began to scribble little verses, but, like Thomson, he always threw them into the fire soon after they were written.

His mother rescued some of these from the flames, and was proud and delighted. Oliver was a *genius*, she was sure, and would be a real poet some day. A boy who could write like that, when only eight years old, should not be tied to a trade; he must be educated. His father had already spent more than he could well afford on his oldest son, Henry, who was doing well at the university, and had other plans for his second boy, but the mother was in earnest, and, as usual in such cases, gained her way.

That year the small-pox went through Europe like a scourge, and the parsonage at Lissoy was not passed over. Little Oliver recovered from the terrible disease, but the roses were gone from his cheeks, and he was sadly scarred and disfigured.

This seemed especially hard, as he was very plain before, and had an intense longing for personal beauty. He was sent after this illness to the home of his uncle, John Goldsmith, where he was placed in another school. Here, as usual, he studied very little, played a great deal, was continually getting into all sorts of scrapes, and yet a general favorite.

One evening, when dancing with a number of young folks, he undertook a hornpipe, in which he made such a ridiculous appearance, with his short clumsy figure, and pitted, discolored face, that the musician, who was one of the party, laughingly called him " his little Æsop." Now this famous maker of fables, which we have all read and enjoyed, was a very ugly man, so tradition tells us, with a badly-shaped head and distorted limbs; and Goldsmith, whose greatest desire seemed to be to be considered handsome, did not relish the joke. For once his wit did not fail him, and, stopping short in his awkward flourishes, he looked for a moment at the fiddler, and then exclaimed:

> " Our herald hath proclaimed this saying,
> See Æsop dancing and his monkey playing."

This repartee completely turned the laugh, and he was thenceforth the acknowledged wit of the family.

He was blessed with a wonderfully kind uncle, Contarine, who, having made up his mind that his nephew was an uncommon child in spite of all his peculiarities, took him under his protection, with a kindness and forbearance as beautiful as it was rare. And so he went through his school-days, " doing as little work as he could; robbing orchards, playing at ball, and making his pocket-money fly about, whenever fortune sent it to him."

There is a funny and very characteristic story told of his last journey home from school, of which I will give Irving's charming version :

" His father's house was about twenty miles distant; the road lay through a rough country, impassable for carriages. Goldsmith procured a horse for the journey, and a friend furnished him with a guinea for travelling expenses. He was but a stripling of sixteen, and, being thus suddenly mounted on horseback, with money in his pocket, it is no wonder that his head was turned. He determined to play the man, and to spend his money in independent traveller's style. Accordingly, instead of pushing directly for home, he halted for the night at the little town of Ardagh, and, accosting the first person he met, inquired, with somewhat of a consequential air, for the best house in the place. Unluckily, the person he had accosted was one Kelly, a notorious wag, who was quartered in the family of one Mr. Featherstone, a gentleman of fortune. Amused with the self-consequence of the stripling, and willing to play off a practical joke at his expense, he directed him to what was literally ' the best house in the place,' namely, the family mansion of Mr. Featherstone. Goldsmith accordingly rode up to what he supposed to be an inn, ordered his horse to be taken to the stable, walked into the parlor, seated himself by the fire, and demanded what he could have for supper. On ordinary occasions he was diffident and even awkward in his manners, but here he was ' at ease in his inn,' and felt called upon to show his manhood and enact the experienced traveller. His person was by no means calculated to play off his pretensions, for he was short and thick, with a pock-marked face, and an air and carriage by no means of a distinguished cast. The owner of the house, however, soon discovered his whimsical mistake, and, being a man of humor, determined to indulge it, especially as he accidentally learned that this intruding guest was the son of an old acquaintance.

"Accordingly, Goldsmith was ' fooled to the top of his bent,' and permitted to have full sway throughout the evening. Never was schoolboy more elated. When supper was served, he most condescendingly insisted that the landlord, his wife, and daughter, should partake, and ordered a bottle of wine to crown the repast and benefit the house. His last flourish was on going to bed, when he gave especial orders to have a hot cake at breakfast. His confusion and dismay, on discovering the next morning that he had been swaggering in this free and easy way in the house of a private gentleman, may be readily conceived. True to his habit of turning the events of his life to literary account, we find this chapter of ludicrous blunders and cross-purposes dramatized many years afterward in his admirable comedy of ' She Stoops to Conquer, or the Mistakes of a Night.' "

Irving wrote of Goldsmith with a loving hand, and makes his constant blunders seem less ridiculous than where they are exaggerated by the curious, gossiping Boswell.

On the 17th of June, 1745, at the age of seventeen, Goldsmith entered Trinity College as a sizar, a position in those days little better than that of a servant. These students worked for their board, and wore a different dress from the others, that no one might mistake their position. It must have been constant torture to a sly and sensitive boy like Goldsmith, to wear the coarse, sleeveless gown, and untasselled cap, badges of his poverty; and wait upon the lazy idlers in the dining-hall, overhearing their sneering comments on his dress and manner.

He lost his good father in 1747, and was in consequence poorer than ever. He now began to make use of his poetical talent, writing street ballads for five shillings apiece, and strolling through the city at night to watch their success.

Whimsical stories are told of his benevolence while at college, which endear him to us in spite of their absurdity. For instance, he was once engaged to breakfast with a classmate, but did not appear. His friend went to his room, and found his expected guest, not only in bed, but immersed to his very chin in the feathers! It seems that a widow with five small children, had touched his heart with her piteous tale, and, having no money to relieve her wants, he brought her to the college gate, and gave her most of his clothing, and the blankets from his bed. He was so cold in the night, that he cut the tick open and crept into the feathers!

He never studied well at college, and was the lowest in his class. He had a very disagreeable tutor, unreasonable

and ill-tempered, who insisted on his devoting his time to
mathematics and logic, both of which he abhorred; who
thought him ugly and stupid, and did not hesitate to tell
him so. And it must be owned that he was not only idle,
but riotous; but this was owing to his love for gay company, more than wrong impulses. At last, after gaining
one of the minor prizes, he celebrated the unusual occasion by a supper and dance in his chamber. In the midst
of the revelry, the fierce tutor appeared, knocked his
pupil down, and turned his guests all out of doors. To be
thus disgraced in the eyes of his friends was more than
Goldsmith could endure, nor could he longer live under
such insulting tyranny. So he sold his books and clothes
the next day, and ran away. He had a vague idea of
sailing to America, or some more distant shore, but lin-
gered about Dublin till he had spent his last shilling, and
was compelled, by absolute hunger, to let his brother
Henry know of his distress. He treated him most affec-
tionately, supplied his wants, soothed his excited feelings,
and induced him to return to college.

He took a very low B. A., in 1749, and then went home
to his mother's little cottage, at Ballymahon. His career
as a student had disappointed his friends, and none were
now inclined to help him but his faithful uncle, who urged
him to prepare for holy orders, the only opening for a
younger son, with no special bent, no plans of his own,
and very little ambition.

Goldsmith himself disliked this plan, and said he was
not good enough for the position; but I really think his
greatest objection was the prescribed dress of a curate,
such a love had he for gay colors. "To be obliged to
wear a long wig, when I liked a short one, or a black
coat, when I generally dressed in brown, I thought such
a restraint upon my liberty, that I absolutely rejected the
proposal." As he could not be ordained until he was

twenty-one, he loitered away the intervening time in the most lazy way, reading biographies, novels, travels, plays, every thing that fed his imagination; wandering on the banks of the Inny; joining in the rustic sports of the villagers, in which he at once became an expert; getting up a convivial club at the little inn at Ballymahon, where he told amusing stories, and sung jolly songs—any thing but studying divinity.

When the time came to apply for orders, he appeared before the bishop, luminous in a pair of *scarlet breeches*—failed in his examination—and was rejected. His friends now began to shake their heads, and were both vexed and discouraged. Even his uncle did not talk much of his future; he was no longer a genius, simply good-natured, and apparently—good for nothing!

It would take too long to tell you minutely of his life and adventures for the next six years; a confusing, ludicrous, and yet pitiable series of blunders, failures, bad bargains, ill-luck at the gaming-table, absent-minded freaks, and all kinds of absurd and unlooked-for predicaments.

During these years, he attempted to be a tutor, a lawyer, and a physician, and failed in all; travelling also through France, Germany, Switzerland, and Italy, often on foot, with nothing to depend on but his flute, playing merry tunes at night before some peasant's cottage, to earn a supper and a bed. During these wanderings he gained in some way the degree of M. B., at Padua, and deserves in future the title of—" *Dr.* Goldsmith."

Until this time he had been constantly assisted by his uncle Contarine, who died while he was lingering in Padua. Lack of means compelled him now to turn his steps homeward; and, after two years spent on the Continent, " pursuing novelty and losing content," he landed at Dover early in 1756, with no plans whatever for his future life.

His dear uncle in his grave, his friends cold and distrustful, a penniless stranger in a foreign land, his condition was indeed forlorn. At last, he determined to go directly to London, and find some sort of employment.

"You may easily imagine," he said in a letter of some years later to his brother-in-law, "what difficulties I had to encounter, left as I was, without friends, recommendations, money, or impudence, and that in a country where being born an Irishman was sufficient to keep me unemployed. Many in such circumstances would have had recourse to the friar's cord or the suicide's halter. But with all my follies I had principle to resist the one, and resolution to combat the other."

These were, indeed, dark days in that great city, without a friend to aid or cheer him. It is a sad history—a lonely struggle. We first find him making a desperate attempt to do something in his own profession; first, as an apothecary's drudge, unable, after all his studies, to manage the pestle and mortar; afterward, assisting a chemist in his laboratory; and, at last, commencing practice in a small way, with small pay, among the poor at Southwark—only the poor, because he lacked the tact, address, polish, which would make him a favorite among the rich.

An old acquaintance, who happened to meet him in the streets about this time, describes him as decked in a second-hand coat of green and gold, his linen looking as if "clean shirt-day" came to him only once a fortnight. But his blessed "knack of hoping" had not forsaken the luckless doctor, who smilingly assured his friend that he was "practising physic, and doing *very well*," while at the moment he was suffering from poverty from which he saw no escape; hungry, perhaps, as well as tawdry and dirty.

Another describes him in a rusty suit of black velvet, to which was added a big wig and cane. A forlorn patch on the left breast he tried to conceal by pressing his three-cornered hat against his side, in the then fashionable style, sternly resisting all inducements to lay it aside when visiting a patient.

We also hear of him correcting proof for the press—always a most tedious task; even reduced to figuring in low comedy in a country town; and, hardest of all, as usher for a short time in a boy's boarding-school. He never failed to make use of his various experiences: we find them all woven into exquisite prose and verse in after-years, and laugh over his well-told tale of miseries—no laughing matter to him.

In the "Vicar of Wakefield" he makes George Primrose undergo the following catechism. The simple youth is questioned as to his qualifications for an usher:

"Have you been bred apprentice to the business?" "No." "Then you won't do for a school. Can you dress the boys' hair?" "No." "Then you won't do for a school. Can you lie three in a bed?" "No." "Then you will never do for a school. Have you a good stomach?" "Yes." "Then you will by no means do for a school. I have been an usher in a boarding-school myself, and may I die of an anodyne necklace, but I had rather be under-turnkey in Newgate. I was up early and late; I was browbeat by the master, hated for my ugly face by the mistress, worried by the boys."

And here is another description of the hardships of an usher's life:

"He is generally the laughing-stock of the school. Every trick is played upon him; the oddity of his manner, his dress, or his language, is a fund of eternal ridicule. The master himself now and then cannot avoid joining in the laugh; and the poor wretch, eternally resenting this ill-usage, lives in a state of war with all the family."

Now for the climax:

"He is obliged, perhaps, to sleep in the same bed with the French teacher, who disturbs him for an hour every night in papering and filleting his hair, and smells worse than a carrion with his rancid pomatums, when he lays his head beside him on the bolster."

The next four years he spent in a wretched way, toiling as a book hack for a grinding taskmaster, a bookseller by the name of Griffiths, whose fussy old wife undertook to criticise and revise his manuscripts.

He describes himself as in a garret, writing for bread, and expecting to be dunned for a milk score. He also contributed to the "Ledger" a series of essays much admired then as now, which he afterward collected and published under the name of "The Citizen of the World;" purporting to be the letters of a Chinaman, who, visiting London, writes home to his friends what he saw, and how it impressed him. They are full of grave irony, good-natured satire, and sparkling criticisms on English manners and morals.

Mr. Newberry, the proprietor of this paper, was also a bookseller, quite famous for getting up picture-books for the little folks. It is said that we owe "Goody Two Shoes" to Goldsmith, who sent it to Newberry one day when quite out of money. "Mother Goose," whose jingling rhymes we all know from beginning to end, was written in part at least by literary men, who tossed off these nonsensical verses to gain a dinner or a night's lodging. In 1759 he published "An Inquiry into the Present State of Polite Learning," which brought him into notice, and enabled him to move from his miserable quarters into very comfortable rooms in Wine-office Court in Fleet Street.

But his native buoyancy was somewhat crushed by all these trials, and in a letter to his brother Henry, when sending the book to him, says :

"I must confess it gives me some pain to think I am almost beginning the world at the age of thirty-one. Though I never had a day's sickness since I saw you, yet I am not that strong, active man you once knew me. You. scarcely can conceive how much eight years of disappointment, anguish, and study, have worn me down. If I remember right, you are seven or eight years older than me, yet I dare venture to say, that, if a stranger saw us both, he would pay me the honors of seniority. Imagine to yourself a pale, melancholy visage, with two great wrinkles between the eyebrows, with an eye disgustingly severe, and a big wig, and you may have a perfect picture of my present appearance. On the other hand, I conceive you as perfectly sleek and healthy, passing many a happy day among your own children, or those who knew you a child."

He begs him never to let his son touch a romance or novel :

"These paint beauty in colors more charming than nature, and describe happiness that man never tastes. How delusive, how destructive, are those pictures of consummate bliss! They teach the youthful mind to sigh after beauty and happiness that never existed ; to despise the little good that fortune has mixed in our cup, by expecting more than she ever gave; and, in general, take the word of a man who has seen the world, and who has studied human nature more by experience than precept— take my word for it, I say, that books teach us very little of the world. The greatest merit in a state of poverty would only serve to make the possessor ridiculous—may distress, but cannot relieve him. Frugality, and even avarice, in the lower orders of mankind, are true ambition. These afford the only ladder for the poor to rise to preferment. ·Teach then, my dear sir, to your son, thrift and economy. Let his poor wandering uncle's example be placed before his eyes. I had learned from books to be disinterested and generous before I was taught from experience the necessity of being prudent. I had contracted the habits and notions of a philosopher, while I was exposing myself to the approaches of insidious cunning; and often by being, even with my narrow finances, charitable to excess, I forgot the rules of justice, and placed myself in the very situation of the wretch who thanked me for my bounty. When I am in the remotest part of the world, tell him this, and perhaps he may improve from my example. But I find myself again falling into my gloomy habits of thinking."

We now come to a pleasant meeting. Johnson had read Goldsmith's essays with great pleasure, speaking of them to his friends in the highest terms. The author was flattered and delighted, and invited Johnson to a literary supper at his lodgings. Accordingly, on the evening of the 31st of May, 1761, the gruff but kind-hearted lexicographer might have been seen rolling along toward Wine-office Court, looking, strange to say, very trim and *bandboxy*. He wore an entire new suit, a new hat, and the scorched wig was discarded; in fact, his appearance was so striking that one of his friends could not but notice his uncommon spruceness. "Sir," said Johnson, "I hear that Goldsmith, who is a very great sloven, justifies his disregard of cleanliness and decency by quoting my practice, and I am desirous this night to show him a better example."

The "little Irishman and the big Englishman" met and were mutually pleased, and the acquaintance soon ripened into intimacy.

Boswell was jealous of this awkward scholar, who had "such a hurry of ideas, and such laughable confusion in

expressing them," and was willing to exaggerate his defects. He avers that he was so eager to shine, so desirous of notice and approbation, that he seemed unhappy
when travelling with two very beautiful young ladies, because they received more attention than himself!—and
that he even grew angry at the praise bestowed on a
puppet, which tossed a pike with great dexterity, saying,
"Pshaw! I can do that better myself!" He also adds,
that, going home with Burke to supper, after the show,
he broke his ankle in attempting to out-do the puppets!•
Goldsmith in his turn despised the fawning parasite, and
disproved Boswell's assertion that "he talked carelessly,
without knowledge of his subject," when he answered
some one who inquired, "Who is this Scotch cur at Johnson's heels?" "He is not a *cur*," said Goldsmith, "you are
too severe; he is only a *burr*. Tom Davies flung him at
Johnson in sport, and he has the faculty of *sticking!*"

We find a double pleasure in a happy retort from him,
because he so often blundered, and one instance of his
success in this direction is positively exhilarating, for the
"Great Cham" himself is the victim. They were enjoying a cosy *tête-à-tête* supper one evening, and Johnson
expatiated on a dish of rump and kidneys, which he was
causing rapidly to disappear.

"These," said he, "are pretty little things, but a man
must eat a great many of them before he is filled."

"Ay, but how many of them," asked Goldsmith, with
affected simplicity, "would reach to the moon?"

"To the *moon?* Ah, sir, that, I fear, excels your cal
culation."

"Not at all, sir. I think I could tell."

"Pray, then, sir, let us hear."

"Why, sir—*one*, if it were long enough!"

Johnson growled for a time, at finding himself caught
in such a "trite, school-boy trap."•

Through the influence of his new friend, Goldsmith was now admitted to the celebrated literary club which used to meet every Monday night, at the Turk's Head, Gerard Street, Soho. The number was limited to nine, and among the original members were Sir Joshua Reynolds, the founder of the English school of painting; and Burke, the orator and statesman, of whom Johnson said that "no man of sense could meet Mr. Burke by accident under a gateway to avoid a shower, without being convinced that he was the first man in England." The others, though not so well known, were all men of culture and wit.

Goldsmith's appearance was against him; he was, to most of them, a mere literary drudge, and must have suffered under their satirical supervision. Although no man of his age could surpass him in smooth, graceful, and attractive composition, he was vanquished in conversation by men who did not possess a tithe of his genius, for he was blundering and illogical, seldom able to tell what he knew.

Of course, he never did himself justice at these meetings, and was often the subject of ridicule. Johnson said of him that "no man was more foolish when he had not his pen in hand, or more wise when he had;" and Garrick, who never liked him, afterward paraphrased this idea in an epitaph, when, as usual, he was the last to arrive at the club :

> "Here lies poet Goldsmith, for shortness called Noll,
> Who wrote like an angel, but talked like poor Poll."

But Goldsmith talked on, often laughed at, seldom listened to, and yet, when in a happy mood, charming all by the thoughtless outpourings of a fertile fancy. He was busily writing, at this time, no one knew what. He was, as usual, in debt, and always in trouble, but he had a firm friend and sincere adviser in Johnson, who discerned his real merit. He would scold him like a child, yet allow no one else to speak of him with disrespect, and was ever ready to help him out of his embarrassments.

"I received one morning," says Johnson, " a message from poor Goldsmith that he was in great distress, and, as it was not in his power to come to me, begging that I would come to him as soon as possible. I sent him a guinea, and promised to come to him directly. I accordingly went as soon as I was dressed, and found that his landlady had arrested him for his rent, at which he was in a violent passion. I perceived that he had already changed my guinea, and had a bottle of madeira and a glass before him. I put the cork into the bottle, desired he would be calm, and began to talk to him of the means by which he might be extricated. He then told me he had a novel ready for the press, which he produced to me. I looked into it and saw its merit; told the landlady I should soon return; and, having gone to a bookseller, sold it for sixty pounds. I brought Goldsmith the money, and he discharged his rent, not without rating his landlady in a high tone for having used him so ill."

The novel was "The Vicar of Wakefield," that captivating story many of whose phrases have passed into household words; which has been translated into various languages, and is just as much read and admired now as ever. The first genuine novel of *domestic* life; like Goldy himself, full of contradictions, blunders, absurdities, yet winning our hearts, and holding a place there. "No bad man could write a book so full of the soft sunshine and tender beauty of domestic life—so sweetly wrought out of the gentle recollections of the old home at Lissoy."

And this delightful story was actually kept by the stupid publisher for two years! Let us be thankful that he did not lose it during the time.

In December of 1764, "The Traveller" appeared, and the slow-witted public began to think that they had a genius among them. It had a remarkable success, and proved a rich prize to the publisher, who doled out twenty guineas to the author for his share of the profits. Even this seemed a golden windfall to the needy poet. He distrusted his power of verse-making, and had published this poem in fear and trembling. He said, "I fear I have come *too late* into the world; Pope and other poets have taken up the places in the Temple of Fame."

But Goldsmith's reputation was now rising rapidly, and he was one of the lions of the day. Charles Fox pronounced "The Traveller" to be one of the finest poems in the English language. Johnson declared it was better than any thing since the days of Pope. Everybody wondered how the homely, dumpy Irishman, full of "brogue and blunder," could have produced such a gem. Some doubted whether it was really his work, he answered so stupidly when questioned as to the meaning of any particular passage.

Miss Reynolds, who had toasted him as the ugliest man she ever saw, exclaimed, after some one had finished reading the poem to her—"Well, I shall never think Dr. Goldsmith ugly any more!"

His presence was now courted in elegant drawing-rooms; but he made a sorry presence there. He was now forty years of age—too old to adopt new manners, with his new mode of life, and he disappointed all who had their ideas of the man, from the ease and grace of his poetry.

It was now considered safe to bring out "The Vicar of Wakefield," which had been slumbering for two years in the hands of the publishers. It came out on the 27th of March, 1766; three editions were exhausted in as many months, and its popularity has never flagged. Goethe,

the greatest genius of Germany, said that this book had
formed part of his education, influencing his taste and
feelings through life, and that he read it at twenty and
at eighty with the same delight.

As an illustration of the humor which runs through
the story, let me give you the description of the picture
of the Primrose family:

"My wife and daughters, happening to return a visit
to neighbor Flamborough's, found that family had lately
got their pictures drawn by a limner, who travelled the
country, and took likenesses for fifteen shillings a head.
As this family and ours had long a sort of rivalry in point
of taste, our spirit took the alarm at this stolen march
upon us, and notwithstanding all I could say, and I said
much, it was resolved that we should have our pictures
done too. Having, therefore, engaged the limner—for
what could I do?—our next deliberation was, to show the
superiority of our tastes in the attitudes. As for our
neighbor's family, there were seven of them, and they
were drawn with seven oranges, a thing quite out of taste,
no variety in life, no composition in the world. We desired to have something in a brighter style, and, after
many debates, at length came to a unanimous resolution
of being drawn together in one large historical family
piece. This would be cheaper, since one frame would
serve for all, and it would be infinitely more genteel; for
all families of taste were now drawn in the same manner.
As we did not immediately recollect an historical subject
to hit us, we were contented each with being drawn as
independent historical figures. My wife desired to be
represented as Venus, and the painter was desired not to
be too frugal of his diamonds in her stomacher and hair.
Her two little ones were to be as Cupids by her side;
while I, in my gown and band, was to present her with
my books on the Whistonian controversy. Olivia would

be drawn as an Amazon sitting upon a bank of flowers, dressed in a green joseph, richly laced with gold, and a whip in her hand. Sophia was to be a shepherdess, with as many sheep as the painter could put in for nothing; and Moses was to be dressed out with a hat and white feather. Our taste so much pleased the Squire, that he insisted as being put in as one of the family in the character of Alexander the Great, at Olivia's feet. This was considered by us all as an indication of his desire to be introduced into the family, nor could we refuse his request. The painter was therefore set to work, and, as he wrought with assiduity and expedition, in less than four days the whole was completed. The piece was large, and it must be owned he did not spare his colors; for which my wife gave him great encomiums. We were all perfectly satisfied with his performance; but an unfortunate circumstance had not occurred till the picture was finished, which now struck us with dismay. It was so very large that we had no place in the house to fix it. How we all came to disregard so material a point is inconceivable; but certain it is, we had been all greatly remiss. The picture, therefore, instead of gratifying our vanity, as we hoped, leaned, in a most mortifying manner, against the kitchen wall, where the canvas was stretched and painted—much too large to be got through any of the doors, and the jest of all our neighbors. One compared it to Robinson Crusoe's long boat, too large to be removed; another thought it more resembled a reel in a bottle; some wondered how it could be got out; but still more were amazed how it ever got in!".

Goldsmith next tried comedy. "The Good-natured Man," after much delay, was brought out at Covent Garden. Owing to mean wire-pulling by his enemies, it was in a measure a failure, though bringing five thousand

11

pounds to poor Goldy, who now dashed out into most extravagant expenditure.

In the books of his tailor we see an entry of a suit—"Tyrian bloom, satin grain, and garter blue silk breeches," and of another "lined with silk, and furnished with gold buttons."

He leased three rooms on the second floor of Brick Court, Middle Temple, and adorned them with mirrors, Wilton carpets, bookcases, and card-tables. Here he gave brilliant dinner-parties and jolly suppers, a thoughtless spendthrift, enjoying in butterfly fashion his transient summer of prosperity. His purse was soon emptied, and then he ran deeply in debt, hoping soon to turn up another trump, and pay all he had borrowed.

In 1769 he published his "History of Rome," for the use of schools and colleges. Though not a work that he enjoyed, it is compiled with taste and skill, and was well received. He also wrote a history of England, in the same style.

About this time he made the acquaintance of two charming young ladies, the Misses Horneck, meeting them one evening at Joshua Reynolds's. The younger sister, Miss Mary, called by her friends "The Jessamy Bride," particularly fascinated him, and both were his firm friends through life.

At the house of Mrs. Bunbury, the older sister, he spent many a happy week, leading the games at Christmas, and romping with the children during his summer holidays.

He always indulged in a gay suit when invited to Barton, doubtless hoping to make an impression on the fair Miss Horneck, who laughed, as did every one else, at his love of finery. He was not allowed to enjoy his silk coats, and dainty ruffles, and bag-wig, when with that merry party. They disarranged his beautiful curls, and daubed his bloom-colored coat with paint, which mortified him greatly.

But they all appreciated his talent, and were really fond of him, and I think his happiest days were spent with this pleasant family, forgetting debts and duns, and rejoicing in the sweet smile of the Jessamy Bride.

"The Deserted Village" appeared in May, 1770, and sold rapidly; by the 16th of August the fifth edition was hurried through the press. It is his finest poem, written in the same measure and style as "The Traveller;" like that, a mirror of his own heart, and equally true to nature. Loitering among the green lanes and hedge-rows that are found in the environs of London, his mind went back to childish days, and the poem is a faithful pen-photograph of the dear old hamlet at Lissoy, where he spent his careless, happy boyhood.

How touching the contrast between his feelings then and the yearnings of his solitary heart, as expressed in these pathetic lines:

> "In all my wanderings round this world of care,
> In all my griefs—and God has given my share—
> I still had hopes my latest hours to crown,
> Amidst these humble bowers to lay me down;
> To husband out life's taper at the close,
> And keep the flame from wasting by repose:
> I still had hopes, for pride attends us still,
> Amidst the swains to show my book-learned skill—
> Around my fire an evening group to draw,
> And tell of all I felt, and all I saw;
> And as a hare whom hounds and horns pursue,
> Pants to the place from whence at first he flew,
> I still had hopes, my long vexations past,
> Here to return—and die at home at last."

The emphatic words of poor, dying Gray, who heard "The Deserted Village" read at Malvern, where he spent

11

his last summer in a vain search for health, must be echoed by every feeling heart: "That man *is* a poet."

Many wondered why Goldsmith should ever write any thing but poetry, but stern necessity compelled him to devote himself to prose, which brought better pay.

Poetry never satisfies an impatient creditor, and when Earl Lisburn asked Goldsmith why he wasted his time compiling histories, he said: "My lord, by courting the Muses I shall starve, but by my other labors I shall eat, drink, have good clothes, and enjoy the luxuries of life."

His affairs were now in a terrible condition; he owed more than he dared to think of, and had spent money given in advance for what was not written. Distressed and heart-sick, he appeared at times unnaturally gay, and then completely down. Alarmed at last, he began to retrench, and went into the country for the summer, to work on a natural history he had undertaken at a hundred guineas a volume, most of which he had already wasted. It would have seemed preposterous for Goldsmith to undertake this task, if he had not been blessed with the power that Stella said Swift possessed—"*of writing well on a broomstick*"—for he had no knowledge whatever of his subject, hardly knowing one animal from another, only able to distinguish a turkey from a goose, when they were cooked on the table; but Johnson prophesied that the work would be as entertaining as a Persian tale, and so it is.

In a letter to a friend, at this time, he mentions that he is writing a comedy, "trying these three months to do something to make the people laugh; strolling about the hedges, studying jests, with a most tragical countenance."

From various reasons this did not appear on the stage for some time after it was written; but on the evening of the 15th of May, 1773, Johnson, Burke, Reynolds, and a phalanx of tried and trusty friends, were seen at the Covent Garden Theatre, seated in different parts of the house, ready to applaud Goldy's new play. Many feared a failure, but Johnson was sure of success. He sat in the front row of a side box, where every one could see him, and it was arranged that, whenever he laughed, all the rest were to roar as heartily and naturally as possible. One Adam Drummond, who had a loud, rattling, and perfectly contagious laugh, was placed in an upper box, just over the stage, but as he was something like a *cannon*, very noisy, but ignorant when to "go off," some one sat by him to give him a *jog*, as a signal to begin.

The plan worked well; the *élite* laughed when the lexicographer shook his clumsy sides over the jokes, and no one could resist the uproarious cackle of the good-natured Adam in the front box. The audience laughed till they cried, and "She Stoops to Conquer, or The Mistakes of a Night," was the "hit" of the season.

You remember the plot of this popular play was suggested to the author by his own mistake so many years before, when he spent a night at the Featherstone mansion, and ordered hot cakes for breakfast.

·I told you of Garrick's epitaph on Goldsmith, which, containing more truth than epitaphs in general, was not relished by the subject, who had serious objections to being considered an inspired parrot. Some time after, he produced a little poem, one evening, at the club, which he begged to read for the pleasure of the members.

This was "Retaliation," in which he retorted upon several of his friends, who had been in the habit of making him the butt of their jokes.

His humor was always *good-humor*, his satire never caustic, but the account was now even. Garrick's epitaph is a perfect description of the man:

> "Here lies David Garrick, describe him who can,
>   An abridgment of all that was pleasant in man;

As an actor, confessed without rival to shine;
As a wit, if not first, in the very first line:
Yet, with talents like these, and an excellent heart,
The man had his failings, a dupe to his art.
Like an ill-judging beauty, his colors he spread,
And beplastered with rouge his own natural red.
On the stage he was natural, simple, affecting;
'Twas only that when he was off he was acting.
With no reason on earth to go out of his way,
He turned and he varied full ten times a day:
Though secure of our hearts, yet confoundedly sick,
If they were not his own by finessing and trick:
He cast off his friends as a huntsman his pack,
For he knew, when he pleased, he could whistle them back.
Of praise a mere glutton, he swallowed what came,
And the puff of a dunce he mistook it for fame;
Till his relish, gown callous almost to disease,
Who peppered the highest was surest to please.
But let us be candid, and speak out our mind,
If dunces applauded, he paid them in kind.
Ye Kenricks, ye Kellys, and Woodfalls so grave,
What a commerce was yours, while you got and you gave!
How did Grub Street reëcho the shouts that you raised,
While he was be-Rosciused and you were be-praised!
But peace to his spirit, wherever it flies,
To act as an angel and mix with the skies:
Those poets who owe their best fame to his skill,
Shall still be his flatterers, go where he will;
Old Shakespeare receive him with praise and with love,
And Beaumonts and Bens be his Kellys above."

This poem was never finished; the portraits are not complete, for Goldsmith, who had long been ill, both body and mind, was attacked by a nervous fever in the spring of 1774, which his constitution had not the power to resist, and he died on the 4th of April, in the forty-fifth year of his age.

When Burke was told of his death, he burst into tears. Reynolds was in his painting-room when the sad news came to him. He at once laid his pencil aside, which, in times of great family distress, he had not been known to do, and left his work for the day. His faithful friend Johnson felt the blow deeply. On the stairs leading to his chamber, sat the old and infirm, mourning their loss; many poor women sobbing bitterly for their generous friend. After his coffin was closed, it was reopened, and a lock of hair taken for a lady, who wished to preserve it as a remembrance. It was his old friend, the beautiful Jessamy Bride, who desired this token.

He deserved a place in Westminster Abbey, and his friends at first intended to honor his memory in that way. A public funeral was planned, Reynolds, Burke, and Garrick, among the bearers; but when they discovered that he died very deeply in debt, owing more than two thousand pounds, such a display seemed inappropriate. Five days after his death, at twilight on Saturday evening, the 9th of April, 1774, he was quietly interred in the burying ground of Temple Church.

A fine bust of the poet was soon after placed in the abbey, by the club of which he had been a member, and Johnson wrote a Latin epitaph, which was inscribed on a white marble tablet underneath. He wrote of Goldsmith as "a poet, naturalist, and historian, who left scarcely any style of writing untouched, and touched nothing that he did not adorn." He also spoke of his power to move us to smiles or tears, and this is as true of his life as his writings.

Irving says that "he seemed from infancy to have been compounded of two natures, one bright, the other blundering." Shy, awkward, sensitive, eager for praise, fond of display, always doing or saying the most ridiculous things, we cannot help laughing at his absurdities; but he was so generous, so noble in his impulses, so forgiving and gentle, so sad-hearted and restless beneath all his merriment and foolish display, that a sigh of tenderness and pity involuntarily follows the smile. His very faults and foibles rather attract than repel, and I doubt if there is a writer in the whole range of English literature who is regarded with more sympathy and affection than—" Poor Goldy."

GOLDSMITH AND JOHNSON.

COWPER.

"And now what time ye all may read through dimming tears his story;
How discord on the music fell, and darkness on the glory.
And how, when one by one sweet sounds and wandering lights departed,
He wore no less a loving face, because so broken-hearted."

WILLIAM COWPER, whom his best biographer, Southey, speaks of as "the most popular poet of his generation, and the best of English letter-writers," was the son of Dr. John Cowper, a royal chaplain, rector of Great Berkhampstead, in Hertfordshire. He could boast of his ancestry on both sides, as his father was the son of a judge, and nephew of a lord chancellor, and his mother was descended by four different lines from Henry III. of England. He was born at the parsonage, on the 15th of November, 1731. His early days were made bright and happy by the tender love of his mother. "Her hand it was that wrapped his little scarlet cloak around him, and filled his little bag with biscuits every morning, before he went to his first school. By her knee was his happiest place, where he often amused himself by marking out the flowered pattern of her dress on paper with a pin, taking a child's delight in this simple skill. He was only six years old when this fond mother died; thus early upon the childish head a pitiless storm began to beat."

The delicate, diffident boy was old enough to know his great loss, and has recorded his feelings at that sad time in one of his most beautiful poems, on the receipt of her picture more than fifty years after:

ON THE RECEIPT OF HIS MOTHER'S PICTURE.

" O that those lips had language! Life has passed
With me but roughly since I heard thee last.
Those lips are thine—thy own sweet smile I see,
The same that oft in childhood solaced me;
Voice only fails, else how distinct they say,
' Grieve not, my child, chase all thy fears away!'
The meek intelligence of those dear eyes
(Blest be the art that can immortalize,
The art that baffles Time's tyrannic claim
To quench it!) here shines on me still the same.
    Faithful remembrancer of one so dear,
O welcome guest, though unexpected here!
Who bidd'st me honor with an artless song,
Affectionate, a mother lost so long.
I will obey, not willingly alone,
But gladly, as the precept were her own:
And, while that face renews my filial grief,
Fancy shall weave a charm for my relief;
Shall steep me in Elysian reverie,
A momentary dream, that thou art she.
    My mother! when I learned that thou wast dead,
Say, wast thou conscious of the tears I shed?
Hovered thy spirit o'er thy sorrowing son,
Wretch even then, life's journey just begun?

Perhaps thou gavest me, though unfelt, a kiss;
Perhaps a tear, if souls can weep in bliss—
Ah, that maternal smile! it answers—Yes.
I heard the bell tolled on thy burial-day,
I saw the hearse that bore thee slow away,
And, turning from my nursery window, drew
A long, long sigh, and wept a last adieu!
But was it such?—It was.—Where thou art gone,
Adieus and farewells are a sound unknown.
May I but meet thee on that peaceful shore,
The parting word shall pass my lips no more!
Thy maidens grieved themselves at my concern,
Oft gave me promise of thy quick return.
What ardently I wished, I long believed,
And, disappointed still, was still deceived.
By expectation every day beguiled,
Dupe of to-morrow, even from a child.
Thus many a sad to-morrow came and went,
Till, all my stock of infant sorrow spent,
I learned at last submission to my lot,
But, though I less deplored thee, ne'er forgot."

He said, when quite an old man, in speaking of her:
"Not a week passes (perhaps I might with equal veracity
say a day) in which I do not think of her; such was the
impression her tenderness made upon me, though the
opportunity she had for showing it was so short."

He was at once taken from the nursery, and sent from
home to a boarding-school, where the timid, homesick child
suffered much from loneliness and the cruelty of a boy
many years older, practised so secretly that no one suspected it for a long time, but it was at last found out, and
the tyrant expelled.

Cowper retained through life a painful recollection of
the terror with which this boy inspired him. He says:
"His savage treatment of me impressed such a dread of
his figure upon my mind, that I well remember being afraid
to lift my eyes upon him higher than his knees, and that I
knew him better by his shoebuckles than by any other

11*

part of his dress.   May the Lord pardon him, and may we meet in glory."

This experience gave him a lasting dislike for schools of all kinds, which he afterward forcibly expressed in a poem called " Tirocinium, or a Review of Schools."   His eyes now troubled him so much that he was placed under the care of an eminent oculist, where he remained two years, and was much relieved, though not wholly cured. At the end of this time, at the age of ten, he was removed by his father to Westminster, where, though often morbid and low-spirited, he enjoyed a good deal.   He was a fine scholar, a favorite with his teachers, and very fond of out-door games, excelling in cricket and foot-ball.   He speaks of this period as one in which, if not thoroughly happy, he was never really sad.   He has given us a picture which proves that he looked back with pleasure on that part of his boyhood :

" Be it a weakness, it deserves some praise,
    We love the play-place of our early days :
    The scene is touching, and the heart is stone
    That feels not at that sight, and feels at none.
    The wall, on which we tried our graving skill,
    The very name we carved subsisting still ;
    The bench on which we sat while deep employed,
    Though mangled, hacked, and hewed, yet not destroyed.
    The little ones, unbuttoned, glowing hot,
    Playing our games, and on the very spot,
    As happy as we once to kneel, and draw
    The chalky ring, and knuckle down at taw ;
    To pitch the ball into the grounded hat,
    Or drive it devious with a dext'rous pat ;
    The pleasing spectacle at once excites
    Such recollections of our own delights,
    That viewing it, we seem almost to obtain
    Our innocent, sweet, simple years again.
    This fond attachment to the well-known place,
    Where first we started into life's long race,

Maintains its hold with such unfailing sway,
We feel it e'en in age, and at our latest day."

"At the age of eighteen," says Cowper, "being tolerably well furnished with grammatical knowledge, but as ignorant of all kinds of religion as the satchel on my back, I was taken from Westminster, and, having spent about nine months at home, was sent to acquire the practice of law with an attorney." And here comes a really sunny spot in the poet's life. With his fellow-apprentice, a refractory but clever boy, afterward Lord-Chancellor Thurlow, he pretended to study, but accomplished very little. Writing to his cousin, Lady Hesketh, many years afterward, he says: "I did actually live three years with Mr. Chapman, a solicitor, that is to say, I slept three years in his house, but I *lived*, that is to say, I spent my days in Southampton Row, as you very well remember. There was I and the future lord chancellor employed from morning to night in giggling and making giggle, instead of studying the law. Oh, fie, cousin! how could you do so?"

This profession had been selected for him by his father, because his connections were such that he would, without doubt, be well provided for by them; and he had given proof at Westminster of two qualifications for success—talent and application. Sometimes he attributed his failure to lack of fitness for the study. He says: "Whatever Nature expressly designed me for, I have never been able to conjecture, I seem to myself so universally disqualified for the common and customary occupations and amusements of mankind." Again, he would blame himself for his idleness; and, writing to a young friend who was studying law, he says: "You do well, my dear sir, to improve your opportunity; to speak in the rural phrase, this is your *sowing*-time; and the sheaves you look for can never be yours unless you make that use of it. The color of our whole life is greatly such as the first three or four years in which we are our own masters make it. Then it is that we may be said to shape our destiny, and to treasure up for ourselves a series of future successes or disappointments. Had I employed my time as wisely as you in a situation very similar to yours, I had never been a poet perhaps, but I might by this time have acquired a character of more importance in society, and a situation in which my friends would have been better pleased to see me. The only use I can make of myself now—at least the best—is to serve as a terror to others, when occasion may happen to offer, that they may escape (as far as my admonitions can have any weight with them) my folly and my fate."

Called to the bar in 1754, he lived rather an idle life in his Temple chambers; more employed with literature than law; writing often for the serials of the day: but more, perhaps, with *love* than literature; for he was fascinated by one of those pretty cousins with whom he used to "giggle" in Southampton Row—Theodora, a younger sister of his constant friend, Lady Hesketh. The attachment was mutual; but when the affair became more serious, her father refused his consent to the marriage, on the ground that they were too nearly related. Perhaps he might have seen in Cowper's moody, morbid temperament another reason for breaking up the romance. At any rate, his determination was unalterable, and the cousins soon parted, never to meet on earth.

Cowper apparently conquered this unfortunate sentiment, which at first threw a darker coloring over his life and spirits; but neither time nor absence diminished Theodora's constancy to her first and only love.

His life in those airy chambers in the Inner Temple was not probably as dissipated as his own words would lead us to think, but still misspent, wasted in frivolous amusements and desultory reading. In his thirty-second year, he began to think seriously of his future. His father was dead, his patrimony nearly spent, and real poverty seemed before him. Major Cowper, a relative, who was anxious to help him, presented to him, in the year 1763, a valuable clerkship in the House of Lords, which required the holder to appear frequently before the House. The idea of thus appearing in public was, in his own words, "mortal poison." His friend then gave him a more private position, that of clerk of the journals, which he resolved to accept, although he felt at the time as if he were receiving a "dagger in his heart." But, owing to some political and party opposition, the major's right of nomination was called in question by his enemies, and a public examination of each candidate was demanded; and this future horror so preyed upon his morbidly-sensitive mind, that melancholy at last became madness, and death seemed better than the prospect before him. He tried to kill himself in various ways, but was wonderfully preserved by God's mercy. His brother, terrified at his condition, placed him at once in a private asylum at St. Alban's, where he remained for eighteen months, enduring mental agonies which words fail to interpret. He felt that his soul was eternally lost, and describes himself as "in a strange and terrible darkness, my conscience scaring me, the avenger of blood pursuing me, and the city of refuge out of reach." Some verses composed in the asylum show his state of mind. They are so painfully sad, I will quote but two:

> " Hatred and vengeance, my eternal portion,
> Scarce can endure delay of execution;
> Wait with impatient readiness to seize my
> Soul in a moment!

> " Man disavows, and Deity disowns me,
> Hell might afford my miseries a shelter;
> Therefore Hell keeps her ever-hungry mouths all
> Bolted against me!"

At last there came a revulsion of feeling; peace and happiness took the place of despair. In his own words: "Unless the Almighty arm had not been under me, I think I should have died of gratitude and joy. My eyes filled with tears, and my voice choked with transport; I could only look up to heaven in silent fear, overwhelmed with love and wonder." But the work of the Holy Spirit is best described in His own words: it was "joy unspeakable and full of glory. For many succeeding weeks tears were ready to flow, if I did but speak of the Gospel, or mention the name of Jesus. To rejoice day and night was all my employment. Too happy to sleep much, I thought it was lost time that was spent in slumber. Oh, that the ardor of my first love had continued! But I have known many a lifeless and unhallowed hour since—long intervals of darkness, interrupted by short returns of peace and joy in believing."

How beautifully he describes the healing of his wounded spirit by the Saviour:

> " I was a stricken deer, that left the herd
> Long since. With many an arrow deep infixed
> My panting side was charged, when I withdrew
> To seek a tranquil death in distant shades.
> There was I found by One who had Himself
> Been hurt by the archers. In His side he bore,
> And in His hands and feet, the cruel scars.
> With gentle force soliciting the darts,
> He drew them forth, and healed and bade me live."

In that hymn so familiar to us all—

> " Oh for a closer walk with God—"

he alludes to that period of peaceful hope. After his recovery he did not wish to return to London, and his friends thought his decision a wise one, and subscribed among themselves an annual allowance, on which he could live frugally in retirement.

" Far from the world, O Lord, I flee,
From strife and tumult far ;
From scenes where Satan wages still
His most successful war.

" The calm retreat, the silent shade,
With prayer and praise agree,
And seem by Thy sweet bounty made
For those who follow Thee."

He soon found a quiet home, congenial and delightful, in the family of Rev. Mr. Unwin, clergyman at Hunting-don. He has given minute descriptions of the family and his life there. He says of Mrs. Unwin : " That woman is a blessing to me, and I never see her without being the better for her company. She has a very uncommon understanding, has read much to excellent purpose, and is more polite than a duchess."

Here is an account of the way in which he spent his time in that excellent household : "We breakfast commonly between eight and nine ; till eleven, we read either the Scripture, or the sermons of some faithful preacher of these holy mysteries ; at eleven, we attend divine service, which is performed here twice every day ; and, from twelve to three, we separate and amuse ourselves as we please. During that interval, I either read in my own apartment, or walk, or ride, or work in the garden. We seldom sit an hour after dinner, but, if the weather permits, adjourn to the garden, where, with Mrs. Unwin and her son, I have generally the pleasure of religious conversation till tea-time. If it rains, or is too windy for walking, we either converse in-doors, or sing some hymns of Martin's collections, and, by the help of Mrs. Unwin's harpsichord, make up a tolerable concert, in which our hearts are, I hope, the best and most musical performers. After tea, we sally forth to walk in good earnest. Mrs. Unwin is a good walker, and we have generally travelled about four miles, -

before we see home again. When the days are short, we make this excursion in the former part of the day, between church-time and dinner. At night, we read and converse as before, till supper, and commonly finish the evening either with hymns or a sermon."

In July of 1767, this pleasant home was broken up by the sudden death of Mr. Unwin, who was killed by a fall from his horse, while on his way to church. Cowper says: "The effect of this awful dispensation will only be a change of the place of my abode. For I shall still, by God's leave, continue with Mrs. Unwin, whose behavior to me has always been that of a mother to her son."

They decided upon a removal to Olney, where the Rev. John Newton was curate; indeed, the only motive which directed them in their choice, was a wish to be under his pastoral care. But this was hardly the best atmosphere for Cowper, always inclined to religious melancholy. The good doctor insisted on his taking an active part in the prayer-meetings, and going with him to the bed of the dying sinner. This kept him in a constant state of anxiety and trepidation, and more than balanced the benefit to be gained from his society. He also urged the poet to write those hymns which we all love to read and repeat; and I fear that, brooding over his own experiences, indulging in introspection and retrospection, as he did when composing them, with the death of his brother, which occurred at this time, were the causes of a return of his insanity.

It was a review of the interpositions of Providence to save him from committing suicide, which led him to write

"God moves in a mysterious way,"

and, looking back on the ecstasy which followed the gloom, he imagined himself sadly changed.

Lady Hesketh spoke her mind very frankly on this

point: "Mr. Newton is an excellent man, I make no doubt," said she, "and to a strong-minded man like himself, might be of great use, but to such a mind, such a tender mind, and to such a wounded, yet lively, imagination as our cousin's, I am persuaded that eternal praying and preaching were too much; nor could it, I think, be otherwise. I do not mean to give you my sentiments upon this conduct generally, but only as it might affect our cousin, and, indeed, for him, I think it could not be either proper or wholesome."

In January, 1773, he was again decidedly insane, going over the dreary path he trod at St. Alban's, Mrs. Unwin devoting herself to him with unceasing vigilance and unwearied devotion. Three years passed away before the cloud was removed. In his convalescence, he amused himself in various ways, petting pigeons, drawing landscapes, making bird-cages, and taming three hares, one of which he has celebrated in "The Task":

> " Well, one at last is safe. One sheltered hare
> Has never heard the sanguinary yell
> Of cruel man, exulting in her woes.
> Innocent partner of my peaceful home,
> Whom ten long years' experience of my care
> Has made at last familiar; she has lost
> Much of her vigilant, instinctive dread,
> Not needful here, beneath a roof like mine.
> Yes, thou mayst eat thy bread, and lick the hand
> That feeds thee; thou mayst frolic on the floor
> At evening, and at night retire secure
> To thy straw couch, and slumber unalarmed.
> For I have gained thy confidence, have pledged
> All that is human in me to protect
> Thine unsuspecting gratitude and love.
> If I survive thee, I will dig thy grave,
> And when I place thee in it, sighing say,
> I knew at least one hare that had a friend."

With returning health, the love of reading and writing

also came back to him, and Mrs. Unwin now urged him to write a poem of some length, giving as his subject, "The Progress of Error." It was soon accomplished, and was speedily followed by three other poems of the same kind, "Truth," "Table Talk," and "Expostulation," all being done within three months. The volume was issued in 1782, but did not sell very well. Johnson, however, and Franklin, saw real merit in the modest volume, and prophesied better things from the pen of the gentle recluse. He says of "Table Talk," in a letter to Dr. Newton: "It is a medley of many things, some that may be useful, and some that, for aught I know, may be very diverting. I am merry, that I may decoy people into my company; and grave, that they may be the better for it. Now and then I put on the garb of a philosopher, and take the opportunity, that disguise procures me, to drop a word in favor of religion. In short, there is some froth, and here and there a bit of sweetmeat, which seems to entitle it justly to the name of a certain dish the ladies call a trifle. Whether all this management and contrivance be necessary, I do not know, but am inclined to suspect, that if my Muse was to go forth, clad in Quaker colors, without one bit of ribbon to enliven her appearance, she might walk from one end of London to the other, as little noticed as if she were one of the sisterhood indeed."

In this same year Lady Austen came to Olney—a sparkling, witty, accomplished woman; and to her we owe the warmest thanks for inspiring Cowper with a more cheerful spirit. Her conversation had as happy an effect upon him as the harp of David upon Saul. "Whenever the cloud seemed to be coming over him, her sprightly powers were exerted to dispel it. One afternoon, October, 1782, when he appeared more than usually depressed, she told him the story of John Gilpin, which had been told her in her childhood, and which in her relation tickled his fancy as much as it has that of thousands and tens of thousands since in his. The next morning he said to her that he had been kept awake during the greater part of the night by thinking of the story and laughing at it, and that he had turned it into a ballad.

"I little thought," said Cowper, "when I was writing the history of John Gilpin, that he would appear in print. I intended to laugh, and to make two or three others laugh. Strange as it may seem, the most ludicrous thing I ever wrote has been written in the saddest mood; and but for that saddest mood, perhaps, had never been written at all."

He also wrote verses for "Sister Anne," as he called his new friend, to suit some of her favorite airs for the harpsichord and guitar. His "Dirge for the Royal George" was composed in this way.

Here is a playful song, celebrating a walk in muddy weather, taken by Mrs. Unwin and himself:

"THE DISTRESSED TRAVELLERS; OR, LABOR IN VAIN.

"*An excellent new Song to a Tune never sung before.*

"I sing of a journey to Clifton,
　　We would have performed if we could,
　Without cart or barrow to lift on
　　Poor Mary and me through the mud.
　　　　Slee sla slud,
　　　　Stuck in the mud;
　Oh, it is pretty to wade through a flood!

"So away we went, slipping and sliding—
　　Hop, hop, à la mode de deux frogs;
　'Tis near as good walking as riding,
　　When ladies are dressed in their clogs.
　　　　Wheels, no doubt,
　　　　Go briskly about;
　But they clatter, and rattle, and make such a rout!

SHE.

"Well; now I protest it is charming;
 How finely the weather improves!
That cloud, though, is rather alarming—
 How slowly and stately it moves!

HE.

 "Pshaw! never mind,
 'Tis not in the wind:
We're travelling south, and shall leave it behind.

SHE.

"I am glad we are come for an airing,
 For folks may be pounded and penned,
While they grow rusty, not caring
 To stir half a mile to the end.

HE.

 "The longer we stay,
 The longer we may;
It's a folly to think about weather or way.

SHE.

"But now I begin to be frighted;
 If I fall, what a way I should roll!
I am glad that the bridge was indicted.
 Stop! stop! I am sunk in a hole!

HE.

 "Nay, never care!
 'Tis a common affair;
You'll not be the last that will set a foot there.

SHE.

"Let me now breathe a little, and ponder
 On what it were better to do—
That terrible lane I see yonder,
 I think we shall never get through!

HE.

 "So think I;
 But, by-the-by,
We never shall know if we never shall try.

SHE.

"But should we get there, how shall we get home?
  What a terrible deal of bad road we have passed!
Slipping and sliding; and if we should come
  To a difficult stile, I am ruined at last!
      Oh, this lane!
      Now it is plain
That struggling and striving is labor in vain!

HE.

"Stick fast there, while I go and look.

SHE.

"Don't go away, for fear I should fall.

HE.

"I have examined it every nook;
  And what you have here is a sample of all.
      Come, wheel around,
      The dirt we have found
Would be an estate at a farthing a pound.

"Now, Sister Anne, the guitar you must take;
  Set it, and sing it, and make it a song.
I have varied the verse for variety's sake,
  And cut it off short, because it was long.
      'Tis hobbling and lame,
      Which critics won't blame,
For the sense and the sound, they say, should be the same."

His spirits were buoyant when not affected by the malady which influenced him in *winter* more than any other season. January was the hardest month for him: he always looked forward to it with dread. He loved the summer months, when he could write and lounge in the myrtle-shaded summer-house, and work in the garden. He says: "In summer-time, I am as giddy-headed as a boy, and can settle to nothing. Winter condenses me, and makes me lumpish and sober, and then I can read all day long."

His letters were often written in rhyme; and he said events were as rare at Olney as cucumbers in December. He had the rare power of investing the simplest topic with a charm. - Here is an example of this:

"*July* 12, 1781.

"To the Rev. John Newton—

"My very dear Friend: I am going to send, what, when you have read, you may scratch your head, and say, I suppose, there's nobody knows, whether what I have got, be verse or not; by the tune and the time, it ought to be rhyme; but if it be, did you ever see, of late or of yore, such a ditty before? The thought did occur, to me and to her, as madam and I, did walk and not fly, over the hills and dales, with spreading sails, before it was dark to Weston Park.

"The news at *Oney* is little or noney; but such as it is, I send it, viz.: Poor Mr. Peace cannot yet cease, addling his head with what you said, and has left parish-church quite in the lurch, having almost swore to go there no more.

"Page and his wife, that made such a strife, we met them twain in Dog-lane; we gave them the wall, and that was all. For Mr. Scott, we have seen him not, except as he passed, in a wonderful haste, to see a friend in Silver End. Mrs. Jones proposes, ere July closes, that she and her sister, and her Jones mister, and we that are here, our course shall steer, to dine in the Spinney; but for a guinea, if the weather should hold, so hot and so cold, we had better by far, stay where we are. For the grass there grows, while nobody mows (which is very wrong), so rank and long, that so to speak, 'tis at least a week, if it happens to rain, ere it dries again.

"I have writ Charity, not for popularity, but as well as I could, in hopes to do good; and if the Reviewer should say 'To be sure, the gentleman's Muse, wears

Methodist shoes; you may know by her pace, and talk
about grace, that she and her bard have little regard, for
the taste and fashions, and ruling passions, and hoidening
play, of the modern day; and though she assume a borrowed plume, and here and there wear a tittering air, 'tis
only her plan, to catch if she can, the giddy and gay, as
they go that way, by a production on a new construction.
She has baited her trap in hopes to snap all that may
come, with a sugar-plum.'

"—— His opinion in this, will not be amiss; 'tis what
I intend, my principal end; and if I succeed, and folks
should read, till a few are brought to a serious thought,
I shall think I am paid, for all I have said and all I have
done, though I have run, many a time, after a rhyme, as
far as from hence, to the end of my sense, and by hook or
crook, write another book, if I live and am here another
year. I have heard before, of a room with a floor, laid
upon springs, and such-like things, with so much art, in
every part, that when you went in, you was forced to begin a minuet pace, with an air and a grace, swimming
about, now in and now out, with a deal of state, in a figure of eight, without pipe or string, or any such thing;
and now I have writ, in a rhyming fit, what will make you
dance, and as you advance, will keep you still though
against your will, dancing away, alert and gay, till you
come to an end of what I have penned; which that you
may do, ere madam and you are quite worn out with jig-
ging about, I take my leave, and here you receive a bow
profound, down to the ground, from your humble me,

"W. C.

"P. S.—When I concluded, doubtless you did think
me right, as well you might, in saying what I said of Scott;
and then it was true, but now it is due to him to note, that
since I wrote, himself and he has visited me."

12

Soon after the publication of "John Gilpin," Lady Austen begged him to try blank verse.

"But," said he, "I have no subject."

"Oh! you can write on any thing," was the quick reply—"take this sofa."

Hence the beginning of "The Task," which took all English hearts by storm. •

> "I sing the sofa.—
> The theme though humble, yet august and proud
> The occasion—for the fair commands the song."

The poem came out just at the right time, when the public mind was prepared to receive it, having been trained by Gray and Thomson to love *Nature*, and simple descriptions of common things. Then, too, there was no other distinguished poet on the field to compete with him. He says: "My descriptions are all from nature; not one of them second-handed. My delineations of the heart are from my own experience."

Southey says: "Were I to say, that a poet finds his best advisers among his female friends, it would be speaking from my own experience, and the greatest poet of the age (Wordsworth) would confirm it by his. But never was poet more indebted to such friends than Cowper. Had it not been for Mrs. Unwin, he would probably never have appeared in his own person as an author; had it not been for Lady Austen, he would never have been a popular poet."

Cowper next undertook to translate Homer into English verse, working regularly at the rate of forty lines a day. He was dissatisfied with Pope's version, saying he had failed to catch Homer's spirit. But his effort to interpret him more happily was not successful, although the translation was well received.

In 1796 he lost his dearest friend, Mary Unwin, his

second mother, to whom he has written two beautiful poems. I will give you the sonnet—one can hardly read it without tears:

> "Mary, I want a lyre with other strings,
>   Such aid from Heaven as some have feigned they drew,
>   An eloquence scarce given to mortals, new
> And undebased by praise of meaner things,
> That ere through age or woe I shed my wings,
> I may record thy worth, with honor due,
> In verse as musical as thou art true,
>   And that immortalizes whom it sings;
> But thou hast little need. There is a Book,
> By seraph writ, with beams of heavenly light,
> On which the eyes of God not rarely look—
> A chronicle of actions, just and bright.
> There all thy deeds, my faithful Mary, shine,
> And since thou own'st that praise, I spare thee mine."

A pension of three hundred pounds from the king comforted his declining days, which were clouded by the old sorrow. Kind friends drew around him in those last sad years, which he described as a "universal blank."

On the morning of April 25, 1800, he expired — so peacefully that, though surrounded by friends, no one perceived the moment of his departure. The last expression on his countenance was that of calmness and composure, mingled with holy surprise. Death seemed a blessed release to the lifelong sufferer; all doubts removed—safe home at last—

> "Secure in Jesus' love."

I cannot close this sketch more appropriately than with these words from Collier:

"If we compare our English literature to a beautiful garden, where Milton lifts his head to heaven in the spotless chalice of the tall white lily, and Shakespeare scatters his dramas round him in beds of fragrant roses, blushing with a thousand various shades—some stained to the core as if with blood, others unfolding their fair pink petals with a lovely smile to the summer sun—what shall we find in shrub or flower so like the timid, shrinking spirit of William Cowper, as that delicate sensitive-plant, whose leaves, folding up at the slightest touch, cannot bear even the brighter rays of the cherishing sun?"

COWPER'S COTTAGE.

BURNS.

"Through all his tuneful heart how strong
The human feeling gushes,
The very moonlight of his song
Is warm with smiles and blushes!
Give lettered pomp to teeth of Time,
So 'Bonnie Doon' but tarry;
Blot out the epic's stately rhyme,
But spare his 'Highland Mary.'"

THE greatest poet, beyond all comparison, that Scotland has produced, was ROBERT BURNS, born on the 25th of January, 1759, in a clay-built cottage, raised by his father's own hands, on the banks of the Doon, at the hamlet of Alloway, in Ayrshire. His father, though a hard-handed peasant-farmer of the humblest class, was every inch a man, an earnest Christian, and fully impressed with the importance of an education for his children. Yet his life was not a sunny one; cramped by poverty, and made despondent by ill-luck, there was an almost habitual gloom on his brow.

"Mighty events turn on a straw; the crossing of a brook decides the conquest of the world. Had this William Burns's small seven acres of nursery-ground any wise prospered, the boy Robert had been sent to school, had struggled forward, as so many weaker men do, to some university; come forth not a rustic wonder, but as a regular, well-trained, intellectual workman, and changed the whole course of British literature, for it lay in him to have done this! But the nursery did not prosper; poverty sank his whole family below the help of even our cheap school system; Burns remained a hard-worked ploughboy, and British literature took its own course."

He did, however, attend school for a few years, and made good use of his time. His teacher tells us that he excelled all boys of his own age, and took rank above several who were his seniors. The New Testament, the Bible, the English Grammar, and Mason's "Collection of Verse and Prose," laid the foundation of devotion and knowledge. He says of himself: "At those years I was by no means a favorite with anybody. I was a good deal noted for a retentive memory, a stubborn, sturdy something in my disposition, and an enthusiastic idiot piety. I say *idiot* piety, because I was then but a child. Though it cost the schoolmaster some thrashings, I made an excellent English scholar, and by the time I was ten or eleven years of age, I was a critic in substantives, verbs, and particles. The first two books I ever read in private, and which gave me more pleasure than any two books I ever read since, were the 'Life of Hannibal,' and the 'History of Sir William Wallace.' Hannibal gave my young ideas such a turn that I used to strut in raptures after the recruiting-drum and bagpipe, and wish myself tall enough to be a soldier; while the story of Wallace poured a Scottish prejudice into my veins, which will boil along them, till the flood-gates of life shut in eternal rest."

Those who are familiar with "Bruce's Address" (and who is not?) will see how those early influences became a part of himself. Carlyle says: "Why should we speak of 'Scots wha hae wi Wallace bled,' since all know it from the king to the meanest of his subjects? This dithyrambic was composed on horseback, in riding in the middle of tempests, over the wildest Galloway moor, in company with a friend, who, observing the poet's looks, forbore to speak—judiciously enough—for a man composing 'Bruce's Address' might be unsafe to trifle with. Doubtless this stern hymn was singing itself as he formed it, through the soul of Burns, but, to the external ear, it should be sung with the throat of the whirlwind. So long as there is warm blood in the heart of Scotchman or man, it will move in fierce thrills under this war-ode, the best, we believe, that was ever written by any pen."

But by far the greater part of Burns's education was gained at home. His mother, a truly religious woman, with a warm heart and remarkably even temper, was devoted to her son "Robbie," who inherited her large, lustrous eyes, black as the night and brilliant as its stars.

The sweet old ballads she used to chant for him, all wore a religious hue, and from them he learned the art of adding a moral to his verses in a way unobtrusive and graceful. And an ignorant, superstitious old woman, who lived in their family, furnished him another school of poetry. He says: "She had, I suppose, the largest collection in the country of tales and songs concerning devils, ghosts, fairies, brownies, witches, warlocks, spunkies, kelpies, elf-candles, dead-lights, wraiths, apparitions, cantraips, giants, enchanted towers, dragons, and other trumpery. This cultivated the latent seeds of poesie, but had so strong an effect upon my imagination, that to this hour, in my nocturnal rambles, I sometimes keep a lookout in suspicious places."

Let us speak the name of Jenny Wilson with reverence, ignorant and credulous though she was, for there is no doubt that her wonderful tales gave color and character to many of Burns's finest effusions.

Edna Dean Proctor, whom Whittier, I think, pronounces the finest female poet in America, has given a very pretty version of his early associations:

" With his head upon her bosom,
    In the firelight's ruddy glow,
Plaintive songs his mother sung him,
    Airs of Scotland, long ago ;
And he thrilled at tales of heroes,
    Or of ghosts and warlocks grim,
Till he felt a chilly horror
    Creeping over every limb.
And he shuddered as the tempest
    Shook the window with its moan,
Lest the sobbing and the sighing
    Were a murdered victim's groan ;
Now his name is linked with story,
    And his life is set to song—
All that Scotland was of glory
    Floats with Robert Burns along.
And King of Hearts he reigns to-day,
    While the noble throng around him ;
God be praised that a man has sway,
    And the wide world's love has crowned him ! "

The Scottish peasantry of that time were much better informed than you would suppose, and the father of Burns was unusually intelligent. Sitting in his easy-chair by the ingle-side, he taught his son, not lessons of morality alone, but the traditionary history of Scotland—all, in fact, that he was able to impart of useful knowledge.

It was a recollection of his happy home, and his good father's domestic devotions, that enabled Burns to charm the world with those faithful, faultless pictures in the "Cotter's Saturday Night." Any sketch of this poet would be incomplete without the whole of this charming tribute to the pleasures found in the peasant's cottage, which I will copy from "Cleveland's Compendium," where the Scotch is explained in foot-notes:

"THE COTTER'S SATURDAY NIGHT.

" Inscribed to Robert Aiken, Esq.

" My loved, my honored, much respected friend !
   No mercenary bard his homage pays ;
With honest pride I scorn each selfish end ;
   My dearest meed, a friend's esteem and praise:
   To you I sing, in simple Scottish lays,
   The lowly train in life's sequestered scene ;
The native feelings strong, the guileless ways ;
   What Aiken in a cottage would have been ;
Ah ! though his worth unknown, far happier there, I ween.

" November chill blaws loud wi' angry sugh ;
   The shortening winter-day is near a close ;
The miry beasts retreating frae [1] the pleugh ;
   The blackening trains o' craws to their repose ;
The toil-worn Cotter frae his labor goes ;
   This night his weekly moil [2] is at an end,
Collects his spades, his mattocks, and his hoes,
   Hoping the morn in ease and rest to spend,
And weary, o'er the moor, his course does hameward bend.

" At length his lonely cot appears in view,
   Beneath the shelter of an aged tree ;
Th' expectant wee [3] things, toddlin,[4] stacher [5] through
   To meet their dad, wi' flicterin' [6] noise an' glee.
His wee bit ingle,[7] blinkin [8] bonnily.
   His clean hearth-stane, his thriftie wifie's smile,
The lisping infant prattling on his knee,
   Does a' [9] his weary carking [10] cares beguile,
An' makes him quite forget his labor and his toil.

" Belyve [11] the elder bairns come drappin in,
   At service out, amang the farmers roun' ;

---

[1] From.   [2] Labor.   [3] Little.   [4] Tottering in their walk.   [5] Stagger.
[6] Fluttering.   [7] Fire.   [8] Shining at intervals.   [9] All.   [10] Consuming.   [11] By-and-by.

Some ca'[1] the pleugh, some herd, some tentie[2] rin
   A cannie[3] errand to a neebor town:
Their eldest hope, their Jenny, woman grown,
   In youthfu' bloom, love sparkling in her e'e,
Comes hame, perhaps, to show a braw[4] new gown,
   Or deposit her sair-won[5] penny-fee,[6]
To help their parents dear, if they in hardship be.

   "Wi' joy unfeigned, brothers and sisters meet,
     An' each for other's weelfare kindly spiers;[7]
The social hours, swift-winged, unnoticed fleet;
     Each tells the unco[8] that he sees or hears;
The parents, partial, eye their hopeful years;
     Anticipation forward points the view;
The mother, wi' her needle an' her sheers,
     Gars[9] auld claes look amaist as weel's the new;
The father mixes a' wi' admonition due.

   "Their master's and their mistress's command,
     The younkers a' are warned to obey;
An' mind their labors wi' an eydent[10] hand,
     An' ne'er, though out o' sight, to jauk or play:
'An', O! be sure to fear the Lord alway!
     An' mind your duty, duly, morn an' night!
Lest in temptation's path ye gang astray,
     Implore His counsel and assisting might:
They never sought in vain that sought the Lord aright!'

   "But hark! a rap comes gently to the door;
     Jenny, wha kens the meaning o' the same,
Tells how a neebor lad cam' o'er the moor,
     To do some errands, and convoy her hame.
The wily mother sees the conscious flame
     Sparkle in Jenny's e'e, and flush her cheek;
With heart-struck anxious care, inquires his name,
     While Jenny hafflins[11] is afraid to speak;
Weel pleased the mother hears it's nae wild worthless rake.

---

[1] Drive.   [2] Cautious.   [3] Kindly dexterous.
[4] Fine, handsome.   [5] Sorely won.   [6] Wages.
[7] Asks.   [8] News.   [9] Makes.   [10] Diligent.   [11] Partly.

" Wi' kindly welcome Jenny brings him ben ;[1]
    A strappan[2] youth, he taks the mother's eye ;
Blythe Jenny sees the visit's no ill-ta'en ;
    The father cracks[3] of horses, pleughs, and kye.[4]
The youngster's artless heart o'erflows wi' joy,
    But blate[5] an' laithfu',[6] scarce can weel behave ;
The mother, wi' a woman's wiles, can spy
    What maks the youth sae bashfu' and sae grave,
Weel pleased to think her bairn's respected like the lave.[7]

" O, happy love ! where love like this is found !
    O heartfelt raptures ! bliss beyond compare !
I've paced much this weary, mortal round,
    And sage experience bids me this declare,—
' If Heaven a draught of heavenly pleasure spare,
    One cordial in this melancholy vale,
'Tis when a youthful, loving, modest pair,
    In other's arms breathe out the tender tale,
Beneath the milk-white thorn that scents the evening gale.'

" Is there, in human form, that bears a heart,—
    A wretch ! a villain ! lost to love and truth !
That can, with studied, sly, ensnaring art,
    Betray sweet Jenny's unsuspecting youth ?
Curse on his perjured arts ! dissembling smooth !
    Are honor, virtue, conscience, all exiled ?
Is there no pity, no relenting ruth,[8]
    Points to the parents fondling o'er their child ?
Then paints the ruined maid, and their distraction wild ?

" But now the supper crowns their simple board !
    The healsome parritch,[9] chief o' Scotia's food :
The soupe[10] their only hawkie[11] does afford,
    That 'yont[12] the ballan[13] snugly chows her cood :
The dame brings forth, in complimental mood,
    To grace the lad, her weel-hained[14] kebbuck,[15] fell,[16]
An' aft he's pressed, an' aft he ca's it good ;

---

[1] Into the parlor.   [2] Tall and handsome.   [3] Converses.   [4] Kine, cow.
[5] Bashful.   [6] Reluctant.   [7] The rest, the others.
[8] Mercy, kind feeling.   [9] Oatmeal pudding.   [10] Sauce, milk.
[11] A pet name for a cow.   [12] Beyond.   [13] A partition wall in a cottage.
[14] Carefully preserved.   [15] A cheese.   [16] Biting to the taste.

The frugal wifie, garrulous, will tell,
How 'twas a towmond [1] auld,[2] sin [3] lint was i' the bell.[4]

" The cheerfu' supper done, wi' serious face,
They round the ingle form a circle wide ;
The sire [5] turns o'er, wi' patriarchal grace,
The big Ha'-Bible,[6] ance his father's pride ;
His bonnet reverently is laid aside,
His lyart [7] haffets [8] wearin' thin an' bare ;
Those strains that once did sweet in Zion glide,
He wales [9] a portion with judicious care ;
And ' Let us worship God,' he says, wi' solemn air.

" They chant their artless notes in simple guise ;
They tune their hearts, by far the noblest aim ;
Perhaps Dundee's [10] wild warbling measures rise,
Or plaintive Martyrs,[10] worthy of the name ;
Or noble Elgin [10] beats the heavenward flame,
The sweetest far of Scotia's holy lays :
Compared with these, Italian thrills are tame ;
The tickled ears no heartfelt raptures raise ;
Nae unison hae they with our Creator's praise.

---

[1] Twelve months.   [2] Old.   [3] Since.   [4] Flax was in blossom.
[5] This picture, as all the world knows, he drew from his father. He was himself, in imagination, again one of the " wee things " that ran to meet him ; and
" the priest-like father " had long worn that aspect before the poet's eyes, though
he died before he was threescore. " I have always considered William Burns "
(the father), says Murdoch, " as by far the best of the human race that I ever had
the pleasure of being acquainted with, and many a worthy character I have
known. He was a tender and affectionate father, and took pleasure in leading
his children in the paths of virtue. I must not pretend to give you a description
of all the manly qualities, the rational and Christian virtues of the venerable
Burns. I shall only add, that he practised every known duty, and avoided every
thing that was criminal." The following is the " Epitaph " which the son wrote
for him :

          " O ye, whose cheek the tear of pity stains,
              Draw near, with pious reverence, and attend !
          Here lie the loving husband's dear remains,
              The tender father, and the generous friend :
          The pitying heart that felt for human woe ;
              The dauntless heart that feared no human pride ;
          The friend of man, to vice alone a foe,
              ' For e'en his failings leaned to virtue's side.' "

[6] The great Bible kept in the hall.   [7] Gray.
[8] The temples, the sides of the head.   [9] Chooses.
[10] The names of Scottish psalm-tunes.

" The priest-like father reads the sacred page,
How Abram was the friend of God on high ;
Or, Moses bade eternal warfare wage
With Amalek's ungracious progeny ;
Or, how the Royal Bard [1] did groaning lie
Beneath the stroke of Heaven's avenging ire ;
Or, Job's pathetic plaint and wailing cry ;
Or, rapt Isaiah's wild, seraphic fire ;
Or other holy seers that tune the sacred lyre.

" Perhaps the Christian volume is the theme,
How guiltless blood for guilty man was shed ;
How He, who bore in heaven the second name,
Had not on earth whereon to lay His head :
How His first followers and servants sped,
The precepts sage they wrote to many a land :
How he,[2] who lone in Patmos [3] banished,
Saw in the sun a mighty angel stand,
And heard great Babylon's doom pronounced by Heaven's command.

" Then kneeling down to Heaven's Eternal King,
The saint, the father, and the husband prays :
Hope ' springs exulting on triumphant wing,'
That thus they all shall meet in future days ;
There ever bask in uncreated rays,
No more to sigh, or shed the bitter tear,
Together hymning their Creator's praise,
In such society, yet still more dear,
While circling time moves round in an eternal sphere.

" Compared with this, how poor Religion's pride,
In all the pomp of method and of art,
When men display to congregations wide
Devotion's every grace, except the heart !
The power, incensed, the pageant will desert,
The pompous strain, the sacerdotal stole ; [4]
But haply, in some cottage far apart,
May hear, well-pleased, the language of the soul ;
And in His book of life the inmates poor enroll.

---

[1] David.   [2] St. John.
[3] An island in the Archipelago, where John is supposed to have written the
book of Revelation.   [4] Priestly vestment.

" Then homeward all take off their several way;
    The youngling cottagers retire to rest;
The parent-pair their secret homage pay,
    And proffer up to Heaven the warm request
That He, who stills the raven's clamorous nest,
    And decks the lily fair in flowery pride,
Would, in the way His wisdom sees the best,
    For them and for their little ones provide;
But, chiefly, in their hearts with grace divine preside.

" From scenes like these old Scotia's grandeur springs,
    That makes her loved at home, revered abroad;
Princes and lords are but the breath of kings,
    'An honest man's the noblest work of God;'
And certes,[1] in fair virtue's heavenly road,
    The cottage leaves the palace far behind:
What is a lordling's pomp? a cumbrous load,
    Disguising oft the wretch of human kind,
Studied in arts of hell, in wickedness refined!

" O Scotia! my dear, my native soil!
    For whom my warmest wish to Heaven is sent!
Long may thy hardy sons of rustic toil
    Be blest with health, and peace, and sweet content!
And, O! may Heaven their simple lives prevent
    From luxury's contagion, weak and vile!
Then, howe'er crowns and coronets be rent,
    A virtuous populace may rise the while,
And stand, a wall of fire, around their much-loved isle.

" O Thou! who poured the patriotic tide
    That streamed through Wallace's[2] undaunted heart,
Who dared to, nobly, stem tyrannic pride,
    Or nobly die, the second glorious part,
(The patriot's God peculiarly Thou art,
    His friend, inspirer, guardian, and reward!)
O never, never, Scotia's realm desert:
    But still the patriot, and the patriot bard,
In bright succession raise, her ornament and guard!

---

[1] Certainly.   [2] Sir William Wallace, the celebrated Scottish patriot.

It is the true poet alone who finds such beauty and dignity in the humblest scenes of life, and Burns *felt* all that he expressed.

His father had a choice though limited selection of books, all of which he read eagerly and thoroughly. These, with a fortnight's French, in which he advanced as far as Telemachus, gave him a better education than many young men possess when they enter the university. But he had yet other teachers: "Out on the fields of Mossgiel, amid the birds and wild-flowers of a Lowland farm, he learned his finest lessons, and conned them with all his earnest heart, as he held the handles of the plough. A little heap of leaves and stubble, torn to pieces by the ruthless ploughshare, one cold November day, exposes to the frosty wind a poor wee field-mouse, that starts frightened from the ruin. The tender heart of the poet-ploughman swells and bubbles into song. And again, when April is weeping on the field, the crushing of a crimson-tipped daisy beneath the up-turned furrow, draws from the same gentle heart a sweet, compassionate lament, and exquisite comparisons. Poems like those to the Mouse and the Daisy, are true wild-flowers, touched with a fairy grace, and breathing a delicate fragrance, such as the blossoms of no cultured garden can ever boast."

I long to give you both of these, but must content myself with the latter, which contains so sad, so truthful a prophecy of his own fate:

"TO A MOUNTAIN DAISY.

" Wee, modest, crimson-tipped flower,
  Thou's met me in an evil hour;
 For I maun crush amang the stoure
    Thy slender stem:
To spare thee now is past my power,
    Thou bonnie gem.

" Alas ! it's no thy neibor sweet,
  The bonnie Lark, companion meet,
  Bending thee 'mang the dewy weet,
      Wi' spreckled breast,
  When upward-springing, blithe, to greet
      The purpling east !

" Cauld blew the bitter-biting north
  Upon thy early, humble birth;
  Yet cheerfully thou glinted forth
      Amid the storm,
  Scarce reared above the parent earth
      Thy tender form.

" The flaunting flowers our gardens yield,
  High sheltering woods and wa's maun shield ;
  But thou beneath the random bield
      O' clod or stane
  Adorns the histie stibble-field,
      Unseen, alane.

" There, in thy scanty mantle clad,
  Thy snawie bosom sun-ward spread,
  Thou lifts thy unassuming head
      In humble guise ;
  But now the share uptears thy bed,
      And low thou lies !

" Such is the fate of artless maid,
  Sweet flow'ret of the rural shade !
  By love's simplicity betrayed,
      And guileless trust,
  Till she, like thee, all soiled, is laid
      Low i' the dust.

" Such is the fate of simple bard
  On life's rough ocean luckless starred !
  Unskilful he to note the card
      Of prudent lore,
  Till billows rage, and gales blow hard,
      And whelm him o'er.

" Such fate to suffering worth is given,
  Who long with wants and woes has striven,

By human pride or cunning driven
        To misery's brink,
Till wrenched of every stay but Heaven,
        He, ruined, sink !

" Even thou who mourn'st the daisy's fate,
That fate is thine—no distant date ;
Stern Ruin's ploughshare drives, elate,
        Full on thy bloom,
Till crushed beneath the furrow's weight
        Shall be thy doom ! "

It was Love's young dream which really roused the poetic fire.

"For my own part," he observes, "I never had the least thought or inclination of turning poet, till I once got heartily in love, and then rhyme and song were, in a manner, the spontaneous language of my heart. You know our country custom of coupling a man and woman together, as partners in the labors of harvest. In my fifteenth autumn, my partner was a bewitching creature, a year younger than myself. My scarcity of English, denies me the power of doing her justice in that language, but you know the Scottish idiom—'she was a bonnie, sweet, sonsie lassie.' In short, she altogether, unwittingly to herself, initiated me in that delicious passion, which, in spite of acid disappointment, gin-house prudence, and bookworm philosophy, I hold to be the first of human joys, our dearest blessing here below. How she caught the contagion, I cannot tell. You medical people talk much of infection from breathing the same air, the touch, etc., but I never expressly said I loved her. Indeed, I did not know myself why I liked so much to loiter behind with her, when returning in the evening from our labors ; why the tones of her voice made my heart-strings thrill like an Æolian harp, and, particularly, why my pulse beat such a furious rattan, when I looked and fingered over her little hand, to pick out the cruel nettle-stings and thistles. Among her other love-inspiring qualities, she sang sweetly, and it was her favorite reel to which I attempted giving an embodied vehicle in rhyme. Thus with me began love and poetry."

He owns that his heart was completely tinder, always lighted up by some goddess or other, and it would be no easy matter to count the "Marys, Bellas, and Elizas," the Peggys and the Nannies O, who, in turn, captivated the susceptible poet, before he settled as a prosy Benedict. He had the same creed in love-affairs that we find in one of Moore's melodies:

> " Then, oh what pleasure, wherever we roam,
>   To be *doomed* to find something still that is dear;
>   And when far away from the lips that we love,
>   We've but to make love to the lips that are near !"

" Highland Mary," however, who inspired several of his best songs, and Jean Armour, who afterward became his dearly-loved wife, are the most prominent names in the long list.

He was an awkward, ungainly youth, with no beauty but his eyes, which shone, as some one said, like coach-lamps in a dark night; but his eloquence rarely failed to produce the desired effect.

One of the many pretty maidens, upon whom he had tried his power, said: "Open your eyes and shut your ears wi' Rob Burns, and there's nae fear o' your heart; but close your eyes and open your ears, and you'll lose it."

He was now working on the farm with his father and his brother Gilbert, "toiling like a galley-slave," until both soul and body were in danger of being crushed (like the daisy he has immortalized) beneath the weight of the furrow. Gilbert touchingly describes those many anxious days:

" My brother, at the age of fifteen, was the principal

laborer on the farm, for we had no hired servant, male
or female. The anguish of mind we felt at our tender
years, under these straits and difficulties, was very great.
To think of our father growing old—for he was now
above fifty, broken down with the long-continued fatigues
of his life, with a wife and five children and in a declining
state of circumstances—these reflections produced in my
brother's mind and mine sensations of the deepest distress."

Burns was so ambitious to *excel* in every thing, that
although this life was far from his taste, he used to love
to outdo all his neighbors; and it is said that he could
draw the straightest furrow on his field, sow the largest
quantity of seed-corn in a day, and mow the most rye-grass
and clover of any farmer in the dale. If ever equalled,
he would conquer by a witty repartee.

After a hard strife on the harvest-field one day, his
rival said, " Robert, I'm no sae far behind this time, I'm
thinkin'." " John," said he, in a whisper, " you're behind
in something yet. I made a *sang* while I was a *stookin!* "

But sadder experiences were in store for the poet-
ploughman. His father, who had long been in ill-health,
was deeply in debt and harassed by constant duns from
merciless creditors, and it was the hand of death alone
that saved him from the horrors of a jail. The old home
passed at once into other hands, and the afflicted family
leased a neighboring farm, hoping by their united efforts
to at least make a comfortable living. But fortune did
not smile. Frosty springs and late summers, for four
years in succession, put them back sadly: the land itself
was poor, and all went wrong. Burns worked well, and
did not dislike a farmer's life; but his soul was full of
music that must have expression in words: so he composed while guiding the plough, or with the reaping-hook
in his hand. Some of his best poems and songs were

produced in this way. Of course, this did not benefit the crops, or fill his empty purse.

"He who pens an ode on his sheep, when he should be driving them forth to pasture; who stops his plough in the half-drawn furrow, to rhyme about the flowers which he buries; who sees visions on his way from market; who writes an ode on the horse he is about to yoke, and a ballad on the girl who shows the whitest hands and brightest eyes among his reapers, has no chance of ever growing opulent, or of purchasing the fields on which he toils."

Quite discouraged at last, Burns resolved to give up the farm, and try his fortune in the West Indies. To meet the expenses of the journey, he collected his poems, and they were published by subscription, many kind friends standing by him in this trying hour. Although the want of money induced him to make himself known as a poet, yet he appreciated the worth of his rhymes, and believed in their success. He said afterward to Moore: "I thought they had merit; and it was a delicious idea that I should be called a clever fellow, even though it should never reach my ears—a poor negro-driver, or perhaps a victim to that inhospitable clime, and gone to the world of spirits."

You see he took rather a blue view of life, as was but natural, with absolute want staring him in the face. He even suffered for food: a piece of oat-cake and a bottle of twopenny ale often made his dinner when correcting the proof-sheets of his volume. He had been long attached to Jean Armour; but her father, a rigidly devout man, disliked the connection; and when he discovered that they had been privately married, without his sanction or that of the kirk, his anxiety changed to anger, and, tearing the marriage-certificate from his daughter's trembling hands, threw it into the fire.

Jean obeyed her father, and refused to see her lover,

who now became utterly despondent and wretched. He forgot how greatly he had sinned in deceiving her parents, forgot her distress, and indulged in the wildest grief. He said: "I have tried often to forget her; I have run into all kinds of dissipations and riots, mason-meetings, drinking-matches, and other mischiefs, to drive her out of my head, but all in vain. And now for a grand cure: the ship is on her way home that is to take me out to Jamaica; and then farewell, dear old Scotland! and farewell, dear, ungrateful Jean! for never, never, will I see you more! His good-by to the "Bonnie Banks of Ayr" is very pathetic. You may like to recall the last verse:

> "Farewell, old Coila's hills and dales,
> Her heathy moors and winding vales;
> The scenes where wretched fancy roves,
> Pursuing past, unhappy loves!
> Farewell, my friends! farewell my foes!
> My peace with these, my love with those—
> The bursting tears my heart declare,
> Farewell the bonnie banks of Ayr."

He was a mason, and addressed a farewell also to the brethren of his lodge, which produced a great effect upon them. An old farmer of Ayrshire, thus tells the story of that leave-taking:

"He was quite late in coming that night—a thing quite uncommon wi' him. He came at last. I never in my life saw such an alteration in ony body. He looked bigger-like than usual and wild-like. His een seemed stern and his cheeks fa'n in. He sat down in the chair as master. He looked round at us. I thought that he looked through me, and I lost the grip of the beginning o' my speech; and no, for the life o' me, could I get it again that night. He apologized for being late. He had been getting a' things ready for going abroad. · He could get to us no sooner. He intended to say something to us, but it had gone from him. He had composed a song for the occasion, and would sing it. He looked round on us, and burst into a song, such as I never heard before or since. If ever a song was sung, it was that ane. Oh, man, when he came to the last verse, where he says:

> 'A last request permit me here,
>   When yearly ye assemble a':
> One round, I ask it wi a tear,
>   To him, the bard, that's far awa,'

that last sight of him will never leave my mind. He arose and burst into tears. They were na sham anes. It was a queer sight to see sae mony men burst out like bubbly boys and blubber in spite o' themsels. Soon after the song, he said he could stay no longer. Wishing us all well, he took his leave, as we thought, forever. We sat and looked at each other; full as we were, wi' great speeches, nane o' them came to the light that nicht. The greatness of Burns was not understood by ony body; but there is a feeling remains, I wad no like to part wi'."

There were additional reasons for Burns's sadness, in the thought that his good father died full of anxiety for his future. On his dying bed, as Robert and his sister were weeping near him, he gave him a few words of earnest Christian counsel, and then, after a pause, said "there was only one member of his family for whose conduct he feared." He repeated the expression, when the young poet said, "Oh, father, is it me you mean?" The old man replied, "It was." Robert turned to the window, the tears streaming down his cheeks and his bosom swelling as if it would burst.

I have given you these circumstances, as a key to his conduct. His thoughts were now turned toward Jamaica, and he was just about to take his passage, when his poems appeared in print, and produced a perfect *furore* through all Scotland. "Old and young, high and low, grave and gay, learned or ignorant, all were alike delighted, agitated, and transported."

A kind letter from a gentleman in Edinburgh, who had enjoyed his book, and strongly advised a second edition, changed all his plans. He spent part of the money intended for his journey, for a new suit of clothes; left as much as he could for his dear mother's support, and, with an almost empty purse, went at once to Edinburgh, where he was most cordially received. His poems were a passport to the finest drawing-rooms, and earls and nobles were proud to know him. He was at once the lion of the day. It was the fashion to pet and flatter the poet-ploughman, and a subscription was soon raised for a second edition of his poems; such men as Blair, Robertson, and Dugâld Stewart, carrying lists in their pockets, to obtain the names of their acquaintances. He bore the ordeal well; was unaffected and manly; was ready to listen or to talk, and his conversation, brilliant and powerful, was considered by many even more wonderful than his poetry.

Scotland could now boast of a *national* poet, and was glad to do him honor. He seldom blundered or lost his self-possession. His heavy boots and buckskin breeches were excused or forgotten by the fair ladies, listening with delight to his wonderful flow of language, and nobles and sages were alike charmed by his untrained eloquence. But, alas for him, and the honor of his country! this was but a temporary enthusiasm, and he was soon pushed aside. Some were envious of his fame and popularity; others preferred some new pet; his politics were not those of the ruling party; his habits were known to be irregular, and he was absolutely shunned by those who had pursued and caressed him. He had expected this "contemptuous neglect," but it was hard to bear!—all his high hopes crushed in two short years, and the fires of ambition were now too strongly kindled to be easily put out.

He resolved to unite the farmer and the poet once more, and, remarrying his beloved Jean, he leased a fine farm and settled quietly at Ellisland, in 1788. The land was good, the scenery beautiful, but his home was little better than a hovel. Yet love was there, and, for a time, Burns was both busy and happy. He longed for the cultivated society, however, of which he had enjoyed such a brief taste—feeling that he was now at "the very elbow of existence," away from all congenial companionship—his visions of future glory fast disappearing. This made him restless and dissatisfied, and he was constantly on the move. "In the course of a single day, he might be seen holding the plough, angling in the river, sauntering with his hands behind his back, on the banks, looking at the running water, of which he was very fond; walking round his buildings or over his fields; and if you lost sight of him for an hour, perhaps you might see him returning from Friar's-Carse, or spurring his horse through the Nith, to spend an evening in some distant place, with such friends as chance threw in his way."

During these solitary walks and rapid rides he composed some of his best songs. "Auld Lang Syne" was written about this time. He loved to read these heart-gems to his friends as old songs—the labors of forgotten bards, or lyrics that he had taken down from some old woman's song.

A few years after, some friend obtained for him the office of exciseman for the district in which he lived, with a salary of seventy pounds a year, and much hard work—a pitiful position for the man whom his country should have delighted to honor.

But he tried to make the best of his lot, saying: "I dare to be honest, and I fear no labor; nor do I find my hurried life greatly inimical to my correspondence with the Muses. I meet them now and then as I jog among the hills of Nithsdale, just as I used to do on the banks of Ayr."

He was occasionally remembered in these days by his Edinburgh acquaintances in some pleasant way. He had a few good friends among them with whom he corresponded, and many more visitors than he cared for found their way to his humble cottage. His farm did not prosper; neither his wife nor himself knew how to manage it with thrift and skill. His excise duties took him often away; and the gay companions he found on these frequent excursions did him no good.

In 1791 he relinquished the lease of the Ellisland property, and removed his family and their humble furniture to Dumfries, where they tried in earnest to economize, but that was impossible. Friends and admirers must be fed and entertained; new books must be purchased; even the wandering poor must be cared for: no one was ever turned from his door.

In his family he was ever gentle and affectionate; helping his bright boys in their lessons; listening to Jean's sweet voice as she tried his last song; or writing in their midst, cheered rather than disturbed by their presence. A third edition of his poems, containing "Tam O'Shanter," as a new delight for his admirers, now came out. But his end was near. Suspected by the government of unpatriotic sentiments, distressed for means, crushed by disappointments, injured by constant dissipation, he died of a nervous fever, on the 21st of July, 1796—only thirty-seven.

The question is yet to be answered—asked by some one when he heard of his death—"Who do you think will be our poet now?"

13

Burns's great mistake in life was his lack of aim and principle. He drifted without helm or rudder—tossed about by passion and temptation—until dashed upon the cruel rocks.

His short, sad life is a lesson in itself—no moralizing could increase its effect. In judging his character and conduct, there is a tendency toward extremes. He is either condemned too severely, or extolled to the skies. Let us pass lightly over his faults, except as they may injure those who read his poems, and dwell thankfully, lovingly, on the happiness he has given to the world. The depths of one's heart are stirred by the very mention of his name.

As Beecher says, in his own inimitable way: "If every man that, within these twenty-four hours the world around, should speak the name of Burns with fond admiration, were ranked as his subject, no king on earth would have such a realm; and if such a one could change a feeling into a flower, and cast it down to his memory, a mountain would rise, and he should sit upon a throne of blossoms, now at length without a thorn!"

Carlyle's wonderful essay on this poet closes with these words:

"With our readers in general, with men of right feeling anywhere, we are not required to plead for Burns. In pitying admiration, he lies enshrined in all our hearts, in a far nobler mausoleum than that one of marble; neither will his works, even as they are, pass away from the memory of men. While the Shakespeares and Miltons roll on like mighty rivers through the country of Thought, bearing fleets of traffickers and assiduous pearl-fishers on their waves, this little Valclusa Fountain will also arrest our eye. For this also is of Nature's own and most cunning workmanship, bursts from the depths of the earth, with a full gushing current, into the light of day; and often will the traveller turn aside to drink of its clear waters, and muse among its rocks and pines!"

A tourist, who writes very graphically in an *Atlantic Monthly* of 1860, on "Some of the Haunts of Burns," thus describes his grave and his early home:

"There was a footpath through this crowded church-yard, sufficiently well worn to guide us to the grave of Burns; but a woman followed behind us, who, it appeared, kept the key of the mausoleum, and was privileged to show it to strangers. The monument is a sort of Grecian temple, with pilasters and a dome, covering a space of about twenty feet square. It was formerly open to all the inclemencies of the Scotch atmosphere, but is now protected and shut in by large squares of rough glass, each pane being of the size of one whole side of the structure. The woman unlocked the door, and admitted us into the interior. Inlaid into the floor of the mausoleum is the grave-stone of Burns — the very same that was laid over his grave by Jean Armour, before this monument was built. Stuck against the surrounding wall is a marble statue of Burns at the plough, with the genius of Caledonia summoning the ploughman to turn poet. Methought it was not a very successful piece of work; for the plough was better sculptured than the man, and the man, though heavy and cloddish, was more effective than the goddess. Our guide informed us that an old man of ninety, who knew Burns, certifies this statue to be very like the original.

"The next morning wore a lowering aspect, as if it felt itself destined to be one of many consecutive days of storm. After a good Scotch breakfast, however, of fresh herrings and eggs, we took a fly, and started at a little past ten for the banks of the Doon. On our way, at about two miles from Ayr, we drew up at a roadside cottage, on which was an inscription to the effect that Robert Burns was born within those walls. It is now a public-house, and of course we alighted, and entered its little sitting-room, which, as we at present see it, is a neat apartment, with the modern improvement of a ceiling. The walls are much scribbled with the names of visitors, and the wooden door of a cupboard in the wainscot, as well as all the other wood-work of the room, is cut and carved with initial letters. So, likewise, are two tables, which, having received a coat of varnish over the inscriptions, form really

BURNS AND HIS HIGHLAND MARY.

curious and interesting articles of furniture. On a panel, let into the wall in a corner of the room, is a portrait of Burns, copied from the original picture by Nasmyth. The floor of the apartment is of boards, which are probably a recent substitute for the ordinary flag-stones of a peasant's cottage. There is but one room pertaining to the genuine birthplace of Robert Burns—it is the kitchen—

into which we now went. It has a floor of flag-stones, even ruder than those of Shakespeare's house, though perhaps not so strangely cracked and broken as the latter, over which the hoof of Satan himself might seem to have trampled. A new window has been opened through the wall, toward the road; but on the opposite side is the little original window of only four panes, through which came the first daylight that shone upon the Scottish poet. In that humble nook, of all places in the world, Providence was pleased to deposit the germ of the richest human life which mankind then had within its circumference."

And now, dear reader, we must part, at the door of Burns's homely cottage. If you have enjoyed this brief excursion in the field of English literature half as much as your garrulous *cicerone*, we may take another ramble together some bright day in the future.

THE END.

www.ingramcontent.com/pod-product-compliance
Lightning Source LLC
Chambersburg PA
CBHW020857020726
47497CB00005B/1453

* 9 7 8 3 3 3 7 2 5 5 4 2 8 *